*Praise for*
# THE SUGAR CUP
*(Written as Annie Sims, Harlequin Worldwide)*

"[Ann Simas] brings a charming new voice to the romance genre. THE SUGAR CUP is a delight. Everyone should have a dog like Daisy."
— Sherryl Woods, author of *Wind Chime Point*

"Get ready for [Ann Simas], a wonderfully fresh new voice in romance. THE SUGAR CUP was delightful, with characters I rooted for, a puzzle that was fun to solve and the perfect blend of comedy, mystery and old-fashioned enchantment. I loved it."
— Eileen Dreyer, author of *It Begins with a Kiss*

"In THE SUGAR CUP, [Ann Simas] stirs up a fine concoction of ingredients: a strong hero, an equally strong heroine, mystery, spookiness…and romance."
— Stella Cameron, author of *Darkness Bred*

■

*Praise for RWA Golden Heart Finalist*
# CHLOE'S SPIRIT

"I found [CHLOE'S SPIRIT] to be a delightful story and even shed some tears! I was drawn into the story quickly and found it hard to put it down. I highly recommend it for a fun and stimulating read."
— Nancy J (Reader, Amazon Kindle)

"I just loved [CHLOE'S SPIRIT]. Chloe and Marsh were incredible and Mary was just awesome. I had never read this author before but I'm going to see what else she has to offer. Such a great book."
— Trish Roberts (Reader, Amazon Kindle)

# CHLOE'S SPIRIT
# *Afterstories*

*Second Chance*

*Foolish Heart*

# ANN SIMAS

MAGIC
MOON
PRESS

# CHLOE'S SPIRIT AFTERSTORIES
## Second Chance • Foolish Heart

## June 2013

**Chloe's Spirit Afterstories: Second Chance and Foolish Heart** is a work of fiction. Names, characters, places, and incidents are either the product of the author's imagination or are used fictitiously. Any resemblance to actual persons, living or dead, or events described herein, is entirely coincidental.

ISBN 978-0-9885460-3-5 (print book)

Magic Moon Press . POB 41634 . Eugene, OR 97404-0386

**Printed in U.S.A.**

072413/11pthyph
CS4302491

This book is for Nancy Jankow.
We've known each other a long time—
and thank goodness for that!
I'm both blessed and honored
to call you my friend.

∎

Thanks again to Suzan Greenlee.
Editors don't come any better!

Thanks also to Father John Costanzo,
who graciously answered all
my priestly questions.

∎

And to Frank—
You are always my first reader
and biggest supporter.
Without you, I just couldn't do it.
✗♥

# Second Chance

**Luce Maguire & JD Kemp**

# chapter 1

*L*uce Maguire opened the door to her chambers, passed through, and closed it firmly behind her. She removed the black robe that served as the iconic uniform of her profession, carefully draping it over the extra-wide hanger on the hook attached to the back of the door.

Sluggish, she moved toward her desk—not because of physical exhaustion, but rather from mental fatigue—and sank down into the rolling leather chair, anxious to get the Ferragamos off her feet. She kicked them away and reached inside the top drawer for the bottle of ibuprofen. Not that a few pills would solve her ongoing internal quandary, but they might do something about the headache raging inside her skull.

God, she was so sick of sitting on that bench, day in and day out. Listening to fabricated arguments from defense attorneys, mendacious testimony from so-called witnesses, and self-important assurances from slimeball defendants that they hadn't done *it*.

Some days the prosecutors, police, and forensic people weren't much better.

She popped the tablets into her mouth and swallowed

them with water from her Starbucks insulated drink cup.

Maybe her disgust, her angst, the general feeling of discontent she'd been experiencing, had been festering for some time, even before this, the worst case she'd heard in the three years she'd been on the bench.

Not for the first time, she wondered how she could pursue a run for the state supreme court when she suddenly felt nothing but contempt for the law, in general, and something akin to hate for the criminal justice system, overall. They say you have to love something to hate it, and oh, how she had loved the law! *Had* being the operative word.

She sank back in her chair, rubbing her temples. She'd heard murder cases before. Some were crimes of passion, others well-planned. All were heinous. But this?

God help her, this was an aggravated murder case, which in Oregon meant the death penalty. At last count, the primary charges had totaled twenty, but the number of bodies continued to grow, not just in Oregon, but in three abutting states. The defendants, who had insisted on being tried together and defended by only one attorney and his team, were as crazy as any two men could get, yet they had passed all their psych evals with flying colors. No mental hospital or insanity pleas for these animals.

Instead, they came into court every day in shackles because no one wanted them loose and cutting up attorneys, court personnel, jurors, or observers into tiny little pieces and doing whatever with them, like they had done to their twenty-and-counting victims. Never mind that they had no cutting implements in the courtroom. They had teeth, and teeth could gnaw and cut well enough for their purposes. Just ask victims four, eight, and eleven.

Surprisingly, the jury had been selected in a matter of days. But by the end of the first week, one juror had experienced a panic attack that sent her to the hospital. Another had tripped on her chair leaving the jury box for lunch break, fracturing her arm, an injury as yet un-substantiated by a physician though it kept her from returning to the courtroom.

By the middle of the second week, another juror had developed hives that didn't respond to creams, anti-histamines, or other oral medications. He, too, went to the hospital. Two days later in the morning, another juror fainted dead away and hit her head on the jury box railing, further exacerbating whatever her condition was with a concussion. She, too, had been taken to the hospital. In the afternoon, the oldest juror on the panel began to babble incessantly and had to be removed. Within an hour, the court had been informed that the stress of the trial had been too much for him. He was sedated at home under doctor's orders.

They had run out of alternate jurors in two weeks. And this week, just today, three jurors had come in and said they were unwell and needed to leave. A prosecutor, one of the defense attorney's assistants, and the court reporter also said they were ill. All speculated they were coming down with a serious flu bug.

Luce knew damned good and well that flu season had arrived, thereby providing a convenient excuse to cut and run for those who had no other medical malady at their disposal. How could she lecture people on their civic duty when two of the world's most sadistic bastards leveled four soulless eyes on them for hours every day, plotting only God knew what against them. Anyone with half a brain knew the twosome enjoyed killing—you could almost hear their sick, evil minds churning out new and inventive ways to accomplish their goals.

More than once, Luce had wanted to pull out the gun in the holster attached under her bench and shoot them both dead.

The only thing that stopped her from succumbing to that secret desire was knowing she'd have to spend the rest of her days in prison. She was more of an outdoor girl, averse to metal bars and concrete walls and razor wire (except for criminals). She preferred, if not designer labels, at least the designer look in her attire. Prison garb just wouldn't suit her at all.

She pulled a pair of sensible but stylish flats out from under her desk and slipped them on. With a glance toward the window, she noted the sky was cloudy, but not dark. With luck, no rain in the forecast. She retrieved the three-inch heels and shoved them into a canvas bag she kept in the bottom drawer. From another drawer she withdrew her purse.

Court was cancelled for today. It wouldn't resume until the following Monday, what with the attorneys all scuttling to complete motions dealing with either mistrial or dismissal, or both. Quite honestly, Luce had no idea how she was going to rule. She'd never had a case fall apart before due to lack of jurors.

The next few days wouldn't be a vacation, but at least she wouldn't be confined to her office or the courtroom, surrounded by everything law enforcement. No scum-bags, perverts, murderers, child molesters, psychopaths, burglars, *ad nauseum*. She could push all thoughts of this trial aside until she was back on the bench.

For now, she had something fun to think about. She was invited to a baby shower for twins. Today, she'd be playing Auntie Luce, in title, if not in actual fact, and she was looking forward to visiting the baby store more than she'd looked forward to anything in the recent past.

It would be normal, and she honestly couldn't re-member the last time she'd felt life was normal. Certainly not her life, anyway. Not in the courtroom, not in the bedroom. She was happy for her friends, Marsh and Chloe Fielding, but she wished more than anything that she had a baby of her own to shop for.

She left her office through the door to the back hall-way and exited via the rear stairs, a sense of freedom building in her with each step she took downward.

Briefly, she pondered calling her fiancé, JD Kemp, to see if he wanted to play hooky for a couple of hours, then decided not to. She loved JD, no doubt about it, but she found herself experiencing discontent of a different nature where he was concerned these days. In fact, she hadn't seen or talked to him in over a week.

That reminder brought a frown to her face. During the two years of their engagement, they'd never had an argument that didn't involve her chosen career path—sitting on the highest court in the state. JD didn't favor the idea but would never specifically say why. Whatever the reason, he used it to avoid setting a wedding date. Always it was the same, but he'd never stayed away before, at least not this long.

What would he say now if she told him that she'd changed her mind? That she hated every single thing about being a judge, about the judicial system, about anything related to crime, and that included cops?

Being a cop, he might take offense.

Besides, how could you hate the man you loved, just because he was a cop? How could you break it to him that you didn't want to see him for a while, at least until you got your head straightened out about all this *stuff* rattling around in your brain that was making you crazy?

At first she'd thought JD selfish and inflexible. But then she'd wonder if he feared some horrible event the future had in store for her if she didn't run as fast as she could from the law. Hadn't she experienced a dark foreboding herself once this stupid trial had gotten underway?

Was it possible that JD's gut instinct, his secret fears, somehow translated into her own anxious thoughts?

Possible, but not likely, she conceded. She had a gut instinct of her own, a sneaking suspicion that his ill-defined resistance to her wanting to be on the Oregon Supreme Court had no real substance. He didn't foresee any trauma in her life as a result of pursuing advancement in the judicial system.

She suspected that JD Kemp, grown man, former psychologist-turned-cop, feared commitment, pure and simple. Any excuse to *avoid* it would do. A hero on the streets of Salem, Oregon, a coward in personal relationships.

She pulled her key fob from her purse and clicked it, unlocking her Lexus sedan. As usual, she perused her surroundings, always expecting the worst in this day and age, relieved when nothing happened. She climbed in and tossed the canvas bag and her purse onto the passenger seat, locking the car doors immediately after.

She put the key in the ignition and was about to start the car when she noticed a barely discernable writing on the windshield, written in reverse so she could read it: BOOM!

# chapter 2

*L* uce sat paralyzed in the leather seat of her car for several moments. Her first reaction was to leap out of the vehicle, but if BOOM! really meant BOMB! then she might activate it by getting out of the car.

She reached for her purse and the smartphone tucked inside, but her fingers hesitated over the keypad. She remembered reading about the cops at the Boston Marathon telling people to stay off their cell phones after bombs had gone off near the finish line. Had they done that to keep the airways clear, or had they worried about setting off other devices? If there *was* a bomb in her vehicle, would dialing 9-1-1 detonate it?

*Think!* she screamed in silence, her fingers trembling just above the key pad.

She parked in a secure facility, with locks and fences and a guard at the gate. No unauthorized person could have entered to put a bomb in or under her vehicle.

And yet, *someone* had finger-written BOOM! faintly on her windshield.

Luce decided to take a chance. First, she closed her

eyes and said a quick and fervent prayer to anyone up there who was listening, then she dialed.

She might be called a fool later for reading more into the message than some idiot's idea of a prank, but on the other hand, judges had died not taking things like this seriously. Judges— made enemies after verdicts came in, at sentencings, or even when they alone made findings if no jury had heard the case. And sometimes, it was as if the nature of the job generated hate.

She might be a fool, but she was not stupid.

A few minutes later, Salem PD's bomb squad pulled up in their big black step van. Two officers in protective gear approached her vehicle, while another stood back and called her on her cell phone. With a deep breath and a sigh of relief, Luce said, "Thank God nothing exploded."

"Don't worry, Your Honor. We'll have you out of there in a jiffy."

"I hope so," Luce said. "I didn't use the ladies room before I left the building."

A moment of silence met her comment, then the officer laughed. "Good one, Luce."

Thank goodness Sgt. Blake Halloran had a sense of humor. "I'm glad you're here, Blake. It slipped my mind that you're both bomb squad and SWAT."

He shrugged. "They often go hand-in-hand, that's for sure."

She nodded at him through her window. "Would you mind giving JD a call so he doesn't freak out if he catches this over the radio?" "Sure, no problem. You hang tight. My guys are going to give your ride a once-over and see if anything's there that shouldn't be. Soon as I can get you out, I will." He paused for a moment. "Since you're technically a state employee, the Oregon State Police bomb squad is also on the way."

*I wish that made me feel better,* Luce thought, but said, "I hope this doesn't turn into a pissing match."

"It won't. We were here first." He grinned at her and

shot a thumbs-up her way.

Luce half-heartedly grinned back, disconnected the call, and tried to relax against the soft leather of the driver's seat. Fortunately, the ibuprofen had begun to kick in, but she felt far from tranquil. It would be a doubly bad day if Connie, her court secretary, had to hear that both her husband, Blake, and her judge, Luce, had been blown to smithereens in the parking lot. *JD probably wouldn't like it, either*, she thought with grim humor.

First, the undercarriage of the car was examined. When that apparently netted nothing, the hood was raised slightly, and what Luce presumed was a camera on the end of a slim metal pole was inserted. As one officer held the hood up, the other inched around the front end of her car.

Luce's phone rang twice. The first call was from her mother, and since her mom would have expected her to be in the courtroom, she felt comfortable letting the call go to voice mail. The second call was from Unknown.

A shiver coursed down Luce's back. She knocked on the window, trying to get Blake's attention. He happened to glance her way and she pointed anxiously toward the smartphone she held up next to her window glass. The urgency of her pantomime registered with him immediately. He shouted out to the officers conducting the bomb search.

The phone stopped ringing, but a moment later it began again. She looked toward Blake, then toward the two officers in protective gear. They raised her hood completely, then one of them came and opened her car door and urged her out.

"Did you find—?"

"Please step away from the vehicle, ma'am."

"Luce, quickly, over here!" Blake called.

Her phone continued to ring. She ran toward the gate, where Blake pulled her away to safety. The phone stopped ringing. "Did they find a bomb?" she asked, breathless.

"They found something."

Luce frowned. "But you don't know what?"

"Not yet."

The phone began to ring again. "This 'Unknown' keeps calling. What if it's whoever wrote BOOM! on my windshield?"

Blake pushed his Salem PD ball cap back on his head, scowling down at her phone. "Let's get inside the van where it's quiet and you can put the call on speaker. Maybe he'll think you're still in your vehicle, if it *is* him."

Bombs weren't a woman's choice of destruction, so Luce didn't bother to correct his pronoun assumption. They hurried to the van and climbed in, but the phone stopped ringing before they were completely inside.

"Damn!" Luce swore, agitated when the phone didn't ring again.

"He may be watching," Blake said.

"Or it was a junk caller who gave up."

"Possible."

They turned, ready to climb back out, when the phone began to ring again.

"Answer it on speaker," Blake instructed, pulling the van door shut.

"Hello," Luce said, cursing the slight warble in her voice.

A mechanical-sounding voice said, "Scared the shit outta ya, didn't we, bitch? This is only the beginning. You better start watching every step you take from here on out, and if I were you, I'd never go back into a court-room again."

"Who—?" she began, but the line went dead.

"Fuckin'-A," Blake said. "We're going to need to check your carrier and see where that call came from."

"Anyone who makes the effort to put a voice synthe-sizer on his phone is not going to call from a traceable number."

"I'm sure you're right, but we're going to check it anyway." He paused. "I couldn't get hold of JD. Left him a voice mail message, but...." His shoulders lifted in a shrug.

Luce bit her bottom lip. "Try Marsh."

Marsh Fielding was JD's partner. If they were on a case, they were most likely together. She extended her phone to Blake, thinking it would save time if he used her speed dial to reach Marsh, but the phone rang again.

"Unknown caller," Luce said, hitting the speaker function to activate the call. "Hello?"

"I forgot to tell you," said the synthesized voice. "We're coming after your boyfriend, too. Tell him to watch out." A horrible cackle screeched across the line, then it went dead.

"Ohmygod," Luce whispered. It was one thing if someone was coming after her, but quite another if JD were made to suffer for something she had done to piss off some degenerate. She felt her knees begin to give way and reached out to steady herself against an odd looking component nearby.

"Careful," Blake warned, sliding an arm around her waist to support her as he guided her toward a stationary chair at a small built-in counter. "That's Babs, our bomb robot. Don't want to knock anything out of whack on this baby."

"Oh, sorry," Luce said, completely numb. She thanked Blake, then raised her phone and dialed Marsh. His phone also went straight to voice mail. "Shit!" she muttered, then when Marsh's message completed, said into the phone, "Marsh, it's Luce. This is urgent. Call me as soon as you can."

# chapter 3

*L*uce disconnected and tapped the phone against her open palm. "Think, *think*," she muttered to herself. After a moment, she hit another speed dial. "Chloe, thank God! Is Marsh there?"

"No," came Chloe's response. "He and JD went up to Rose's for the day to do yard cleanup." After a brief pause, she asked, "What's wrong?"

Luce didn't want to alarm Chloe, who, after less than two years of marriage to Marsh, was still a newlywed. Cops' wives walked on pins and needles regularly. Telling one that her husband might be with a man who had a bull's-eye on his forehead, especially one who was eight months pregnant with twins, didn't seem like a good call, psychologically or physically.

"Luce, buck up!" Chloe said. "I know something's wrong. I had lunch with Sarajane yesterday and her aunt has been warning her about some bad *juju* in the air. Just tell me!"

Despite the severity of the situation, Luce gave a bark of laughter, even though she wasn't amused. "Being the Deputy Medical Examiner," she said, her voice quavering, "our friend Sarajane Nichols should know better than to put stock in her aunt's dire warnings."

"Where are you?" Chloe demanded. "I'm coming over."

"You will not!" Luce almost shouted.

"Okay, then tell me what's going on."

Luce looked at Blake, who was hearing only one side of the conversation. She put her hand over the phone and said to him, "Will you get that phone records check started, then please find out the situation outside, so I can have something to tell JD when I reach him?" She rattled off her number for him.

He nodded, opened the van door and stepped out. Through the open door, Luce saw quite a crowd of law enforcement personnel gathered outside, including the OSP guys. A wave of relief overcame her—they wouldn't let anything happen to her *or* JD. They were here to protect their own.

"Luce? Luce, are you there?"

"Sorry, Chloe. Listen, I'll give it to you straight. The case I'm hearing is continued until Monday because of, well, because too many people are out sick. I left early, and when I got into my car, I noticed someone had lightly written BOOM! on the windshield. Whoever it was wrote it backward so I'd be sure to be able to read it. I didn't know whether or not to take it literally, so I called the bomb squad. They're checking over my car now, but in the meantime, I've had a couple of phone calls. One threatened me."

"And the other one?"

"Threatened JD."

"And JD is with Marsh."

Luce heard the catch in Chloe's voice, but her strength also came through.

"So, you're at the courthouse?"

"Yes."

"I'll call Rose, and one of us will get right back to you." A brief pause. "Hang tough, Luce. Don't let the bastards get you down."

"I wont. You know, Chloe, I love you like a sister."

"Me, too," Chloe said, "and I want to keep you safe. After I talk to Marsh, I'm coming down there to get you."

"Chloe, no—"

"I am, and I won't take any argument about it."

"I'm not putting a pregnant woman in danger!" Luce argued anyway.

"You're not. Really. I'm sure my house will be swarming with cops if you're here, and it will help JD rest easier knowing that you're at our house instead of alone at yours."

"But—" she said to a dial tone.

"Rose, hi, it's Chloe."

"As if I wouldn't recognize the sweet sound of my first grandbabies' mother's voice!" Rose chided.

Chloe had never known a grandmother, but she cherished Marsh's as if she were her own.

"How are you and the precious little ones?" Rose asked.

Since it had only been two days since she had spoken to Rose, Chloe answered ruefully. "Still the same, only bigger. Brenden or Mary Kate is kicking me like a little soccer player, or else they're fighting already."

Rose chuckled. "So, you decided on names, but not Jamie for the boy."

"That will be his middle name," Chloe said, impatient to talk to Marsh, but unwilling to scare his seventy-eight-year-old grandmother by demanding to speak to him immediately.

"I like Brenden," Rose said. "It's a good strong Irish name." Marsh's grandmother took a breath. "They haven't come back again, have they? I forgot to ask the other day."

"No." Chloe also didn't want to get into a discussion

right at the moment about the ghost who had lived in her house for over a hundred years, not when someone might be trying to blow up Luce Maguire and maybe do something equally bad to JD, and subsequently Marsh, just because they were together. "I need to speak to Marsh, Rose. Is he still there?"

"Sure. They're just loading up the truck with yard debris to take over to the disposal place. Let me get him for you."

Chloe began to pace, impatient for Marsh to come on the line.

"Hey, sweetheart, what's up? Sorry, I left my phone in the truck."

As always, a warm feeling of content surged through her at the sound of her husband's voice. It gave her the courage to blurt out, "Marsh, Luce went out to her vehicle and someone had written 'boom' on the windshield, so she called the bomb squad, who're there with her at the courthouse now. She's also received a couple of phone calls, one threatening her life, the other threatening JD. I'm going over there to pick her up and bring her back here now, but you and JD need to haul it back to Salem as soon as you can."

A moment of shocked silence greeted her outburst. "You can't bring Luce back to our house if she's being threatened!"

"Yes, I can. You know as well as I do that half the PD will be here, and probably OSP, too."

From his lack of response, she knew he agreed, albeit grudgingly. His silence had *that* kind of sound to it.

"What's your ETA?" she asked. "Do you have to go to the dump or something?"

"I've got a tarp, so I'll cover the load, and dump it later. We should be there in about fifty."

"Okay, good. JD should call Luce and let her know he's okay and that you're on your way."

"Yeah," Marsh said, but with hesitance.

"What?"

"It's awkward."

"Tell me later, but for now, make sure your partner calls the woman he's engaged to so she knows he's alive. And, Marsh?"

"Yeah, babe?"

"Be extra super careful, okay?"

"I will, Chloe. I've got too much to live for not to be."

"Love you."

"Ditto."

Chloe disconnected and grabbed her sweater and purse as she waddled her way to the back door, and out to the garage. She thought about calling Luce again, just to let her know she was on her way, then decided against it.

Surely, JD was already on the phone with her.

# chapter 4

Marsh filled JD in on what was happening in Salem, then gave his grandmother an abbreviated version as the two men tied the tarp over the yard debris.

Once they climbed in the truck, JD said, "I'll call Luce. You call Blake and see what the real story is."

JD was thankful he had Luce on speed dial, because his hands were shaking so badly, he didn't know if he could have punched in ten digits to save him. She answered on the first ring.

"JD, thank God! Are you okay?" she said before he had a chance to utter a greeting.

"I'm fine, darlin'. Are you?"

"A little shaken. They've found some kind of device, but I don't think it's actually a bomb. Just something to scare the crap out of me."

"Marsh says Chloe is coming down to pick you up. Blake's there, right?"

"Yes. And OSP, too."

"Okay, Marsh is telling Blake to call the LT and make sure you have an army of Salem PD patrols with you. OSP will probably insist on being included, since technically, you're their judge." He poked Marsh in the arm.

Marsh nodded and kept talking to Blake.

"You and Chloe will be fine, and we'll come directly there."

"Okay, but—"

"No buts!"

"Yes, but!" she shot right back. "Who's going to be watching out for you two?"

"That's why they call us cops, darlin'—we carry guns and we have the eagle-eye out for bad guys."

"Stop trying to make light of this, JD. It's not funny!"

JD doused his sense of humor. "I know that, Luce. Your life is precious to me, and I take it very seriously when some piece of shit thinks he's going to mess with that."

"I love you, JD."

After a moment's hesitation, he said, "I love you, too, darlin'. Keep away from the windows at Chloe's."

She hesitated back, which left him silently cursing himself.

"You *are* a cop," she finally said, her tone dry.

"Damn straight," he agreed, trying to force some levity into his tone again. "See you in about forty-five."

JD disconnected and a minute later, Marsh tapped the Bluetooth in his ear. "So, what does Blake say?"

Traveling at about ninety, Marsh never took his eyes off the road. "I wish I had a blue flasher I could put on top," he muttered.

"Blake?" JD prompted.

"First, get OSP on the line and tell them we're traveling like bats outta hell down I-5 to get back to Salem for this. I don't want to have to deal with some hot dog trying to pull me over."

JD agreed and hit another number in his speed dial. Within minutes, he had finished the call, and about sixty seconds after that, an OSP vehicle pulled out from under an overpass where he'd been clocking vehicles' speed and, with red-and-blue lights flashing, shot ahead of Marsh's Tundra, blazing a path.

With an escort, Marsh pushed the gas pedal down a little further. "Blake said they found a dummy bomb, something anyone who cruised the Internet might build, even if they were an idiot."

JD stared straight ahead, his jaw clenched. "I got a feeling whoever did this, they aren't idiots."

"I got the same feeling."

"We need to get Luce out of your house as soon as possible, and put her someplace where they won't find her."

"Or you, either."

JD grunted.

"I'm not kidding," Marsh said. "Both your lives have been threatened. The problem is, they knew some way to get in that secure parking facility, so what else do they know? *How* do they know?"

"I've been wondering the same thing." He looked at his partner, who still had not taken his eyes off the road. "I was thinking about breaking up with her."

"I know you were."

"But I still love her."

"I know that, too."

"What the hell am I gonna do?"

"I don't know what to tell you, except don't make the mistake I made with Chloe. You and Luce have problems, sit down and talk them out, *rationally*. Then if you still want to walk away, you can do it with a clear conscience."

JD hit his fist against the side door. "I've never liked her goddamned job."

"I don't imagine she likes your job much, either."

"Your point?"

"Give and take. On both sides. You've been pretty hard on her about this supreme court thing. Are you sure you're not just using that as an excuse?"

JD ignored the last question. "So, if Chloe decides

she wants to go interview paroled or convicted felons, you're going stick to your what's-good-for-the-goose theory?"

Marsh took his eyes off the road for a nano second. "You can be a real jackass sometimes, JD."

"Yeah, and you can't?"

"I'm not the one whose woman is being threatened right now."

"Again, your point?"

"I can't spell it out for you any plainer, partner. I'm as close to Luce as I am to my sisters. Any guy treats my sisters the way you've been treating Luce the last few months and I say to him, *fuck off.* Either you love her, and you take her for better or for worse and stop all this bullshit game-playing you've been doing, or do her a favor and take a hike so she can find a guy who will appreciate her for the smart, successful woman she is."

"I didn't know *you* had a goddamned psych degree now," JD snarled.

"I didn't know you'd forgotten *you do,*" Marsh shot back.

# chapter 5

*b*lake notified the patrol units at the outer perimeter of the area that had been cordoned off that Chloe was on her way and gave them her vehicle info.

Chloe eased through the lifted barricade, experiencing a weird sense of otherworldliness, kind of like a big war had taken place, and now only she and an occasional police officer were left on earth. Downtown Salem had never been this quiet before.

She turned a corner and all that changed.

Both the SPD and OSP bomb squads and the SWAT team step vans were onsite, along with about thirty uniformed and plain clothes officers. At the periphery, near the SPD bomb squad van, Luce stood as immobile as a daVinci sculpture. The likeness didn't end there. Her face was so pale against the silky strands of her dark hair, she seemed to be wearing chalk for makeup. A light breeze rippled the stylish shoulder-length cut, but other than that, she didn't even appear to blink.

Chloe parked and climbed out of her brand new Sienna van, somewhat laboriously. Blake, whom she'd met at several social events, hurried over. Since one of the babies chose that moment to give her a good swift kick in the kidney, she didn't mind the assistance. Man, did she have to use the bathroom bad. "Thanks," she told him.

"Marsh and JD are about twenty-five out," he said. "They picked up an OSP escort, so they're making better time."

Chloe didn't like to think how fast Marsh must be going to have covered that much distance from Rose's house already.

"You and Luce will proceed back to your house, with patrols in front of and behind you. Three patrols should already be at your place, cordoning off the block."

Chloe grimaced. "I'm sure my neighbors are going to love that."

He pulled a face. "Long as they aren't toting guns when they come into the neighborhood or out of their houses, there won't be a problem."

"Or bombs."

"That, too. If you don't mind, I'll have an officer drive your van."

"But—"

"Sorry, Chloe, this is for your own protection. Our guys have skills in defensive driving that I don't think you do."

"Why would I…?" Her voice trailed off as a light bulb went off over her head. "You think someone may try to attack my van or drive us off the road?" she asked, appalled, thinking about her unborn babies. What had she walked into?

"No, but it's better to be safe than sorry, right?"

Chloe nodded, hoping he was telling the truth.

"I've already gone over this with Luce—there'll be a total of two officers at each end of your block and two at the back door. The two units following you will divide, two at the front door, two inside. It'll be a mix of OSP and SPD guys."

"That's a lot of coverage."

"When a judge and a cop have threats against their lives, we take it seriously. You wrote a book about it, so you remember the incident in Woodburn a few years back with a bomb that resulted in dead and injured officers."

Chloe nodded. "You're right. I'm quite familiar with how badly things went that day."

They met Luce halfway between the two bomb vans and Chloe's vehicle. "Ready to go?" she asked Luce.

"Yes, and the sooner the better." Luce shivered, rubbing her arms as if to keep warm. "Blake, thanks to you and your men for all you've done here today."

"Not a problem, Your Honor. It's what we're here for." He tapped his fingers to the brim of his cap.

She stepped closer and gave him a hug.

Chloe knew that Blake's wife and Luce were not only old friends from college days, but Connie was Luce's court secretary. He'd take it personally that someone was on a mission to harm Luce.

"Be safe," he said as they walked away. "I'll keep you informed of what we learn about this contraption."

Luce waved over her shoulder at him.

As soon as she climbed into Chloe's van, Luce belted up, then clasped her arms around her torso, shivering so badly she was certain Chloe could hear her teeth chattering. "I'd offer to drive, but I'm afraid I'd run into the nearest pole."

"Don't worry about it. I'm pregnant, not incapacitated, and besides, Blake says a patrolman is going to taxi us."

Chloe went around and climbed in through the sliding door on the other side of the vehicle.

Once she was settled, Luce reached over and grabbed her hand. "I'm lucky to have such good friends."

Chloe returned the squeeze. "Likewise. There's a blanket in the back."

Luce reached over the seat to retrieve it. A moment later, an OSP patrol officer opened the front door and climbed in.

"We'd better get going or your guys will beat us to the house and then they'll go ballistic turning the town upside down trying to find you."

Chloe belted in. The officer started up the engine and maneuvered out of the lot, following the first patrol car. "Any ideas who might be trying to…?" she asked Luce.

"Kill me?"

"Yeah."

"My brain is going in a thousand different directions right now, so it's hard to think. When we get to your place, I think the first thing I'd better do after I use the bathroom is sit down and start compiling a list of people who hate my guts."

"It can't be that long," Chloe protested.

"Maybe not, but then it would only take one person, wouldn't it?"

"Tell me again what the caller said."

Luce repeated both calls almost verbatim. She'd always had excellent retentive skills, especially for spoken words, which had served her well on the bench.

"I guess your list would have to be at least two names long."

"What?"

"They guy said 'we' which infers at least one other person, maybe more."

Luce turned in her seat and stared at Chloe. "You are absolutely right."

"Does that change anything?"

"Yes, the list gets shorter," Luce said.

"How so?"

"Until this current trial, I've never had multiple defendants."

"But they're in jail, right?"

Luce bit her lower lip. "I've been kind of going crazy during this trial, hearing the testimony, every last gruesome, horrible, goddamned detail of the crimes these lunatics have been committing, the places they've been committing them—they're worse than Hannibal Lechter—and something about it has been bothering me like crazy. Now I know what it is."

The driver signaled to turn into Chloe's neighborhood.

"What?" Chloe asked.

Luce lowered her voice and leaned nearer Chloe. "There's more than two of them. They're working in pairs. Maybe in more than two pairs."

For a brief moment, Chloe gave her the owl eyes. "Holy shit!"

A bit startled because Chloe didn't swear, Luce said, "Yes, exactly,"

The officer nosed into her neighborhood behind the lead patrol car, went down to the corner, then turned left onto her street. As Blake had promised, the block where she and Marsh lived was barricaded and two officers, armed with shotguns, stood at each end.

The OSP officer driving the van pulled into her driveway, shut off the engine, and got out. He drew his weapon and went around to Luce's side and opened her door.

"We're going to have to discuss this further while we wait for the guys to get here," Chloe said, unbuckling her seatbelt, "but I have a plan in the meantime."

"Plan?" Luce asked, not wanting to involve Chloe any more than she already had in this dangerous situation.

"Yes, I *really* have to pee, too, so if you wouldn't mind taking the upstairs bathroom, I'd sure appreciate it."

Luce laughed. For the first time in months, she was actually amused.

# chapter 6

O nce both women had taken care of their bladder needs, they and the two uniformed officers stationed inside the house, congregated in the kitchen.

Luce paced the room like a mad woman. The two officers stood to the side, trying to keep out of her way. She was, after all, a judge, and you didn't get in the way of a judge, even if you were protecting her.

"I'm Chloe Fielding," Chloe said, introducing herself. "And I guess you know Judge Luce Maguire?"

The cops nodded and the older one stepped forward. "Pleased to meet you ma'am, Judge. I'm Tiger Conway, and yes, I had the name before Tiger Woods, but I wasn't born with it. My mama—" He broke off as though realizing he was giving TMI, too much information.

"Your mama what?" Chloe asked, shaking his hand as Luce continued to pace. She went to turn on the burner under the tea kettle.

"Well," he went on, a little red in the face, "my mama said I sounded more like a little tiger growling than a baby when I cried, so she kinda gave me that nickname early on and it stuck."

"I like it," Chloe said, nodding her approval as she checked to make sure the coffee pot was full. "Don't you, Luce?" She moved on to the cupboard and withdrew a gallon-size container half-full of *biscotti*.

Luce looked from Chloe to Tiger and back to Chloe. "Yes." She turned and made her way toward the other side of the kitchen. Again.

"I'm Dave Jernigan," said the younger officer.

Chloe stopped midstride, on her way to the kitchen table. "No way! Marsh told me you'd been hired into patrol, but I didn't know you were on the street already." She put the cookies down and approached the young man. "I'm so glad to finally meet you in person," she said, extending her hand.

Luce stopped her mad pacing and stared at Chloe. Tiger's head went back and forth between Chloe and Dave, question marks in his eyes.

"Dave was interning in Persons Crimes when I was investigating Mary MacFee's murder," Chloe explained. "He helped me do some research."

Luce got it right away because Chloe had shared the story of her haunted house with both her and Sarajane one night over too many glasses of wine, pre-pregnancy.

"How's patrol?" Chloe asked Dave.

"Good. Tiger's teaching me a lot."

"Kid's got brains," Tiger said, puffed up like he was Dave's father. "He's going to make detective before you know it."

Chloe gave Dave a thumbs-up. "I have no doubt of that. Hey, if anyone's hungry, help yourself to the *biscotti*."

Dave and Tiger eyed the cookies as she filled a small bowl on the kitchen table.

"If you're thirsty, there's Diet Coke and bottled water in the fridge. Also, coffee and hot tea."

"We're on duty," Tiger explained just before his stomach rumbled.

"Geez, I bet no one's eaten lunch," Chloe said, glancing at the wall clock. "I'll make some sandwiches."

Luce suddenly realized she hadn't eaten anything since the night before.

"We're on duty," Tiger repeated.

Luce stopped her pacing. "Officer Tiger, you're allowed to eat on duty, right?"

"Yes, ma'am," Tiger said.

He opened his mouth to say more, but Luce quelled him with a *look*. She turned to Chloe, who she knew for a fact, did not find the kitchen to be her forte. "*I'll* make some sandwiches."

"Thanks," Chloe said, obviously grateful.

"You sit down and put your feet up," Luce instructed her.

"But—"

"Chloe, you're eight months pregnant. Sit down."

"I'll help make the sandwiches, ma'am," Dave said.

"Good, but please don't call me ma'am."

Dave saluted her and grinned.

"You look in the fridge and see what's there." She looked at Chloe. "Bread still in the same place?"

Scowling, Chloe nodded and pointed toward a drawer to the right of the stove. "I repeat, I am not incapacitated."

Luce leveled her best courtroom stare at her friend. "Let's keep it that way, shall we?"

Chloe padded back to the table and plunked herself down with as much grace as a pregnant woman carrying twins could manage, reaching into the cookie bowl as she went. "I like salami," she said. "Plain white bread, dry, and lots of salami."

"How about you Tiger?" Luce asked. Both cops were busy inspecting the packages Dave had withdrawn from the various compartments of the fridge.

"I'll have ham and cheese with lettuce, tomato, and mayo," Dave said.

"I'll have what he's having," Tiger said.

About that time, the front door banged open. JD and Marsh had arrived.

"With me, that'll make it a threesome," Luce said, turning toward the kitchen doorway.

JD stood in the portal, glaring at her. "A threesome what?" he demanded.

Luce took her time extracting a knife from the block on the counter, then looked pointedly at the vicinity of his manhood as she held the knife aloft. JD blanched, though she knew he'd never admit it. "We're making sandwiches. Want one?"

Marsh went over to his wife and knelt on the floor next to her, putting a hand against her belly. "You're okay?"

"Yes, Luce is making me sit."

"Luce has always been a smart woman," he said.

"You're treading on dangerous ground," Chloe warned. "I am not an invalid."

"Never thought you were, babe, but you've had a lot of excitement today. The kids need their rest and their mommy strong."

Chloe put a hand to his cheek and leaned forward to give him a kiss that almost sizzled. Luce put her gaze back on JD, who apparently had never taken his eyes off of her. She arched an eyebrow at him.

He blinked. "What?"

"Sandwich, or not?"

"Yeah, okay."

"Marsh?"

"Yeah, whatever you're making. Chloe only likes—"

"She told me," Luce said, turning back to the counter. She handed the knife to Dave, who'd located a cutting board for slicing tomatoes.

"I have paper plates," Chloe offered. "In the pantry. That will help keeps things simple."

Tiger followed the finger pointed toward a floor-to-ceiling double-door cupboard at the end of the kitchen.

"What is this, a social gathering?" JD demanded.

"Calm down," Luce said over her shoulder. "People have to eat, and I think we all need to be fortified for the discussion we're going to have about this…thing."

"It's more than just a 'thing,'" JD said, his tone slightly snide.

Luce slammed her hands down on the counter and all conversation ceased in the kitchen. She turned on JD, her eyes blazing. "You think I don't know that? You think I didn't see the word BOOM! written on my window? You think I wasn't scared shitless when I dialed 9-1-1 because I was afraid there was some wireless signal or something that might set off the bomb? Do you think I wasn't freaking out when the bomb squad guy opened my door, the very act of which could have triggered an explosive device?"

She ranted on, barely taking a breath. "You think I didn't wonder if a sniper had me in his sights when I got out of the car. I goddamned well know this is more than a fucking *thing*!" she finished, her voice rising with every word.

She sucked in a deep, shaky breath, exhaling slowly, and then she did it again. "I'm sorry," she said finally, her eyes going around the room to each of them except JD. "That was uncalled for. My nerves are shot." She turned back to the counter and started assembling the sandwiches.

Her fingers began to tremble so badly, she couldn't get the ham slices apart. "You finish, Dave," she said, stepping away from the counter, making her way toward the kitchen doorway.

JD put out a hand to her. "Luce, I'm so—"

"Don't," Luce said, side-stepping him. "And don't anyone follow me. I'm going into the bathroom, and I'm not coming out again until I damned well feel like it."

# chapter 7

$m$arsh stood and faced his partner. "Smooth," he said.

"Fuck you," JD said without heat. He turned and immediately apologized to Chloe.

She shook her head sadly, then said to Marsh, "Let's eat in the dining room. There's more space in there. What does everyone want to drink? JD, make yourself useful and grab some napkins from the pantry, will you? Dave, maybe you should make a couple of extra sandwiches, just in case. I think there's another loaf in the drawer."

JD wanted to kick something. He wanted to punch a wall. He wanted to yell until his throat couldn't take anymore. Instead, he did as Chloe asked. Man, what a jerk he was. Of course Luce knew the events of the day were more than a *thing*. For God's sake, she sat in a courtroom all day. She saw the worst that humanity had to offer.

And yet, facing a threat to her own life, she had remained calm. Until he'd started in on her, and this time not even about her career choices. What the hell was the matter with him? He might as well have hired one of those new digital billboards with four-foot-tall letters begging BREAK UP WITH ME!

And, that, he thought, was the crux of the matter. He didn't want to be the one breaking up with her. He wanted her to break up with him, so he didn't have to face the guilt of having done the deed himself.

In matters of the heart, he was nothing but a chicken. *Bwauk, bwauk.*

Everyone except Tiger took a seat at the big mahogany dining table. Tiger insisted he was supposed to be keeping an eye on Judge Luce Maguire, bathroom or not, and he'd eat standing up outside the bathroom door. Dave could keep an eye on JD well enough at the table.

Conversation over sandwiches and chips was desultory and by the time they'd finished and cleaned up, Luce still had not come out of the bathroom.

"What the hell!" JD muttered, heading for the other room.

Chloe jumped up, or tried to. Her belly got stuck under the table. "Wait! Let me go," she said, pushing away so she could stand. "I think I'll have better luck getting her to come out."

JD stared at her for a moment, then nodded.

The house became so still, a ghost could have floated in and no one would have noticed.

Chloe knocked on the bathroom door. "Luce?"

No answer.

"Luce? Come on. You have a theory. It's time to start figuring out who these guys are and how we can stop them."

No answer.

"Luce?"

"Damn it!" JD stomped in from the dining room.

At the same moment, the doorbell chimed.

"Who the—?" Marsh said. With his hand on his weapon, he pulled open the front door. "Sarajane! What the hell are you doing here?"

"I came as soon as I heard," she said, almost breathless. "And hello to you, too!"

"Sorry. Hi. How did you get through the blockade?"

The Deputy Medical Examiner shot Marsh a look that was part exasperation, part amusement. "I guess they thought someone here had died," she replied, her tone disingenuous. She glanced around at the faces staring at her. "Looks like they were right, judging from the expressions on your faces."

Marsh turned away from the door, muttering. "You and Luce always have been a pain in the ass."

Chloe said sweetly, "I guess you living between their two houses growing up must have made it catching."

Marsh came to a standstill, a scowl on his face. After a moment, he grinned. "Must have." He turned back to Sarajane. "You might as well come in."

"Gee, thanks," the Deputy ME said, closing the door behind her. "Where's Luce?"

"She's shut herself in the bathroom."

"Oh, for God's sake," Sarajane said, heading in that direction. She pounded on the door and shouted, "Luce, get your butt out here!"

"The door doesn't have a lock on it," Chloe pointed out, but before Sarajane could open it, Luce did.

"You people are giving me another headache," Luce said to the group in general.

"I have ibuprofen," Chloe offered.

"Perfect. Now," Luce said, making eye contact with her fiancé, her friends, and the two uniform officers, "let's sit down and try to get this figured out. Is there a sandwich left?"

As they were moving to settle in around the table, the doorbell rang again. Marsh threw up his hands. "Now what?"

He yanked open the door once more to find Blake Halloran and the lieutenant in charge of JD and Marsh's squad, Kerry Schaeffer, standing on the front porch. Behind him was Lt. Derek Hunter, an OSP investigator.

At the same time, Blake said, "I've got something on the device," and Kerry said, "This setup at your house is just not going to work," Derek declared, "OSP is going to take charge of this investigation immediately."

"Welcome to the Funny Farm," Luce commented dryly.

"Your Honor, we need to get you to a safe house," Kerry said.

"Judge, OSP wants to lead this investigation—" Derek began.

Luce held up a hand silencing them. "Lieutenant Schaeffer, Lieutenant Hunter, come in and have a seat. I want to lay out my thoughts about all this, then we'll see about who's in charge, and who needs a safer house than this to be in right now." She looked at each of them expectantly and received no arguments, though both were wrinkle-browed with frowns.

Being both a gentleman and a subordinate to the judge, and the only one who had not argued with her, Blake closed the door and followed the group into the dining room.

Chloe offered everyone beverages. Everyone declined. She asked Dave to bring in the extra sandwiches, just in case. She took the seat Marsh virtually had pushed her into with no complaint.

"What have you got, Blake?" JD asked before Luce could speak.

"First off, it was a dummy bomb. Forensics lifted prints off a piece of tape used to adhere a fake C-4 package to the body of the device. We figure maybe it was a roll previously used and the guy who built the bomb didn't think about that before he put on gloves. Or else, they're someone else's prints. We'll know soon if anything turns up on AFIS."

"So, no other prints," Marsh said.

"Right. But—and this is where it gets really weird— the fake C-4is actually Play-Doh and there was something embedded into the edge of it. Again, probably something that was laying out wherever the faux bomb was assembled."

"What was it?" JD asked.

Blake pulled out a sealed evidence bag from his pocket. Inside was a pierced earring with the post attached.

Luce, JD, and Marsh stood up and bent over the bag to examine the earring. The two men sat down, but Luce remained frozen. She raised her gaze slowly, looking directly into Chloe's eyes.

"What?" Chloe asked.

"It's exactly what I thought."

Chloe gasped.

Luce straightened, looking first to Blake and the two LTs, then to Marsh, and finally to JD. "I recognize that earring."

"How is that possible?" JD asked, his skepticism obvious.

"Are you sure?" Marsh and Blake asked at the same time.

The two lieutenants peered at the evidence bag, then up at the judge. "You *recognize* it?" Derek asked. He looked at his SPD counterpart, then back at Luce. "How?"

Luce sank back down into her chair. "It's mate has been presented as evidence in my courtroom."

# chapter 8

*a*bsolute silence greeted Luce's statement. Then pandemonium broke out around the table. Luce once again held up her hands, trying to quiet the group.

"*Shut up!*" Sarajane finally yelled.

Twenty minutes later, because Luce said she wasn't going to say what she had to say twice, the group grew by two—Marion County District Attorney John Kingman and lead Deputy DA Gio Rossi, who also happened to be prosecuting the case currently under continuance in her courtroom.

Fortunately, the dining room in the Fielding house was roomy. Marsh had brought in extra chairs from the kitchen. Everyone was sitting except for Tiger and Dave, who insisted they had to be "on their toes," so to speak, in case anything happened. There were two entrances to the dining room. Tiger stood in one, Dave the other.

"Can we get this show on the road?" JD asked.

Luce nodded.

"Good. Now please explain," he said.

Luce pushed back her chair, got up, pushed it in, and began to pace the width of the dining room. She ignored

JD. He always got terse when he was stressed, which wasn't often, but happened more and more lately. That was something separate from this, and she'd have to deal with it later.

She stopped once more at the head of the table and put her hands on the back of her chair. "You all know I'm hearing the case dubbed by the media as the Paired-Up Serials."

Everyone nodded, no one spoke.

She straightened, rubbing her temples. The headache was back. Or maybe it had never gone away. She willed herself to "buck up," as Chloe had told her earlier. In the growing silence, she made eye contact with each individual in the room. "The first of what I am about to say can never leave this room. Both my personal and professional lives depend on you, and on this I am deadly serious. I'm not going to threaten you with retaliation through my judicial capacity. I am going to trust you. If I can't, please get up and leave, now."

Once again, she gazed into each set of eyes. No one disappointed her, but the Deputy DA spoke up. "If you think you need legal counsel, Your Honor, maybe you should have your personal attorney present."

Luce almost laughed. "First of all, let's cut the titles for the time being, okay? I'm Luce, you're Gio. That's Tiger in that doorway and Dave over there. Everyone knows everyone now. Secondly, I'm not going to say anything that is illegal. Probably, it does border on unethical. However, since I believe everything that happened today is directly related to the Paired-Up Serials case, I think the assembled group is the logical choice to hear what I have to say and to discuss possible means of resolution."

DA Kingman said, "I think perhaps it's not necessary to have Mrs. Fielding and the Deputy ME here, then."

"I disagree," Luce said. "Chloe and Sarajane are my two closest friends. I trust both of them with my life. They stay."

Luce watched Marsh, who was standing behind Chloe, put a protective hand on his wife's shoulder. Biting back a small twinge of envy, she shot a glance at JD. His expression was impossible to read. She quickly gathered her thoughts and said, "This case has been the worst goddamned experience of my life. The trial is only in its second week and I've already had to call a continuance due to jurors and court personnel literally dropping like flies. On Monday, I'll be barraged with motions to dismiss or declare a mistrial."

She resumed pacing. "Every day, those two lowlifes sit at the defense table, their satanic eyes—honestly, they remind me of that look you see in every photo ever taken of Charles Manson—boring into the jurors, the court staff, the spectators. Hell, their own attorney and his assistants!"

She shook her head in disbelief. "I've been watching the jury members. I knew up front that many of them were reluctant to serve, but surprisingly, selection went quickly, and almost everyone questioned was selected. Nothing any of the potentials said seemed to deter the defense attorney, and I presume their responses to the questions put to them *did* please Gio. He tried to weed out some, but overall, these jurors are decent people who wanted to do their civic duty."

"Agreed," Gio said. "I still don't get it."

"You will," Luce said. "At first, the jurors would look at the two defendants, which is what most jurors do during a trial, but as the days wore on, no one looked at them, much less made eye contact, unless a particularly horrific fact was presented, then they might sneak a glance. Right from the start of the actual trial, Attila and Vlad—" She paused a moment. "I know it's inappropriate, but in my own mind, that's what I call them."

"If the shoe fits," Gio muttered.

Luce nodded. "Anyway, Attila and Vlad began to level a certain *look* on whomever made eye contact with them, and suddenly all kinds of medical issues and injuries began to crop up in the jury. Then today, we exhausted the subs and have no one else to call who has heard the proceedings."

"No more alternates?" Marsh asked, dumbfounded.

"Nope." She took a breath. "In addition, one of Gio's own team and the court reporter went home with the flu." Luce snorted. "Flu my ass! These people, *all* of them, are scared to death of those two, and I don't blame them. Every day I leave that chair and *I* want to go home and shower until the hot water runs out. They are creepy evil and if glaring daggers could kill, I'd be dead from all the holes in my body already."

There, she'd said it, even though she wasn't supposed to discuss the case outside the courtroom, just as she had instructed the jurors not to.

"You never told me any of this," JD said quietly.

"I haven't seen you to tell you anything," Luce said, working hard to keep the accusation out of her tone.

Nevertheless, JD flinched, but to his credit, he did not look away.

"And besides that, you know I don't talk about cases outside the courtroom until the verdict has come in."

"I know you don't, but you're not usually scared on the bench."

For the space of a couple of heartbeats, the room was quiet. "I think you get the picture," she went on, not disputing JD's spot-on remark. "Everyone involved in this case is unnerved."

She glanced at Gio, who nodded. "I've been on some bad shit, but never anything like this," he said.

Luce once again grasped the back of the chair. "Now, today, I get this bomb scare and two phone calls threatening my life and JD's. The bomb was fake, but made to look exactly like the real thing, according to Blake. Instead of C-4, they found Play-Doh and in the Play-Doh, they found an earring. Blake, would you mind showing the earring to Gio?"

Once more, Blake dug the sealed baggie out of his

pocket. Gio leaned over the table and examined the earring through the clear plastic. He looked up with startled eyes. "Motherfu—"

"Exactly," Luce agreed. "We saw an earring exactly like that entered into evidence in the Paired-Up case. It belonged to the young woman we believe is the first victim. Her mother positively identified it, both in evidence and when presented in court—it had passed down from the victim's grandmother, to her, and then to her daughter. It was custom made as an anniversary gift, so no one else ever had one like it. Speculation is that the Paired-Up boys kept one of something from each victim as a trophy. Not uncommon among serial killers."

"And since one had already been submitted into evidence—" Gio began.

"Where the hell did the other one come from?" Marsh finished.

He looked at JD and it was as if identical light bulbs went off over their heads. They both looked at Luce.

"There's more than just the two of them," JD said.

"I think so," Luce said. "I've been listening to the evidence closely and so many things bother me. The geographic area involved, over three states, although we're only prosecuting for Oregon. The alibis provided that, while weak or questionable, nonetheless raise doubts about whether these two could have killed the victims they claim to have killed. The fact that they can give names of victims, but are hazy on where they disposed of those victims' bodies."

"Two more of these predators out there?" DA Kingman asked, his tone incredulous.

"More than two," Luce said. "I think there's a pair in each of the three states where we know about victims being found. Maybe it's a game they play and it crosses state lines. Maybe they have quotas, challenges, even prizes. Maybe they all used to pull bugs apart and set dogs on fire together when they were kids."

JD stared back at her. "If you're right about this, we

have one hell of a clusterfuck on our hands."

# chapter 9

Chloe tugged on Marsh's hand so he'd lean over. She whispered in his ear, "I'm going to go upstairs and lay down for a while."

He put his other arm around her. "Are you feeling okay?"

"Yes, just a little tired. I stayed up too late last night working on edits."

"I'm sorry," he said. He pulled out her chair so she could stand. "I hate it like hell that I get called out late, when I should be here with you, making sure you get to bed early." He wiggled his eyebrows at her.

She punched him lightly on the shoulder.

"I'll clear all these people out so you can rest."

"No, don't do that. I feel better knowing Luce is close by. Our house surely isn't on serial-killer radar, right?"

"I hope not, but I'll feel better when JD and Luce get somewhere where they are completely safe and no one else is in danger." He cupped her face and gave her a kiss. "C'mon, I'll walk you upstairs."

"I don't like to interrupt love fests," Sarajane said, coming up next to them, "but can I tag along? I need to talk to Chloe."

Marsh and Sarajane and Luce had been friends since they were toddlers. He scowled at his childhood pal and said, "You're not going to fill Chloe's head with more of your aunt's *juju* bullshit, are you?"

"Of course not," Sarajane said, but she didn't quite meet his eye.

"You've never been a very good liar, Sarie."

"Well, I'm not quite lying," she retorted. "I already talked to your lovely wife about this, so we'll just be rehashing *old* bullshit, not anything new." This time, she stared him down.

Chloe stood on tiptoe to kiss her husband again, then grabbed Sarajane's hand. "You stay down here with the troops and figure out what needs to be done," she said to Marsh. "Sarie's coming with me."

"We need Luce," Sarajane said.

"Of course you do," Marsh growled, and moved away to retrieve the woman in question.

Upstairs, armed with beverages and more *biscotti*, the three women settled into a spare bedroom that had been converted into an office for Marsh. It held some of the mission-style furniture he'd brought from his other house, which Sarajane now rented, when he and Chloe had married. Luce and Sarajane settled in on the leather-cushioned sofa; Chloe chose the easy chair with the ottoman, so she could put up her feet. "Ahhh," she sighed.

"Comfy?" Luce asked, putting her own feet, sans shoes, up on the coffee table.

"Deliciously so," Chloe said, dipping a chocolate *biscotto* into her milk glass.

Sarajane and Luce did the same with their coffee.

"So I hear your Aunt Gennie has foreseen something bad happening," Luce said. "Does it have to do with carnage?"

"Carnage?" Chloe squeaked.

Sarajane swallowed her mouthful. "Why would you choose that exact word?"

Luce set aside her coffee and the cookie. "I'm not sure."

"Of course, you are," Sarajane scoffed. "Lately, you're like a cat that accidentally stepped onto a hot griddle."

Chloe looked from one to the other of them. "I feel like I missed out on something. What gives?"

"Luce gets these...*feelings*," Sarajane said.

"What do you mean?" Chloe asked.

Sarajane looked at Luce. "How would you explain it?"

Luce looked unhappy. "I don't know! I feel anxiety, apprehension, like it's a foreboding."

Chloe studied her friend. "Doesn't everyone get that sometimes?"

"Not like Luce," Sarajane said. "Tell her."

Luce reached over and yanked on Sarajane's hair.

"Ouch!"

"You deserved it, blabbermouth."

"Wow," Chloe said, wide-eyed. "This must be serious, because you never mentioned it when I spilled my guts to you about the ghost living in my house."

"I guess I hadn't had enough wine," Luce informed her wryly.

Chloe raised her eyebrows in disbelief. "Whatever it is, I can handle it and I can keep it a secret."

Sarajane said, "Chloe has a point. Who would understand *anxiety* like yours better than a woman who lived with a paranormal experience almost her whole life?"

Luce shook her head, rolling her eyes. "I'll try to make it short, because I want to hear what Aunt Gennie said."

Luce began. "Once in a while I get these feelings of...I don't know! A foreboding that *seems* to be connected to certain events." She paused for effect. "*Seems* is the operative word here. Most of the time, the incidents are fairly benign or predictable."

"But?" Chloe encouraged, intuiting that it wasn't that simple.

Luce gave her a baleful look. "You are too observant."

Chloe grinned. "Am I? Gee, maybe I should be a writer."

"You *are* a writer," Sarajane reminded her.

Chloe laughed. "However, not to be distracted. Please continue," she said to Luce.

Luce picked up her coffee and *biscotto*. "As I got older, my anxieties grew, not in frequency, but in intensity. I attributed it to being stressed out about studying, then passing the bar, then running for the judgeship." She set her cup and cookie back down again, frowning.

"Sarie and I wanted to go to a concert once. Springsteen was playing at the Rose Garden in Portland. It was winter and we'd been having excessively rainy weather. We'd be coming back late because we couldn't afford tickets *and* a hotel room. My feelings of dread just kept growing, so we put off buying our tickets and ended up *not* going. Sarie was furious because she thought I was overreacting." She spared a glance for her old friend, who nodded somberly.

Luce toyed with her cookie, turning it over and over on the napkin. "That night, one person was killed and several people were seriously injured by a drunk driver who tore through the parking garage, trying to outrun a traffic stop."

"How awful!" Chloe said.

Luce nodded. "We'd been to concerts there before. The incident took place *exactly* where we always parked."

Chloe's eyes widened.

"*Exactly*," Sarajane said again. "Tell her about your mom."

"My mother was supposed to go to New York for a

conference. As you know, she's really into graphic design, and this was a big deal put on by Adobe that ran for three days. As soon as she told me about it, my anxiety level shot through the roof. Finally, I became so distraught I called and begged her not to go. She promised me she wouldn't, since the same conference was being offered a few months later in Colorado." Her hand shook slightly. "September eleventh. Mom was supposed to be at that hotel next to the World Trade Center."

Goosebumps ran up Chloe's arms. "And now you've had a foreboding of…carnage?"

"Not carnage specifically, but I think the word 'bomb' written on my windshield implies explosion, bodies piled up, twisted metal, complete turmoil, and that *would* be carnage, wouldn't you say?"

"Carnage," Sarajane repeated, a serious look on her face.

"I thought it was a real warning. That's why I didn't screw around calling 9-1-1. I was scared to death that my phone might detonate it, but what could I do? I was in the parking lot, I didn't see anyone else around, the guard was far away in his guard booth. It seemed like, if I was going to be blown to smithereens, at least I wouldn't be taking any others with me."

Luce picked up her cookie and dunked it into her coffee with trembling fingers, then took a bite of it and chewed, her movements seemingly on autopilot, her eyes focused on something that wasn't really there over Chloe's head. "After this trial started, I actually thought my disquiet was because of Attila and Vlad." She shrugged, her eyes back on her friends. "But now with the fake bomb, I'm not so sure."

Chloe and Sarajane studied her in appalled silence. Finally, Chloe whispered, "You have to hear what Aunt Gennie says."

Sarajane cocked her head at Chloe. "Are you sure you're up to hearing this again?"

"Oh, for Pete's sake!" Chloe said. "For about the umpteenth time—I am pregnant, not an invalid!"

"Hey, simmer down," Sarajane said, putting her hand up. "Marsh would flat out kill me if I caused you undue stress."

"Me, too," Luce chimed in.

"Well," Chloe said, "if it makes the two of you feel any better, *I* will kill you if you don't get on with this!"

# chapter 10

*d*ownstairs, the men divided up tasks to be accomplished.

Blake took off to further investigate the fake bomb. The two lieutenants went back to their respective offices to get some balls rolling. The two DAs headed for their office to gather files and electronic gadgetry to take over to Salem PD, which everyone had finally agreed should serve as headquarters for the investigation, regardless of which agency ran it. The SPD conference room was bigger and had a better coffee machine.

After conferring with JD and their lieutenant, Marsh went to Dave Jernigan. "You're a helluva researcher, Dave. We want you back at the station, working with the IT guys. Find us some other crimes outside Oregon, Idaho, and Washington that match the same parameters as the Paired-Ups claim to have committed in the tri-state area."

"Also," JD added, "work with Financial Crimes for another look at the bank accounts and other money trails on these guys. The Deputy DA is going to personally deliver all the laptops and smartphones that were confiscated. Let's take another look at them, see if any anomalies crop up that were missed before. Land-line records, too."

"The FinCrime guys are going to take my word for it, that you want all this done?" Dave asked.

JD assured him, "The LT is there ahead of you. You'll be following up, but you know what we're looking for."

Marsh interjected, "You've got a good brain in your head, Dave. You heard what the judge said." He put a hand on the younger man's shoulder. "I trust you to find something for us."

Dave offered JD and Marsh a rueful smile. "Thanks. I think. Tiger...?"

JD said, "The LT will contact Patrol to send someone back to take your place. You're going to be of more help to Luce, doing what you do best. Getting information."

"Call me on my cell as soon as you find anything, or if you have any more questions," Marsh said.

"Can I get a look at the evidence log, see if anything else crops up like the earring? As we saw today, you never know when some small piece of a puzzle is going to mean something. IT can plug things into databases, maybe make connections."

JD nodded. "Good. The DA's office has a photo library of every piece of evidence that's been collected. I'll give Gio a call and make sure he brings it on CD when he comes. Now get."

"You two will be here?"

"No," JD and Marsh answered at the same time.

"You will be," Marsh said, poking JD in the chest.

"No, I w—"

"Yes, you will. You've been threatened. I haven't. Any legwork to be done, I'll do it."

"Your pregnant wife is upstairs," JD reminded him.

Marsh hesitated, indecision clearly battling his protective instincts. "You're here. Tiger and another officer will be inside, as well, and there are another eight officers around the house and on the street. If Luce's theory is accurate, we'll have the FBI here before we know it, too."

"Look, Marsh—"

"No, you look, JD. You stay here. The boss already gave you the order, I'm just repeating it."

JD's jaw worked furiously. "I can't stay here forever. *We* can't stay here forever."

"Probably not, but you'll stay here for now. We've got the room, it's as secure as any place else will be, and you and Luce will be together."

JD looked away at that. Luce and him together, probably in the same bedroom, as the other three rooms upstairs were spoken for—Marsh and Chloe's room, the nursery, Marsh's office. He gritted his teeth. The sofa in the upstairs office wasn't long enough for a guy his size to stretch out, but he could probably sleep on the floor. He'd do just about anything to keep from sharing a room with Luce right now.

Hell, who was he kidding? There wasn't anything he wanted *more* than being in the same bed with Luce, right now or anytime. It was himself he had to fight, not his attraction to her. He'd have to avoid touching her, comforting her, because every time they made physical contact, all he could think about was the man-woman thing and how good it always was between them, no matter how much they argued about the career thing. "Okay," he agreed.

"Look, I'll let you know if anything crops up," Marsh promised.

JD ran a hand through his hair in frustration. "I know you will. I'm just so pissed because I'll be sitting here doing jack shit while everyone else is doing *something*. I just don't sit on my ass that way!"

"I know you don't, but things aren't the usual right now." He grabbed JD by the elbow and guided him toward Chloe's office and shut the door. "Listen, JD, however you feel about Luce, whatever you're going through, you have to put it all aside for the time being. She needs you and you need her, whether or not you admit it. And if Luce is going to find sanctuary in my home, *I* need you, for Chloe's sake, understand?"

"You're right. I'm a selfish bastard."

Marsh grinned. "I wouldn't go that far, but like I told you before, don't do anything to hurt Luce, and that includes getting your sorry ass killed. Okay?"

"Might be less painful than this turmoil over my love life."

"Too bad you don't have any sweat-inducing hobbies," Marsh said. "That's how I figured out what to do about my life with Chloe."

The only sweat-inducing hobby JD currently had outside a gym was making whoopee with Luce, but he kept that to himself. "Too bad you don't have a gym."

"I've got the elliptical in the little room off the garage. And before you say you don't have workout clothes, you can borrow a T-shirt and a pair of shorts, both of which will be yours forever after because I never, ever want to smell like you when I work out."

JD called him a name.

"Likewise," Marsh said, laughing. "Now let me out of here. I need to see my wife before I take off. I should be back around dinner time. I'll bring pizzas so no one has to cook."

"Chloe's learned to cook?" JD asked.

Marsh grinned. "My point exactly."

# chapter 11

*L*uce got up and closed the door to Marsh's office, apologizing to Officer Tiger as she did so. "All right," she said to Sarajane, "let's have it. What dire prediction does Aunt Gennie have for me?"

Sarajane's only living relative, her aunt Genevieve Laroche, claimed to have descended from a seer who had turned New Orleans on its ear in the 1850s.

"Well...." Sarajane drew the word out for a moment longer than necessary, then glanced at Chloe, as if for help.

"Hey, don't look at me. She's your aunt."

"Quit looming over there," Sarajane said to Luce. "Sit down, would you?"

"Will me sitting down help your story come out any better?"

"It might."

"Oh, just get on with it!" Luce said, starting to feel exasperated.

"Okay, okay! Look, you know Aunt Gennie loves you like you were her niece, too, don't you?"

Luce nodded. "Aside from her voodoo connections,

she's a super nice woman."

"Voodoo," Sarajane muttered. "Sometimes I just want to smack you, Luce."

"I can still beat you up."

"You two are giving me a headache," Chloe said. "Just tell Luce the damned *juju*, will you?"

Still, Sarajane hesitated.

"What's wrong with you?" Luce demanded.

Sarajane seemed to shrink into her corner of the sofa. "I don't know. It was such a ridiculous story when I first heard it, but after today, and what I heard downstairs, it's not silly anymore."

"What is it then?"

"Scary," Sarajane admitted.

Chloe nodded. "And eerie."

"For crying out loud, if you don't tell me right now I'm going to bean you!"

Sarajane took a deep, shuddering breath. "Whatever she saw, she knew it involved you. There was an earring, and she kept seeing deuces, like on cards. Two of spades, two of hearts, two of clubs—"

"I get it," Luce said, somewhat impatiently.

"And she saw a black robe, floating in the air, with nothing attached to it. Down below on the ground, a man was running and jumping, trying to get the robe."

Luce almost choked on the symbolism of it all.

"It didn't mean anything yesterday when I told Chloe about it, but today, it seems to be *full* of meaning."

"Full," Chloe agreed.

"So, let's talk about it," Luce said, though she'd rather poke needles in her eyes than discuss this particular *juju*. "The earring thing is pretty obvious, isn't it? And innocuous. Nothing threatening about it at all."

"Unless you count that it was found in Play-Doh used to simulate C-4 in a bomb," Sarajane inserted sarcastically, "in *your* car."

"There is that," Luce admitted.

"And, its match was found on a dead girl," Chloe

contributed.

"And that, too," Luce granted them. "As for the deuces...."

"This is where it really gets eerie," Chloe said. "You come up with the theory that the Paired-Up Serials are at least three pairs of killers—"

"Maybe four pairs max, if Aunt Gennie saw only the four card suits," Luce said.

"If only," Sarajane added, "but she saw a *lot* of cards with different faces in the four suits."

Luce stared open-mouthed. "More than four?"

"Yes, but I didn't think to ask her how many. Should we call her?"

"Yes," Chloe responded instantly.

Sarajane looked back at Luce, who said, "Go ahead. Unfortunately—and call me crazy because I'm admitting this—maybe Aunt Gennie has an accurate count, and if she does, I think we need to know what that number is."

Sarajane dug her cell phone out of her pocket and speed dialed. When her aunt answered, she quickly told her what she wanted to know, then listened intently to the answer. "Thanks, Aunt G. No, she's fine for now, but if you get anything else, please call me right away, okay?"

"Well?" Luce asked.

"Twelve," Sarajane said, her tone numb. "Twelve deuces. Minimum."

"At least nine other states," Chloe said. "Minimum."

"Not good," Luce added. "Not good at all."

"We need to talk about the floating robe before we're interrupted by the guys," Sarajane said. "Are you and JD having problems? The tension is so thick between the two of you I almost got up to get a knife to cut it."

Luce snorted half a laugh. "You mean other than the fact that he hates what I do and doesn't want me running for the supreme court position? Yes. Hell, yes!" She dropped her head into her hands and began to cry softly.

Luce Maguire *never* cried.

A short time later, Luce raised her head and reached for her napkin to wipe her tears. Sarajane and Chloe watched her with worried eyes. "This morning, before all this happened, I was this close" —she held up her thumb and index finger about an inch apart— "to quitting the law. It's not just this trial, although that has a lot to do with it. It's everything about the law. I worked hard to get to and through law school, to pass the bar, to work as a prosecutor so I could be a judge, and beyond that, a supreme court judge, and you know what? I hate it! I fucking hate it!"

Sarajane and Chloe stared at their friend in shocked silence.

"I don't want to do it anymore," Luce admitted, "and it has nothing to do with JD hounding me." She hung her head again, and when she looked up at them, tears were still coursing down her cheeks. "I don't even know if I'm in love with JD anymore," she said on a whisper. "If we'd gotten married two years ago, we'd probably have started a family by now and I wouldn't be going through this mid-life crisis."

"You're too young to be having a mid-life crisis," Chloe said.

"Next birthday, I'll be thirty-six. If you double that, it's seventy-two. I could be at my mid-life."

"That is so freaking depressing," Sarajane said morosely.

Chloe said, "At least now I understand the robe floating and the man trying to get it down to the ground."

"Me and JD," Luce agreed. "Pathetic, isn't it? But the really weird thing is that I haven't seen or talked to him for over a week—I think he's the one who's getting ready to ditch me, so I really don't get him being the man on the ground chasing my robe."

They would have hashed it out more, but at that moment, a knock sounded on the closed door.

Marsh stepped into his office and went directly to Chloe. He put out a hand to help her up. "Gotta go," he said, "but I need some sustenance."

"Hmmm," she said. "I think there's some leftover chili in the fridge."

"I don't mean *food*."

"Of course you don't," she said, her tone sly. She peeked around her husband and said, "Girls, give us a minute, will you?"

"Love birds," Sarajane groused, unfolding herself from the sofa.

"Let's take a look at the nursery," Luce suggested, wiping her face this time with Sarajane's napkin. "I'm so bummed I never made it baby-shower shopping today." She linked arms with her old friend. They pulled the door closed behind them.

"Luce is all shook up over this bomb thing," Marsh said gravely.

"Yeah, but not so much the bomb as JD."

"He needs to grow up." He pulled Chloe into his arms. "I don't like leaving you here."

"I don't like you going, but almost the entire Salem PD and half the OSP is within shouting distance."

"Not quite."

"You know what I mean."

"I do." He lowered his head and kissed her, long and deep.

When they pulled apart, Chloe said, with a rueful look down at her belly, "I wish I could get closer."

"Hey, I like your bump!"

She grinned. "More like a camel hump."

He grinned back. "JD's staying at the house, under duress, and Dave has gone back to the station to put his brain and fingers to work online trying to find other crimes nationwide that match the Paired-Ups. Someone will be replacing him, but I don't know who."

"That's the *juju* Aunt Gennie was talking about," Chloe told him. "More pairs than just three or four."

"Shit."

"I know. What's JD so grumpy about, anyway?"

Marsh looked at his wife in surprise.

Inside information aside, Chloe said, "A blind woman could see there's something not right between them, Marsh."

# chapter 12

"What do you know?" Marsh asked. "What has Luce told you?"

"I can't say. What has JD told you?"

"I can't say, either."

"So, neither of us can say, but we both know they are in deep do-do."

"I would say that's a fair assessment."

"Should we intervene?"

"No."

"But—"

Marsh leaned down and kissed her again. "It's none of our business, babe."

"They're our friends," Chloe protested.

"True, but you don't get in the middle of other people's love affairs."

Chloe stuck out her bottom lip in a fake pout.

Marsh couldn't resist. He took the lip in between his and nibbled it with his teeth. "Delicious. Better than food."

Chloe put her arms around his neck and did her best to lean into him. "Dessert is ready when you are."

Marsh laughed. "Who knew pregnant ladies could be so inventive?"

Chloe withdrew her arms and turned her butt to him, pressing close.

"Don't start anything we can't finish," he begged.

This time Chloe laughed and grabbed his hand. "C'mon, before we both embarrass ourselves in front of all these people."

At the doorway, she hesitated before opening it, turning back to her husband. "Why is everyone still here? I thought Luce and JD would be ferreted away to some hyper-secure location by now."

"Good question. I've been wondering the same thing myself, and once I'm back at the station, I intend to ask the LT just that."

"No one even mentioned it at the table."

"It was kind of like a decision had already been made before the upper echelon ever got here, even though the LT and the OSP guy both mentioned it when they arrived."

"I'm no expert on protecting people, of course, but my thoughts exactly."

"That's why I married you, because you're so smart."

"Ha!"

"One of the *many* reasons," he said, giving her one last kiss. He reached around her for the door knob. "Promise me you won't do anything rash."

Chloe laughed, patting her belly. "Rash? Really?"

Marsh put his big hand over hers, giving her a serious look. "Really."

Brenden or Mary Kate chose that moment to give his or her mom a big kick. "Wow," Marsh said with reverence.

"I think they play soccer in there," Chloe said. "I'm the ball."

Marsh grinned. "Let's go, soccer ball. I've got a lot to do before I can be back here for dinner."

"Oh, no!" Chloe ground to a halt. "Dinner!"

"Don't worry, sweetheart. I'm going to pick up some pizzas."

"Thank you! Maybe I should go to the grocery store, get some cereals and milk for breakfast."

"You're not going anywhere, remember? Everyone in the house, *stays* in the house."

"Sorry. I forgot I'm grounded."

Marsh chuckled. "You're not grounded."

"Feels like it."

"Do I have to remind you that *you* are the one who insisted on going down to get Luce, then bringing her back to our house?"

"Why do you have to be so sensible?" she grumbled.

"I refuse to answer, for my own safety."

"I married you because you're smart, too," Chloe informed him.

Marsh choked back a laugh.

"Hey, you guys, the nursery is so sweet!" Sarajane said from the end of the hall. "I love the way you've done it all in either-gender décor."

"Very smart," Luce agreed. "And so charming." She looked at Marsh. "Two of everything, including rockers."

Marsh looked at Chloe and grinned. "My wife says, if she has to be up in the middle of the night, so do I."

"Just don't forget, I'm up for babysitting anytime," Sarajane said.

Luce looked at her friend in disbelief. "You?"

"Don't look so shocked," Sarajane said. "I've been reading up on babies and I'm going to take the infant care class with Chloe and Marsh so we all know what we're doing."

"Are you thinking about having a baby?" Luce asked.

A fleeting look of hurt flashed across Sarajane's features. "I just thought Marsh and Chloe might like to go out sometimes, alone, and they'd need someone they could trust to watch the kidlets." Her chin went up a little bit. "You're welcome to join us, if you want to learn how to change a baby diaper."

Luce surprised them all by saying, "Maybe I will, but right now, I have more pressing issues. Marsh, would it be possible for a patrol officer to accompany Sarie to my place to pick up some clothes and sundries for me? I need to get comfortable and I certainly can't sleep in this suit, if I end up spending the night here."

"I don't see why not. As soon as I get back to the station, I'll see about sending someone over. I suppose I could to the same for JD."

"Hey, I don't want to go through his stuff!" Sarajane protested.

"I didn't mean *you*, Sarie. I meant I'd do it for him," Marsh said.

"Thank goodness. I might freak out if I had to start poking through a guy's underwear."

The three of them stared at her.

"What? You all know I am not the dating queen, right? I don't even know what men's underwear looks like, anyway."

"Oh, please," Luce said.

"I don't." Sarajane's eyes flew to Marsh. "Do I?"

"Why are you asking me?" he demanded, but he already knew the answer.

Sarajane Nichols was in love with his brother Dominic. Father Dominic. Dom had taken priestly vows nearly twenty years ago, and Sarajane had taken her own vows of celibacy right along with him. If she couldn't have Dominic, she wouldn't have anyone.

It was sad and poignant at the same time, and if Dom ever decided to come home again, Marsh just might kick his butt over it. Sarajane ought to have an opportunity for happiness.

Sarajane shrugged and retorted. "Maybe I'll just peruse *your* underwear drawer while you're gone."

"Peeping Sarie," Marsh said, trying to keep a straight face. "Whatever fires up your jets, kid."

A moment later, he yelped when his beautiful and

amazing wife pinched him pretty damned hard.

# chapter 13

*t* he afternoon wore on with all the speed of a DMV employee on break.

Luce changed into a sweater and blue jeans that Sarajane had included in her overnight bag. She went barefoot, except for a pair socks, to Chloe's office. There she spent the time reading a draft of Chloe's latest book about Christian Longo, the deranged sociopath who had killed his wife and three children, then thrown their bodies, stuffed in suitcases, into the river at Waldport. Luce was familiar with the case. Who wasn't in Oregon?

She jotted editorial comments in the margin, per Chloe's request, catching an occasional typo or missing word, and in one section, made suggestions for a rear-rangement of the material to make it less confusing for lay readers.

Longo had run to Mexico afterward, where he was soon found and returned to Oregon. A dozen years later, on death row, he had finally admitted his guilt and was now supposedly attempting to "atone" for his crimes by trying to get permission to donate all his organs upon his death by lethal injection. He even had a website set up for the purpose of getting other inmates to do the same.

"Lethal injection, my ass," Luce muttered. No one had been executed in Oregon since 1997, and unless something changed drastically, Longo would die an old man in prison.

Just thinking about the narcissistic, murdering bastard was enough to push Luce's buttons, but the fact that he was granted privileges like Internet access sent her blood to boiling. Probably, he'd bought a TV for his cell, too. Such was the state of justice these days, where punishment included television with cable.

If only the governor of Oregon would lift his moratorium on the death penalty, or someone else was elected who would, justice could finally be served on all those who had committed the monstrous crimes that had landed them on death row.

The inequities and vagaries of criminal justice contributed to Luce's building disillusionment with the system. And yet, what would she do, if not the law, a profession she had trained for and practiced for years? Get a job at a gas station? For crying out loud, she lived in a state where it was illegal to pump your own gas. She'd never even held a nozzle! Flip burgers? Data entry? Telemarketing? Door-to-door sales?

Incredible as it seemed, she had no skills outside the law, even for the most elementary job.

Depressing, that's what it was. Depressing. Luce pushed back all thoughts of it—the law, a second career, her unhappiness, in general—and began to read again.

Chloe was an engaging writer and several times Luce found herself tearful over the events that had transpired in the Longo case. Just seeing the pictures of the sweet little children Chloe had included in the book caused Luce's heart to break. How could a father kill his own children?

No one ever had an answer for that. Not the father. Not the system. And certainly not Luce Maguire.

As she flipped over the final page of Chapter Five,

she had the feeling of being watched. She looked over her shoulder and found JD standing in the doorway, leaning against the jamb, his gaze intent on her, yet his expression giving away nothing.

"Busy?" he asked.

"No, just reading Chloe's book. She asked me to comment as I go. She's an excellent writer."

"She is. Want a cup of coffee or a hot chocolate?"

"Actually, a hot chocolate sounds yummy." She started to rise, but he motioned her down.

"I'll get it," he said. "The teapot's already hot."

"Thanks." She watched him turn and walk away, wondering if this overture was one of consideration or a prelude to the final showdown.

JD returned a few minutes later, a steaming cup in each hand.

She scooted away from the desk and stood. "Thanks."

Chloe had two easy chairs in front of the fireplace, which had been converted to gas when the room had been renovated from a parlor into her office a few years back. Luce settled into one, JD the other.

Chloe was upstairs napping. Dave's replacement, Andy Parr, was at the top of the stairs. Tiger stood at the doorway to Chloe's office. "Want the door closed?" he asked.

With a smile, Luce said, "Thanks," at the same time JD said, "Yes, please."

"Alone at last," JD said, his tone dry.

"Umm." Luce shivered, wishing she had a sweater.

"It's raining again."

"I noticed."

"Are you cold?"

"A little chilled." Knowing an ax was about to drop could do that to a person.

JD put his cup down on the table between them and pushed himself out of the chair. He flipped on the fireplace, then reached for the throw across the ottoman and placed it over her legs. "Better?"

"Yes, thanks." She tilted her head, baffled. As he eased his big body back into the chair, she said, "You're always so solicitous of my comfort, and yet I haven't heard word one from you in at least eight days." She hoped the remark came out without accusation, just a statement of fact.

His gaze, planted on the flames in the fireplace, lingered there for several moments before he spoke. Prefaced by a huge sigh, he said, "Our relationship isn't working."

"No," she agreed, amazed at how calm she sounded, "it isn't."

That brought his head around with a surprised jerk. "What are you saying?"

Her tone chiding, she said, "The same thing *you're* saying. We don't seem to *have* a relationship anymore. Especially when I don't see or hear from you for over a week."

"We have passion in bed," he argued.

Luce blew on her hot chocolate, pleased that he'd remembered a big fluffy marshmallow on top, dismayed because his caring didn't go deep enough to fix what was wrong between them. "A lifelong commitment involves more than passionate sex."

He gave her a crooked smile. "But you do admit it's good between us that way."

Luce didn't return one of her own, even though just the sight of his caused her insides to curl in a way that made her want to do the nasty with him right then and there. She took a sip of the still-too-hot liquid in her cup and it burned her tongue, effectively wiping thoughts of intimacy with JD out of her mind for a moment. "What's not to admit. We screw ourselves senseless, and I've never experienced anything better, but what about support, trust, love?"

"I love you."

"Maybe so, but are you *in* love with me?"

He hesitated a moment too long. "Don't you think we

have trust?"

"It's a package deal. I support you in whatever you decide to do—unless you decide to kill yourself. I trust you implicitly, even with my life. And I used to be in love with you."

His jaw clenched. "Used to be…?"

"Don't sound so shocked, JD. You brought this up. It's been percolating for months. Maybe even since the day we met. No matter how many times I hear it, nothing you've ever said has made sense about why you don't like me being a judge, or why you don't want me to throw my hat in the ring for the state supreme court." She paused, searching for the right words. "Sometimes you're like the little boy who covers his eyes—if he can't see the monster under the bed, the monster can't see him."

JD faced front again, studying the flames intently.

"At first, I thought it was fear *for* me. I can understand fear. I face it every day when you're on the streets, chasing lunatics with guns and knives and whatever other tools they use to kill and do bodily harm. I'm not out on the street, but I face those same people in the courtroom. I have my bailiff and my gun, which make me feel safe while I'm presiding, but outside, I have no protection."

She shrugged. "I may get hit by a car while crossing the street, but I can't live my life in fear for myself or for you. I have to temper that fear, *trusting* that at the end of each day, we'll both still be here, ready to tackle the next day."

She stopped, took a deep breath, plunged on, and couldn't believe she was speaking so rationally and without emotion. "I face my monsters with my eyes open, JD. I *support* your choice and I would never ask you to give up being a cop. You love your work, you're good at it, you take precautions that give me peace of mind, and you have a partner, who I know has your back every day."

He locked gazes with her, his emotions clearly grappling with each other, if the conflicted expressions on his almost too-handsome face and in his eyes were accurate.

Luce steeled her heart to his turmoil and forged on. "You don't want me to run for supreme court judge, but every argument is the same—I won't have time for family, I won't have time for you, I won't have time for myself." She shook her head in disgust. "Stupid arguments. *Ridiculous* arguments. I would overrule them in court! Do you know there's a federal judge in Eugene who has given birth to five sons? Women can hold a baby in both arms and still a have hand free to cook a man's dinner. Could you do that?"

Still he said nothing, but his obvious internal chaos churned on.

"When you asked me to marry you, I went straight to Cloud Nine. You're intelligent, you have a great sense of humor, and—don't let this go to your head—you're fabulous to look at, from the top of that headful of sandy-brown hair all the way down to your little toes."

Luce took another sip from her cup, then set it aside. She licked the marshmallow off her lip, then fiddled with the fringe on the blanket. Finally she said, "Making love with you is always an amazing experience. I never want it to end, but maybe therein lies the problem. For me, it's making love. For you, it's having sex."

She closed her eyes for a moment, fortifying herself, frustrated beyond belief by his silence. When she opened them, he was regarding her intently, suddenly giving nothing away of his feelings. "To me, sex means it's temporary, JD. Making love means permanence. We should have already been married by now, had a least one child, maybe another on the way. You've been reticent all along. I'm starting to feel used, like I'm nothing more than a convenient sex partner for you."

When he still didn't deny it, she went on, not even realizing she was twisting her engagement ring around on her finger. "Let's be amicable about this. No hard feelings." Though she hadn't consciously planned it, she had the ring off and extended it to him. "This should make it easier for you." When he didn't take it, she set the gorgeous two-carat diamond set in platinum next to his cup.

God, she'd loved that ring, from the moment he'd taken it out of the velvet box. She almost felt naked without it. "Easier for both of us."

"So, that's it?"

"You're the one who said our relationship isn't working. I just agreed with you."

He stared at her, his jaw clenched so hard she could see it flexing.

She loved those not-quite-green, oh-so-sexy eyes of his. Loved it when she was the cause of them heating up. That was all over and done with now. "What, you weren't building up to asking for the ring back?"

He looked down at it, uttered the f-bomb, then stood, towering in front of her. "So, you read me like a book, do you?"

She gave him a sad smile. "No, I *don't* read you like a book. If I did, I'd know how to fix your problem. You'd have an instruction manual."

His face tightened with anger. "So, it's only *my* problem?"

"From my perspective, yes."

"How the hell do you get off scot-free?"

"For a former psychologist you can be so dense, JD. It took me a while, but I finally figured it out. You're afraid of commitment and you use every lame-brained argument about my career that you can think of to justify your actions, when all you really have to do is *trust* me. I wouldn't have taken anything from you that I didn't give back twofold. That's what love is all about."

He clenched his big fists, looked like he wanted to argue, but couldn't find the words with which to do the job, telling Luce she'd hit a nerve. Big time.

Having just uttered the hardest words she, herself, had ever had to speak, she glanced pointedly at his cup, then back at him. "Would you mind closing the door behind you?"

And then she prayed she'd be able to keep her tears at bay until he was out of hearing distance.

# chapter 14

*J*D stalked into the kitchen, wishing he had something stronger to drink. A lot stronger. He went to the cupboard where Marsh kept his liquor and withdrew the bottle of Maker's Mark, filling his half-full coffee cup nearly to the rim.

Luce had just beat the shit out of him, figuratively speaking. Not that he didn't deserve it. He had, after all, gone into that room *intending* to end their relationship. He'd expected to break her heart, had gone in prepared for tears, shouting, accusations. He hadn't expected to come out with his balls lopped off.

Luce had been calm, prepared. He hadn't expected her to break up with him, even though he'd told himself repeatedly that's the way he wanted it to happen. So he wouldn't be the one who was guilt-ridden afterward. He also hadn't expected to hurt bone-deep.

The way it had transpired left him shell-shocked, not only with her cool-headed, almost dispassionate delivery of the facts as she saw them, but about what he had just learned about himself.

She had him nailed. Bull's-eye. One hundred percent.

Big Bad JD Kemp was a coward, pure and simple, when it came to commitment. Hell, even Marsh had called it on the drive back just hours ago.

What he'd done to Luce, stringing her along for the past two years, was as rotten as rotten could get. She should have been free to find another man who wasn't terrified of tying himself to one woman for the rest of his life, having kids with her, growing old with her.

Jesus, no wonder he couldn't hack it as a psychologist!

Just how stupid and dense could a guy get? He'd gone in there to break up with Luce, fully expecting they'd still share the bed in the spare room tonight, regardless. To compound matters, he'd done it when she had to be at one of life's low points, and with her life in peril, to boot.

He was worse than dense. He was a total freaking idiot! Clueless! Plus stupid. And a jerk. And let's not forget inconsiderate.

JD looked at his watch. Only five. Marsh had moved bedroom stuff from the spare room that was now his office up to the attic once he'd finished that renovation. Sarajane had delivered the duffel Marsh had thrown together for him. Being Luce's friend, he half-expected to find she'd planted a poisonous snake or a smoke bomb on top to greet him.

JD decided he might as well head up to the attic and get to work now that he had his laptop. The house had wi-fi and he could log into several law enforcement databases and do some searching on his own, even if he wasn't allowed to get back on the street. He'd grab a set of sheets from the upstairs closet on his way.

*You made your bed, sucka, now sleep in it!*

He *was* a sucker. Man, he had to get his head around all of this before it exploded. That probably meant he wouldn't be able to think about anything but Luce, but he had to try.

On his way up the stairs, he passed Chloe coming

down. She'd napped for a couple of hours, but she didn't particularly look rested.

"Anything I can do for you, darlin'?"

She stopped two steps above him, blinked at him a couple of times, then said, "No, thanks. Where's Luce?"

"In your office."

Chloe nodded. "Ah, the book."

"It will keep her busy," JD said. "Keep her mind off of…things."

She arched an eyebrow at him. "I hope it will. Men and bombs don't mix."

She proceeded down, leaving JD wondering if she'd meant him when she'd said *men*, and knew damned good and well she had.

Marsh's wife was too intuitive for her own good sometimes. JD guessed that's what made her such an adept writer, but it played hell on his ego that she might think less of him for the way he'd handled his relationship with Luce. "Give a holler if you need me," he called after her. "I'll be working on my laptop in the attic."

He couldn't be sure, but he thought her reply was, "Good."

The single-syllable word from the woman who made a career out of writing couldn't have been more full of innuendo if she'd put it up in neon.

Even though it was her own office, in her own house, Chloe knocked on the door. She had a feeling, given the thundercloud over JD's head as she'd passed him on the stairs, that Luce might not want to be disturbed.

"Who is it?" came the muffled reply.

Chloe gnawed on her lower lip, thinking. "It's me."

"Can you come back in a little bit?"

Chloe looked at Tiger, standing near the front window, staring at his feet. "Yes. I'll…be in the kitchen."

She stood immobile for several moments. "Rough afternoon?" she asked the patrol officer.

"For some," he answered obliquely.

"Need a bathroom break or a snack?"

"Nah, I'm good Mrs. Fielding."

"Chloe."

He smiled at her, taking ten years off his face.

She smiled back, turning away from office. "I'll just be…." She pointed eastward.

"In the kitchen," he finished for her. "Let me know if you need anything, ma'am."

*I need a crystal ball,* she almost told him. A crystal ball to help figure out this mess between Luce and JD. Officer Tiger would no doubt look at her askance if she whipped out such a device and started rubbing it, gazing into its hazy depths for answers. The thought of helping patch up a broken romance with a crystal ball made her smile. If only! It would be the least she could do, since she had nothing to contribute to the pseudo-bomb investigation. Of course, Marsh would have a cow if he got wind that she was even hypothetically intervening!

And of course, there were ways to detract him….

Chloe grinned and busied herself pulling paper plates and napkins from the pantry, got forks from the drawer and condiments from their various storage places, taking everything to the dining room through the little-used connecting pocket door. She put everything on the sideboard, buffet style, for easier access.

Back in the kitchen, she checked the fridge for beverages. Marsh had replenished the Diet Coke and 7UP before he'd left, and there were several bottles of beer, plus bottled water.

Satisfied that her guests wouldn't die of thirst or starvation since Marsh was bringing pizzas home, Chloe grabbed her cell phone and dialed Sarajane. "Hi," she said when her friend answered. "Will you be coming back tonight?"

"I thought I would. Will that be okay?"

"Yes." She dropped her voice. "I think JD and Luce must have had a split-up talk while I was napping. He's up in the attic making a lot of noise for someone who's supposed to be working on his laptop. She's in my office, crying."

"God, this is so screwed up! They don't need to be distracted with love problems when someone's threatening their lives."

"That's a given, but what can we do about it?"

"I don't know. I have to finish up some paperwork, then I want to go home and change clothes. After that, I'll be over. In the meantime, I'll put what's left of my brain on it."

"Marsh, um, wants me to stay out of it."

Sarajane laughed. "Of course, he does. JD's his partner, Luce is his friend. I'd put money on it that they've *both* been unloading on him for quite some time, poor guy. He'll end up thanking us when we get them back together again."

Chloe frowned. "*If* we can get them back together. And in any case, I'm not so sure he'll *thank* us."

"Don't worry, sweetie. I've known your husband a long time. He never stays angry for very long."

Chloe remembered the first and last time Marsh had gotten angry, *really* angry, with her. Two weeks had sure *seemed* like a long time. Mary-the-Ghostly-Spirit had devised Plan B, in case Chloe's attempt to get pregnant by intrauterine insemination failed, which it did. Mary's Plan B had equaled Marsh, but it wasn't Chloe's plan. It had taken him a while to get that, but he'd finally come to his senses and realized she meant it when she said it was *him* she loved, not his baby-making ability.

Chloe glanced ruefully down at her swollen belly, rubbing it softly. When they met, Marsh had believed he couldn't father children, and now look—he was going to have twins! The miracle of modern medical science was something to behold.

"Chloe, you still there?"

"Chloe, you still there?"

"Sorry, I got side-tracked. See you soon, and by the

way, I'm really craving some ice cream—would you mind picking up a half-gallon of Umpqua strawberry? Hmm, better make it two, since somebody else might want some."

Sarajane laughed. "No problem. Do you want some pickles, too?"

Grinning, Chloe said, "Smart ass," and disconnected.

# chapter 15

*d*inner was a hungry, if fairly quiet, affair. All the pizza got eaten (the two pairs of officers outside the front and back doors each got a box of their own) and an impressive dent had been made in the strawberry ice cream. Even the jar of baby kosher dills stood empty.

Afterward, Luce and Sarajane cleaned up, insisting Chloe go sit down somewhere and put her feet up. Chloe complied, seating herself back down at the dining room table with her feet up on an adjoining chair. She had another bowl of ice cream for company while she watched her friends work through the open doorway into the kitchen.

JD and Marsh headed upstairs to Marsh's office. Officers Tiger and Andy switched places for awhile, so Chloe talked to Andy until the commotion in the kitchen ceased. Then, licking the last drop off her spoon, she got up and went to join her friends around the kitchen table.

Andy hung back in the dining room where he could see but not hear, giving them privacy.

"Okay, give," Sarajane said to Luce, her voice lowered.

Luce's eyes welled, but no tears spilled. She shrugged. "I was reading the draft of Chloe's book, he came in and wanted to talk about our relationship. I basically said, 'What relationship?' and told him how I felt, called him a coward for being a commitment-phope, gave him his ring back, and that was that."

"He didn't argue with you about it?" Sarajane demanded.

"He's been arguing with me forever about my career and the judgeship. He's keen on the sexual aspect of things, but other than that, he had nothing to say. What else was there to discuss?"

"Is there hope you'll reconcile?" Chloe asked.

Luce shrugged again. "I don't know. I don't think so."

"Let me rephrase that," Chloe said. "Do you *want* to reconcile?"

Luce folded her arms on the table and laid her head down for several moments. A few tears had escaped by the time she raised her head and spoke. "I asked JD if he was still in love with me. He said he still loved me, but he wouldn't say he was *in* love. Maybe it's a man-woman thing, but I think there's a difference between loving and being in love."

"I'd have to agree," Sarajane said, her tone somber.

"Me, too," Chloe agreed. "This just sucks."

"I'd drink to that if you had some wine," Sarajane said.

"I have wine," Chloe said.

Sarajane perked up. "You do?" Then, "That wouldn't be right, us drinking in front of you when you can't because you're, you know, *preggers*."

Chloe laughed. "Tell me something I don't know! It's not like I drink regularly anyway."

"Which is why she told us about her ghost the night she got bombed—oops, wrong choice of word!" Luce said. "Substitute *hammered*."

Luce was retrieving wine glasses and Sarajane was getting white wine out of the fridge when Luce's phone rang. Since it was on the table, where Chloe had been relegated to sit and relax, she asked, "Shall I get it?"

"Please," said Luce, digging in a drawer for the corkscrew.

"Hello."

"How was pizza, bitch?"

"What?" Shocked, Chloe pulled the phone away for a moment. Caller Unknown. She pushed away from the table and went to the kitchen swing-door, pushing it open.

Andy Parr immediately trailed her.

"Don't play games, bitch. I know you and your scared little mice friends had pizza for dinner."

"I'm sorry, but you must have the wrong number." She pantomimed frantically toward the top of the stairs for Tiger to get Marsh and JD.

"Listen, your bitchship, don't play fucking games with me."

"No need to get nasty. You have the wrong number." As soon as she saw her husband and JD at the top of the stairs, she disconnected.

"It was him," she said. "Marsh, you said at dinner that the call to Luce's phone had come from a pay phone."

"Yeah. And?"

"They're probably calling from a phone booth this time, too. Close enough to know that we had pizza for dinner." Chloe took a breath. "I know this neighborhood, Marsh. There's only one pay phone in the immediate vicinity, and it's at the gas station." Totally off-topic, she added, "They joke about it being the only pay phone in the country that you can still call from for a dime. Somehow, it's been off the phone company's radar."

Luce's phone rang again.

"One more thing," Chloe said. "He's not using a synthesizer and he's desperate. He's going to keep trying."

The phone rang again.

Luce reached for it, but Marsh stopped her. "Hold on. I get Chloe's drift."

The phone continued to ring. "Okay, sweetheart," he said to Chloe, "keeping 'em calling back as long as you can."

He gave Chloe's arm a squeeze. "Tiger and Andy, you know what to do here. JD, you're with me. Get some units there, no sirens." He rattled off the names of the intersecting streets.

The front door slammed just as Chloe said, "Hello?"

"Don't you fucking hang up on me again, Judge."

"Judge? Hey, are you the same guy who just called about some pizzas? I told you, you have the wrong number. Why don't your recheck your number and dial again?"

"I'm getting sick of your bullshit," the caller screamed.

Chloe tried to inject some emotion into her voice. "Look, I don't know who you are or who you think you called, but I don't know you, and I didn't have any pizza for dinner. Please leave me alone!"

Again, she disconnected.

And sat down. Lying was stressful.

When the phone rang again a few minutes later, everyone jumped, even though they were expecting it. Unknown Caller.

Chloe let it ring several times before she answered. "Hello?"

"I've checked the number, you stupid bitch, and I'm dialing it right! Don't fucking hang up on me again!"

"No offense, mister, but you must be an idiot," Chloe said. "I'm telling you for the final time—I didn't have pizza for dinner, I am not a judge, and I don't know who the heck you are!

"Shut up!" he screamed.

"What number are you trying to call?" she screamed

back, startling even herself.

He recited the numbers as if he was talking to a moron.

"That's your problem, buster. You're inverting the last two numbers."

"*What?*"

"Are you suddenly hard of hearing? Who are you, anyway?"

"None of your goddamned business. Who the fuck are you?"

"None of *your* business."

Standoff. But still connected. The longer, the better. *Please God, let Marsh and JD get there in time. Let them be safe while they get this whack job.*

"You got a mouth on you, bitch."

"I have a brain, too, which you obviously don't." She counted to five, hung up.

The five of them waited in silence. One minute passed, then two.

They all looked at each other.

Three.

Four.

Brenden and Mary Kate took to playing soccer. Chloe's belly was so obviously moving, Luce, Sarajane, and the two officers watched it in fascination.

Five.

Finally, the phone rang again. After three rings, Luce took the call.

# chapter 16

"*h*ello?"

"Who is this?"

"Who's calling?" Luce asked.

The phone was on speaker. Everyone remained stock-still, listening.

"Don't play games with me, you goddamned, ball-breaking bitch!"

Luce had been called worse, but not with such venom. "I take it you're the bomb-making asshole," she retorted.

A brief moment of silence told her he had expected a cowed response from her. "Tread lightly, judge."

"And if I don't, you'll what? Put more Play-Doh under my hood?"

"Play-Doh? What the hell are you talking about?"

Startled, Luce looked up into the faces of the four people hovering at the table.

"Careful," Tiger mouthed.

"What do you want?" Luce asked, instead of answering his last question.

"Where did your boyfriend and his partner take off to

in such a hurry?"

Luce gasped, hoping the caller hadn't heard. Some-one was still watching the house. "A multiple homicide," she improvised, even as Tiger left the room, his cell phone out, motioning Andy to the back door.

Andy took the direction, closing the door softly behind him as he went out. Luce heard the front door open and close.

"Ah, too bad. More people dead," he mocked.

"How many have you killed?" she asked, not feeling as brazen as her tone indicated.

Chloe and Sarajane exchanged worried looks.

"Not as many as I'm going to."

"Your buddies, the Paired-Up Serials, are taking credit for some of yours, aren't they? Is that the way all of you do it? If some get arrested and go to trial, they take the credit for others, so the rest of you can keep killing?"

"You don't know shit!"

"Once we realized how many of you there are, it was easy to figure out—"

"*Fuck, fuck, fuck!*" the caller screamed.

They heard something, probably the handset, banging against something else, which might have been the housing unit, although the sound of breaking glass contributed to the mayhem.

"He's pissed," Sarajane whispered.

A moment later, they heard, "Police! Step out of the phone booth with your hands in the air, where we can see them."

A moment after that, a gunshot rang out, and total pandemonium broke loose.

In front of Chloe's house, a similar outbreak ensued. A couple of gunshots were fired. Andy came back inside. From the radio on his shoulder came, "Dispatch, officer down," but then there was so much commotion, no one could make out the location.

Was it Chloe's front yard, or the gas station?

Luce jumped up and ran to Chloe's office to retrieve her purse. She withdrew a Compact Walther.

"Upstairs," Andy instructed them. He looked down at the gun in Luce's hand.

"I know how to use it," she said.

Sarajane retrieved her purse from the sofa and withdrew a small pistol, as well. "Smith and Wesson. I know how to use this one, too."

Andy looked at Chloe.

"Hey, I don't even know how to load a gun, let alone shoot one!"

"C'mon, let's move," Andy said again. He took up the rear, behind Chloe.

"Marsh's office only has one window," Chloe said. All the others are corner rooms and have two. We could also go on up to the attic."

"Let's start in the office and move if we have to. Is the attic access nearby?" Andy asked.

"Yes," Chloe said. "The attic stairs are past Marsh's office and across from the spare bedroom."

Several minutes later, Chloe was situated in a far corner in one of the easy chairs Luce and Sarajane had pushed over for her. They also moved the mission-style sofa crossways in the corner. Luce and Sarajane were on their knees behind it.

Andy stood beside the closed door, his weapon drawn and aimed at the floor, waiting. He seemed a little agitated, but weren't they all?

An eternity passed before anything happened. No one heard the door open downstairs, but they all heard the clomping of footsteps up the stairs and Marsh shouting Chloe's name.

"Careful, Andy," Luce warned as the young officer reached for the doorknob. "You don't know if someone has him at gunpoint, giving him instructions."

"Yes, ma'am, I know." He opened the door about six inches and stood aside, his weapon aimed at the opening. Whoever came in would not immediately have a direct line of sight toward the sofa and the three women in the corner, two of them with guns pointed at the doorway.

"Chloe!" Marsh called again.

They heard footsteps running toward the master bedroom, then back out and into the nursery. Back out again and down the hall.

Andy lowered his gun and opened the door further. "In here, sir."

"Thank God," they heard Marsh say. They also heard another voice. JD.

Andy raised his arm unexpectedly, taking aim into the hall. Simultaneously, a woman screamed and six shots rang out. Andy Parr fell to the floor.

"Chloe, stay!" Luce ordered, jumping over the back of the sofa. "You, too, Sarie."

Luce approached the doorway and kicked the gun away from the patrol officer's hand.

"Marsh!" Chloe screamed, held back by Sarajane. *"What just happened here?"*

"Give me time to check!" Luce said, her tone terse with fear. *Please, God, not JD, not Marsh.*

She pushed the door all the way open and stuck her head around the jamb. JD was on the floor, sprawled against the stair rail. She didn't see any blood, but he was obviously in pain. Marsh crept silently toward her, his weapon drawn, aimed straight toward her chest. "No more bad guys," she said, lowering her own gun. "We're all okay.

She and Marsh rushed past each other, him toward Chloe, she toward JD.

"I'm okay," she heard Chloe tell her husband. "Are you?"

"Yes, but JD's hit."

"Go," Chloe said.

Luce knelt next to JD, pulling his hand away from his chest. She saw the bullet hole in his shirt right away. Her heart went directly up into her throat. "Ohmygod."

"This goddamned vest...is uncomfortable as

hell...and that hurt...like a bastard." He gasped as he shifted, struggling to draw a regular breath.

Luce quickly unbuttoned his shirt to see for herself. Sure enough, a bullet from Andy's gun had lodged in the Kevlar, roughly in the vicinity of JD's heart.

"Just...give me...a minute," JD said.

Luce bowed her head and thanked God and anyone else up there who was listening for giving her a second chance, for saving the man she loved. The man who had no heart for commitment, but had nearly lost the one he needed to keep on living. How could she have been so foolish, to think she no longer loved him?

In the Marsh's office, Chloe was arguing with him that she didn't need to lay down. Between the two of them, Sarajane and Marsh got her out of the room and onto the landing where JD lay, with Luce hovering over him.

"What the *hell* is going on?" Sarajane demanded. "And by the way, I'm glad you're both still alive!" she said to JD and Marsh.

"Thanks," JD said on a gasp. "I think. Jesus...who knew a...bullet to the Kevlar...could hurt...so goddamn-ed much?"

# chapter 17

"**f**orensics is going to be up here shortly," Marsh said, "Let's take this downstairs. Can you get up, JD?"

JD nodded and Marsh gave him a hand. He holstered his weapon and used the handrail to make his way to the head of the stairs and down with Marsh's help. The women followed.

They made their way into the dining room, where Marsh brought over an ottoman from Chloe's office for her to put feet up. "Everyone okay?" he asked.

At four nods, he said, "Stay put. I'm calling a bus for JD. Tiger will come in to keep an eye on all of you."

"I don't need medical attention," JD protested.

"Shut up!" Marsh snarled. "I'm in no mood to fucking argue with you, and I need your brain on this as soon as possible. They give you the all-clear, and you're back out there with me." He stormed out the door.

JD had his mouth open, but snapped it shut. He unbuttoned his shirt.

Luce put her weapon and JD's, which she'd removed from his holster, on the table. She helped him get out of his shirt and the vest. He didn't complain, but his face flushed with the exertion and sweat began to pour down his brow. "I'm sorry," she kept saying, trying to be as gentle as possible. "Where is that ambulance?" she fretted.

"I'll go see," Sarajane said, even though they hadn't heard a siren. She put the safety on her gun and added to the two already on the table.

Tiger stepped aside so she could pass through the doorway. Looking shell-shocked, he glanced at JD and said, "What the hell? Andy?"

"Did you…know him?" JD asked with a grunt.

Tiger shook his head. "None of us did. He was relatively new. I can't believe he went to Babylon."

"Babylon?" Chloe asked.

"Corrupted. Dirty cop." Tiger almost spat the words. "Little prick dishonored the badge."

Activity at the front door turned Tiger around, his hand on the butt of the gun in his holster. "EMTs," he said, stepping out of the way.

"Busy night," one of the men said. He knelt down beside JD and opened up his kit. "Looks like you caught one in the Kevlar."

"Yeah…lucky me," JD said.

"Lucky or not, you're going in for a check-up. This baby landed too damned near your heart."

"I'm not—"

"You *are*," said Kerry Schaeffer, JD's supervisor.

"LT, where did you…come from?" JD mumbled, still struggling for an even breath.

"I always show up when part of my team starts shooting up the neighborhood."

"Yeah, well part of your team…wants his shirt back so he can get back…out there."

Kerry pointed an index finger at JD. "You will submit to whatever the paramedics tell you, then you're going in the ambulance to the hospital. SOP for all vest hits. Can't have you keeling over later because we didn't get you checked out."

"But—"

"*Goddamnit!*" Kerry shouted, "I'm getting fucking sick and tired of my team arguing with me. Got it?"

JD glared at him. "Got it...*Boss*."

More commotion ensued at the front door. "Forensics," Tiger said and pointed them up the stairs. "Take a left, first door on the right. You'll know it by the dead piece of shit in the doorway."

Kerry clamped a hand down on Tiger's shoulder. "Take it easy, buddy. It's not Andy Parr upstairs."

Startled, Tiger said, "What?"

"Parr was just found by another patrol unit, near the first blockade. He'd been hit on the head, stripped of his uniform and weapon and shoved into the trunk of his car."

"Oh, no," Chloe said. "Is he...is he alive?"

"Barely," the LT said. "The first EMT responder stopped to assist there. The FD had to send out another unit for JD."

Tiger actually teared up. He looked heavenward and said, "Forgive me for my bad thoughts. I rescind them. And I pray for the real Andy to survive." He tipped his head down and was silent. The paramedics kept working, but were quiet, perhaps doing their own praying with the others in the room.

"Where's Marsh?" Chloe asked.

"He's back at the gas station."

"Will he be there long?"

Kerry went around the table and knelt beside her. "This is going to be a long night for all of us, Chloe. We got one guy in the phone booth, and another one in a van in the parking lot. And we got this guy upstairs, who apparently had been texting his buddies from here. That's how they knew about the pizzas."

"Wait a second," Luce said. "Why didn't he text them about phone scam Chloe was pulling on them?"

"He wasn't out of our sight," Sarajane interjected. "Except when he went to the bathroom, or when he left us alone in the kitchen. That's probably when he sent the text about the pizzas. After that, he was close-by, listening to the phone calls. He couldn't do anything about it."

Chloe said, "When we heard gunfire, he was outside the back door."

Sarajane chewed on that for a moment. "He wasn't out there long enough to text, especially in the dark."

"What was all the shooting we heard?"

"Someone got trigger happy, thought he saw someone with a gun and fired." Kerry frowned. "Sorry about disrupting your neighborhood, Chloe. JD and Luce will both be out of here immediately."

Luce stood, wringing her hands. "We should never have come here!"

"They found you here, they could've found you anywhere," Chloe said.

"She's right," Sarajane concurred.

"The ruse was smart thinking on your part, Chloe," Kerry said, giving Chloe's arm a squeeze. "Because of the way you handled that, we were able to get into that block where the gas station is, secure it, and grab two of the Paired-Ups' associates."

"It was brilliant," Luce agreed. "What do you mean by 'associates,' Lieutenant?"

"Not clear yet. All we know so far is that they're driving a van full of electronics."

"This guy's ready to go in the bus," one of the paramedics said. "Want to walk out, or should we bring in the rig?"

"You bring in…the rig and…you'll be the one… going out in it," JD threatened.

The paramedics grinned. One of them said, "Up you go, then, big guy, but don't fight us helping you. Just remember I can put you to sleep in the bus if you're naughty."

"Can I go along?" Luce asked.

The two paramedics consulted each other with a glance. "Ma'am, we're not allowed to—"

"Judge," Kerry said.

"What?"

"Circuit Court Judge Luce Maguire."

"Got'cha."

Kerry rose and glanced toward the three pistols on the table. "I already have Marsh's weapon and I take it that all three of you fired," he said, his gaze going from JD to Luce to Sarajane, who all nodded. "Forensics will run ballistics, yada, yada, yada."

"Marsh went out without a weapon?" Chloe asked, a worried frown on her face.

"He's got his backup piece," Kerry assured her.

"Call us when you know anything," Sarajane said to Luce, giving her a hug.

"I will."

"Tiger," the LT said, "let's get a patrol car or two on the bus."

"Yes, sir."

Sitting by themselves, Sarajane said to Chloe. "I could sure use that glass of wine right about now."

"I could use a dish of ice cream," Chloe admitted.

"What are we waiting for?"

A few minutes later, the two sat at the kitchen table, one nursing a glass of Chardonnay, the other a bowl of strawberry ice cream and a *biscotto*.

"If I eat for the next four weeks like I've eaten today," Chloe said, "my babies will have a blimp for a mama."

"Fat chance of that," Sarajane said, "and please excuse the unintended pun.

Chloe laughed and scooted back from the table a little so she could put her feet up on the chair next to her. She balanced the bowl of ice cream on her belly. "This is feeling slightly decadent, after everything that's happened today."

"I wonder if they'll let you stay in the house tonight?"

Chloe froze, the spoon of ice cream halfway to her mouth. "Surely they will." She glanced at the clock on the wall. "It's not even eight yet. How long will it take them to do their thing upstairs?"

"A couple of hours, at least. There's not really much to do except take measurements and photos. I'm sure they've already pulled in Freddy, the other Deputy ME, since me calling the death might be a conflict, in this instance."

"You think?"

"Be quiet, or I'll finish that ice cream for you."

"I'd like to see you try." Chloe spooned up another bite and said, "Something's bugging me about all this."

"Like what?"

"That's just it. I don't know. But all the pieces aren't coming together right. I'm too exhausted to think straight!"

"Want to discuss it, see if anything shakes loose?"

Chloe heaved a big sigh. "I don't know. Usually when I think I'm forgetting something, it's when I'm writing. The answer invariably comes when I lay down to go to sleep. Then I have to get up and deal with it, so I don't forget it by morning."

"Bummer."

Chloe nodded. "As odd as Marsh's schedule gets sometimes, I don't think he's gotten used to my sometimes erratic sleep patterns."

"The guy loves you so much, it's scary."

Chloe smiled. "Scary good."

"Yep."

They sat in silence, Sarajane finishing her glass of wine and pouring another, Chloe finishing her ice cream and munching on the *biscotto*.

The feeling of unease grew in the pit of Chloe's stomach.

Or maybe it was Brenden and Mary Kate getting ready to play soccer again.

# chapter 18

Marsh called to tell Chloe not to wait up for him, he'd be late working the case. "Ask Sarajane to stay the night," he said, "so I don't worry about you."

"She already volunteered."

"Good." He hesitated. "Are you sure you're okay staying there after what...after the shooting?"

Chloe couldn't help being amused. "Mary? Ghost in the house?"

"I get it. Dead is dead. Have you heard from Luce? I haven't had a chance to phone her."

"I spoke to her just before you called. They want to keep JD overnight for observation. He has a bruised sternum and they want to monitor his heart, just to be on the safe side."

Marsh heaved a sigh of relief. "He's going to be okay."

"Of course, and Luce is going to spend the night in his room."

"Not sure that's such a good idea."

"It might be just what both of them need."

"JD is as stubborn as that proverbial mule."

"He is, but he's going to have to come around, sooner rather than later, if he wants to get Luce back."

"You don't think he's got her back, if she's planning on spending the night in his hospital room?"

"No," Chloe said, "I don't. What JD doesn't know—and you can't tell either one of them I told you this—is that Luce wants to give up the law altogether. Before she tells him, I think she's hoping he'll come around on his own, accept her career and what used to be her dream of sitting on the supreme court. Once he does that, he won't have any excuses to fall back on, and he'll either make that commitment he's so afraid of, or he'll walk."

"*What?* Luce wants to give up law?"

"It's complicated," Chloe said. "I'll fill you in later."

"If JD wasn't already injured, I'd be tempted to go down there and shake some sense into him."

"While we're on the subject of sense—something about this incident tonight doesn't make sense to me."

"What do you mean?"

"I wish I knew! Sarajane and I are just sitting here talking about it, but whatever it is, it's eluding me. I guess because I'm feeling a little tired. It's so frustrating!"

"Look, sweetheart, if anyone can figure it out, it's you." He broke off for a moment, talking to someone with him. "Gotta go, babe. The gang's all here—Oregon State Police, Marion County Sheriff's Office, the FBI, and, if you can believe it, several agencies from Washington, Idaho, Nevada, and California."

"They came because of this? And they're here already?"

"Yeah, some flew in, some drove. The van in the gas station lot had California plates on it. We contacted the California Bureau of Investigation because Dave found similar-crime links there, as well as in Nevada."

"The death toll is rising."

"The entire goddamned mess started like a little snowball that's growing almost faster than we can blink, and it's still rolling down shit hill."

Chloe managed a chuckle. "The visual of that is quite—"

"Shitty," he concluded for her. "Look, give Dave a call for the particulars. He and the IT guys are amazing. And if you need to get hold of me, or if you think of what it is that's bothering you, I'm putting my phone on vibrate, so text me, okay?"

"Sure. I love you."

"Love you, too. Stay cautious."

"You know me."

Marsh laughed, then said, his tone *über* serious, "I mean it, Chloe. The LT is leaving one unit outside our house all night, but make sure everything is locked up tight, including our bedroom windows upstairs."

"You think someone might try to climb in on the porch roof? Even though Luce and JD aren't here?"

"I think better safe than sorry."

As soon as Chloe hung up, she said to Sarajane, "Marsh says Dave Jernigan can fill us in on details." She told her about the California van and that Dave had found similar crimes in California and Nevada.

Before Sarajane could respond, the other Deputy ME popped his head through the swing-door opening. "They're bringing the body out. Want this door closed?"

Chloe, who had lived with a ghostly spirit for almost her entire life, and Sarajane who worked with the dead every day, both said "No," at the same time.

"Freddy, did he have ID on him?" Sarajane asked the other Deputy ME as she pushed away from the table.

"Driver's license—Clifford James Bright, Nebraska. Age thirty-one. We'll run it when we get back."

"Thanks, Freddy." Sarajane looked at Chloe. "I guess he wasn't so *bright* at the end."

"I guess not," Chloe agreed. Nebraska. Just how far did the insidiousness go?

The guys who drove the call-car, otherwise known as the Dead Van, brought the deceased bad guy down the stairs in a body bag, careful not to drag him bumping over each tread. It was either that, or incur the wrath of Cameron Swift, the ME who would be doing the autopsy.

"I thought I counted six shots," Chloe said as the body bag passed by the doorway.

"I think Marsh and Luce must have each got off two. I got off one and JD must have got off one before he went down."

Chloe patted her belly where someone's elbow, or knee, or foot poked out in a little hard lump. "I think I'm going to learn how to shoot and handle a gun."

"Feeling left out?" Sarajane teased.

"No," she responded seriously. "Just feeling reality set in."

Once everyone had gone, and the patrol officer who was assigned first shift outside the house came in to introduce himself—Pat O'Hara—and give them his cell number, Chloe and Sarajane made the rounds in the house, checking every door and window.

By then, it was nearly ten and they decided it was time to call Dave Jernigan. Chloe dialed and put the phone in the center of the kitchen table, on speaker, so they could both hear.

"Holy crap, you are not going to believe what we've found," he started off by saying. "We've got like crimes in California, Nevada, Colorado, Wyoming, Nebraska, Kansas, Oklahoma, Arizona, New Mexico, and Texas."

"The entire West," Sarajane said.

"Almost," Dave agreed. "We still haven't heard back from North and South Dakota or Montana, and we haven't even begun to look at the Midwest states, Alaska or Hawaii, or the South and East. What we're finding out is that once the deaths in each state hit ten, they apparently stop. So the Paired-Ups are taking credit for twenty-plus, but, in fact, they probably only committed the murders in Oregon."

"They got caught before they finished," Sarajane said. "Only seven of the murders they admitted to were in Oregon."

Even though it was exactly what Luce had specu-lated, Chloe was shocked. "To keep the focus off the others who are still out there killing, they've accepted culpability for crimes they didn't commit."

"The pair at the gas station," Dave went on, "had several laptops with them, so IT is digging into their emails. This just gets crazier and crazier—there's some kind of thrill-seeker network of sickos who have hooked up via this blog called Killzone. They have a screening process that narrows to two people from each state who may or may not know each other initially, but then pair up to commit ten murders."

"Killzone!" Chloe said, "Like they're playing some kind of video game or something!"

"Fifty states, five hundred murders! My God, this is…." Sarajane looked at Chloe. "I don't know *what* the hell this is!"

"Crazy, unprecedented, horrific," Dave said. "I never thought I'd be spending time my second month on the job uncovering a serial killer ring that might span the entire United States!"

Left unsaid by all of them was that, if these macabre duos had slithered into all the states, they might also be in Canada, and maybe even Mexico. Or beyond.

"What else have you got?" Chloe asked.

"Lt. Schaeffer and a lead detective from Oregon State Police are interrogating the guy from the phone booth. Captain Swain and someone else from OSP are on the dimwit from the van. Everyone else is in the conference room, trying to figure out what-the-hell. One of the IT guys is due to make a report to the room in about thirty, so I'll try to get back to you after that. If it goes beyond that, check in with me in the a.m."

He went on. "I can't believe that other guy got in to

your house posing as Andy Parr. I wish I'd been there. I'd have made him in a New York minute. Andy's in a coma, bad brain swelling from the blow to his head. The doc doesn't know if they can save him. I heard JD's okay, and you guys are okay, so we have something to be grateful for." He paused for a moment, then said, "Holy shit!"

"What?" Chloe and Sarajane both asked at once.

"These psychos have a website up that is members-only. The IT guys found an email earlier with the URL, but we needed a password. We've been running a pass-word breaker, but independently I've just been plugging in some possibles, thinking it might be something really simple. Damned if it wasn't! GAMEBUDDIES, with a '3' substituted for the 'S'—can you believe it?"

"How did you even *think* of that?" Chloe asked.

"Don't ask me. I've just been keying in stuff, thinking about how cocky serial killers are, and *voilà*, there it was. If they weren't calling themselves Killzone, it probably never would have occurred to me to try game-related passwords." He paused again. "I'd better sign off. This is some bad shit. They have video of their…kills. We need to get some big guns in here to see this."

"Thanks for all your good work, Dave. I knew when Marsh put you on this, we'd see some results," Chloe said.

"That reminds me and totally off the subject," Dave said. "Maybe some day you'll tell me the *real* story behind your interest in a murder over a hundred years old."

"Maybe," Chloe said, slightly amused, but not surprised by the young man's insight. "Sarajane and Chloe, signing out."

Once she'd disconnected, Sarajane said, "If that kid was about ten years older, I'd scarf him up. He has brains, brawn, a sense of humor, *and* good looks, not a common combo these days."

Chloe considered her friend, surprised. "Does that mean you're ready to move on and stop waiting for Marsh's brother to show up again?"

"Nope," Sarajane said. "I will always be in love with Dominic, but I might consider a side trip with a man like Dave, just because...."

"Because?"

Sarajane heaved a particularly deep sigh. "Just because I get so freaking lonely sometimes. I want a man to..." —she shrugged— "well, to be all the things a man should be to a woman who loves him, and who he loves back."

Chloe's heart almost broke for her friend. "Maybe, you should become a nun," she said, only half-joking, "then the two of you can start up some kind of home for lost souls and at least see each other every day."

"Don't think I haven't considered it!" Sarajane retorted. Her gaze dropped to Chloe's belly. "And I would if I didn't want kids so damned bad. I couldn't be around *Father* Dom knowing there wasn't a chance in hell of him ever being the *father* of my children."

A single tear ran down Sarajane's cheek. "It sucks being in love with someone you can't have." On that note, she rose from the table and said, "Bedtime for pregnant ladies and old maids. Grab your phone and head upstairs. I'll shut off the lights."

"Dave said he might call back with more details."

Sarajane glanced at the clock. "It's so late now, they're all going to be wrapped up looking at these videos on the Killzone website."

"Do you think we should log on and see what we're facing?" Chloe asked, easing her feet off the other chair so she could stand.

"No, I absolutely do not! I want to be able to sleep tonight."

"You're right. Just the *thought* of the Killzone sickos filming their kills is already enough to give me nightmares."

"And besides, *we're* not facing it, the cops are."

"Well, actually, we are *sort of* facing it," Chloe said, "if only secondarily." She felt the hairs on her arms stand up, but she didn't think it was because of the idea of sickos filming their kills.

Something tickled at the edge of her consciousness, something she couldn't quite grasp. Something damned important.

# chapter 19

*L*uce thanked the nurse who brought her a warm blanket and a pillow. She pulled a chair up opposite the one she had placed next to JD's bed, and after several minutes of settling in, decided she was as comfortable as she was going to get.

Nighttime in the hospital—lights were dimmed, noises were somewhat muted. Luce tried to doze off, but her eyelids wouldn't stay down, and her eyes wouldn't stay away from the heart or blood pressure monitors at the side of JD's bed.

In the area of his sternum, a nasty-looking bruise had already begun to blossom. The cardiologist had skipped an X-ray and gone straight to a transesophageal echocardiogram, to determine if an aortic dissection had occurred from the violent impact of the close-range, large caliber bullet. "In lay terms," he had told Luce, "I was looking to see if there's a tear in the sac around JD's heart. There isn't. His heart looks fine, but we'll still keep him overnight."

The doctor had given JD something for pain and something to help him sleep. He'd been soundly sawing logs for a couple of hours.

Still, Luce could not sleep. The chair setup was awkward, but she forced her eyes closed, hoping to nod off. When next she opened them, it was to the squeak of nursing shoes against the linoleum.

"You don't look very comfortable," the nurse whispered.

"I'm fine," Luce whispered back, although she knew she'd have aches in new places in the morning.

"Can I get you anything?"

"No, thanks."

Before the nurse pulled the door closed, Luce glimpsed the uniformed officer outside. Her eyes went back to the monitors. JD's blood pressure had dropped from 160/90 to 140/79. That was encouraging. His heart peaks did not look erratic, which the doctor had told her was a good sign.

She repositioned herself, trying not to make any noise as she squirmed in her makeshift bed. She swore once under her breath when the pillow fell to the floor. She picked it up and put it behind her back and head once more, then glanced at JD to make sure she hadn't awakened him.

In the vague light of the monitors, she found his not-quite-green eyes gleaming at her.

"Water," he croaked.

The nurse had already told her it would be okay if he had a little water, but encouraged her to try and get him to go slow and suck on some ice chips instead. His throat was going to be dry and probably a little sore from the echo.

"They want you to start with ice chips," Luce said.

JD blinked at her. "Whatever. Throat's dry, hurts."

Luce untangled herself from the bedding. The nurse apparently had replenished his ice cup, because the spoon stood straight up again.

JD mumbled something raspy that might have been "thanks" around the first spoonful of ice chips. She watched his jaw and stubbly cheeks move as he sucked and chewed, and then he said, "More."

Luce almost smiled. He sounded like a caveman, uttering monosyllabic instructions.

After she repeated the process several times, he seemed satisfied and rested back against the bed. She hadn't even realized he'd been leaning forward, however slightly.

"What are you doing here?" he asked, his voice hoarse.

"I didn't want you to be alone."

He gave her several slow blinks, then his eyes stayed closed. After several moments, she realized he'd fallen back to sleep.

Since she was up, she decided to go down the hall and use the bathroom and splash some water on her face. She felt groggy, but didn't know if she'd be able to doze off again, so she also got a hot chocolate from the dispensing machine in the waiting room. She stood at the window, gazing out at the Salem panorama. The clouds had passed and stars twinkled everywhere.

It was a lovely night.

Too bad the ugly day marred her enjoyment of it.

"Chloe, wake up. There's someone in the house!"

Chloe squirmed in her bed, murmuring in her sleep.

"Chloe, please wake up!"

"Mary...?"

"Yes, it's me. *Wake up!*"

Chloe's eyes flew open. She thought she'd been dreaming about Mary, but Mary was bent over her, talking to her in all her transparent glory.

"Mary! Ohmygod, Mary, it's so good to see you!"

"*Shhh!* Listen, love, I'm glad to see you, too, but you have to get up. Someone's in the house, and he isn't here for a social call."

Suddenly the missing puzzle piece appeared as if by

magic in Chloe's brain. "The other half of the pair. How could I have been so stupid?" she whispered, taking Mary's warning to heart.

"Quickly, get to the hidey-hole!"

"Hidey-hole?" Chloe repeated blankly.

"Yes, remember the hidden door in the closet of your childhood bedroom. We used to have tea parties in there?"

Chloe finally woke up. She hadn't thought of the hidey-hole in years! "Sarajane is in the spare bedroom. I have to get her."

"Hurry and be quiet," Mary urged. "You only have minutes before he comes upstairs."

Chloe grabbed her phone and moved barefoot toward the door.

"Take your blanket and pillow—it's cold in there and you're pregnant."

Chloe ripped both off the bed and dropped them by the door, then hurried to Sarajane's room as quietly and quickly as her pregnant self allowed. She entered not quite on tiptoe and went to the bed. She shook Sarajane, a hand over her friend's mouth.

Good thing, because Sarajane was so startled, she yelped. "Someone's in the house. Grab your pillow and blanket and keep your voice to a whisper."

"What? Where are we going, the attic?" Sarajane asked, awake but obviously disoriented.

"No, just follow me and try not to make any noise."

A nightlight in a hall plug gave enough light for them to see, but Sarajane removed it as they passed by. In total darkness, the two of them made the return trip down the hall, where Chloe grabbed her bedding, and led the way into the nursery, across the hall.

Once the door was closed, she touched a button on her phone, lighting up the panel. "The closet."

Sarajane opened the closet door. "Now what?"

Chloe stepped inside a space that was easily four times longer than it was deep. She turned right and went to the corner where she ran her hand up the wall until her fingers felt a familiar bump. She pushed against it and a small door popped open. "Quick!"

"No way," Sarajane said. "You first, pregnant lady. I'll drag this stuff in."

Chloe decided not to argue. "Be sure to close the closet door behind you."

They didn't waste any more time on whispered words. The set-up of the hidey-hole was like a number nine, with the leg of the nine being about a three-foot hallway leading from the closet. Chloe stooped and entered. Her pillow under one arm, her phone in her free hand, she touched the screen again to activate the light. She hurried as quickly as she could to the middle of a small room approximately six feet deep and about eight feet long.

The closet door clicked shut. Sarajane moved lickety-split through the small opening and into the hidey-hole, her own lighted phone in one hand as she methodically hauled in the bedding.

Chloe moved over to latch the secret door behind her and reached for a towel that hung on a hook next to the entry. She started to squat to press the towel up against the bottom of the door to ensure that no light from their phones escaped, giving them away should the invader happen to examine the closet closely.

"I'll get that," Sarajane said.

Dust from the old towel wafted up and Chloe felt a sneeze coming on. She quickly moved back into the tiny room and grabbed her pillow, shoving it against her face just as the sneeze erupted. *Please, God,* she prayed. *Don't let the intruder have heard. Please!*

"What the hell?" Sarajane said, keeping her voice low. "How did this happen? We have a cop out front."

Satisfied she wasn't going to sneeze again, Chloe said, "I don't know." She didn't even want to think about what might have happened outside to Officer Pat O'Hara. She helped Sarajane make a nest for the two of them against the wall and eased into it with the pillow behind her. "Sit down and get comfortable," she said, patting the space beside her. "We're going to have to be super quiet. And set your phone to vibrate."

Chloe followed her own advice, then texted Marsh: *911. missing piece. half of pair here. hurry. hidey-hole.* She hit send, but half-growled when the message lingered in the outbox. Marsh's office was just on the other side of the wall and they had network wi-fi both there and in Chloe's office below, but cell service was spotty in the old house.

*Please, please, please,* Chloe prayed silently. She had babies to think of. No crazed psychopathic lunatic was going to take them away from her, or vice versa.

A little clumsy in her long nightgown, she half-crawled to the outside wall and finally, the message went on its way.

# chapter 20

*J*D swallowed and it hurt like hell. He searched the semi-darkness for Luce but saw only the two empty chairs beside the bed. He felt his disappointment keenly, but didn't stop to analyze why.

He fumbled for the cup of ice, almost knocking it over, surprised when Luce's hand wrapped around his to steady him.

"Thought you'd gone," he said, trying to minimize his words. Damn, what the hell had they stuck down his throat, a three-inch pipe with spikes?

"I can, if that's what you'd prefer," she said.

"Ice. Please."

Luce came around the table and obliged him. "How do you feel?"

"Like shit…but at least alive."

She gave him half a smile. "We can thank God for that."

"God and Kevlar."

In the faint light cast by the monitoring equipment, he could see her shake her head in amusement.

"What's happening…on the case?"

Luce relayed what she had learned from Dave Jernigan.

"Jesus-H," JD said. "All over the country…filming their kills."

"It's awful," Luce agreed. "I was just talking to Marsh when he got a text from Chloe." She gnawed on her lower lip. "I wonder if I should go over there and see if everything's is okay."

"Don't go. Please."

She studied him for several long, agonizing moments. "Why do you want me to stay?"

"More ice. Please." He sucked enough to ease his aching throat. "I want you to stay because…." He tried to find the right words, couldn't, and said instead, "You're not a cop…you don't have your gun anymore."

"Still…."

"I'm serious. If something's wrong…you'll be in the way. Besides, you rode with me in the ambulance…you don't have your car."

The silence that followed his explanation lay heavy in the room. Why didn't Luce say something?

Why didn't *he*?

JD suddenly realized he didn't *have* to think about why her absence had left him feeling disappointed, even bereft. He knew. Luce gone from his life would be the worst thing that could happen to him and it would be totally avoidable if he wasn't so damned afraid to take a leap, make a commitment, and *trust*. Luce had wrapped it up all nice and neat for him and he'd been too frigging stupid or selfish to accept her explanation. She knew him better than he knew himself.

Finally Luce said, "Is that all?"

"No. I want you to stay because…because I love you." He straightened himself up, grimacing with pain as he did so. He almost said, *I'm* in love *with you,* but decided he couldn't go quite that far. Yet.

"You are such a jack rabbit, JD."

"But a loveable one." He patted the bed beside him.

"Lower the bed rail, darlin'. Climb up beside me. We'll wait to hear from Marsh…together."

"It's cold in here," Sarajane said, still whispering. "I never get cold."

"It's fright," Chloe whispered back, settling in once more. "Let's pull the comforter over us and snuggle together. We'll preserve our body heat."

"What time is it?"

"O-dark-thirty."

"In other words, the dead of night."

"Not literally, I hope."

At that moment, a floor board squeaked at their back. The killer was in Marsh's office. They froze, holding their collective breaths. Had he heard them whispering?

"We dodged the bullet," Sarajane said, as they listened to their unknown assailant move on to make the rounds in other rooms.

Chloe had never been in her hidey-hole when no one else was in the house. She hadn't realized how sound traveled when bodies didn't buffer it, or when the TV wasn't on, or when the radio stood silent.

Her phone chose that moment to vibrate. She held it up so Sarajane could see Marsh's message. *on r way.*

The door to the nursery slammed open.

The killer must be good and pissed right about now, although he hadn't yet searched the attic. For sure, they would have heard him up there. He opened the closet door. They heard him step inside, swear profusely, then step out and slam the door against the wall. The crash, which must have left a hole where the doorknob struck the wall, startled Chloe and Sarajane so badly, they both jumped.

He made a helluva racket, flipping over cribs and dressing tables and rocking chairs on his way out. If Chloe hadn't been so scared, she would have cried.

And then he went to the stairs that led to the attic. He

stormed up the wood risers making enough noise for ten men. By that time, he was beyond pissed or being careful not to make noise. Again, things went flying, and his cursing seemed loud enough to be heard down the block.

He flew back down the attic steps, and they could hear him taking the stairs to the first floor.

And then silence reigned.

After several minutes, Sarajane said, "He's gone."

"Maybe not."

"I wish I had my gun."

"Don't move, Chloe," Mary said, her transparent self appearing out of nowhere. "He's sitting on the bottom step, waiting. He knows you're hiding. He's trying to fool you."

Another minute passed. "Let's get out of here," Sarajane said.

"No, we can't. He's sitting on the bottom step, waiting for us."

"How do you know that?" Sarajane whisper-hissed.

"Mary told me."

Sarajane's shocked silence could be felt in the darkness. "*The* Mary?"

"Yes, and keep your voice down!"

"Is she here, right now?" Sarajane asked, her voice reduced again by many decibels.

Chloe looked to the glimmering phantasm in front of her, frowning with worry. "Yes."

"I can't see her," Sarajane complained.

"Tell her I said 'hello,'" Mary said, "and promise me the four of you won't move until I get Marsh up here."

Like a parrot, Chloe repeated what Mary had said.

"Hello, back," Sarajane said to the air. "I'm really bummed that I can't see you."

"Tell her I'm really glad she's been such a good friend to you."

Chloe did.

"Chloe has been a good friend to me, too." Again to the air.

"Tell her, always listen to Aunt Gennie. She knows things."

"*What?*" Chloe demanded quietly.

"You heard me," Mary said in her sternest tone.

"What 'what'?" asked Sarajane.

"She says to tell you to always listen to Aunt Gennie. She knows things."

"Always?"

"Always," Mary repeated, so Chloe did, too. "And tell Sarajane, she's got the sight, too. She should heed it."

Chloe paraphrased for Mary.

"I do not!" Sarajane protested too vehemently.

"Have to run, Chloe. Marsh is outside."

"Tell him to be careful!"

"I will."

"Mary! Mary, will I see you again? *Mary!*"

But there was no answer.

# chapter 21

Marsh approached his house on foot from the corner. In the patrol car, Officer Pat O'Hara stared blankly at nothing. A small caliber weapon had left a small hole in his left temple and only a small dribble of blood. Small. It didn't matter how small, it had still been fatal.

Marsh felt a wave of both grief and regret wash through him. A fine man had died tonight. And he had died protecting Marsh's family. He owed him big time for that.

Flanked by two other patrol officers and the LT, Marsh motioned the uniforms around to the back. Kerry Schaeffer whispered to him, "You stay behind me."

"My wife—"

"Your wife will appreciate me keeping you safe so your babies have a daddy when they get here."

Marsh understood the importance of that, but Chloe was stuck inside the house with a murderer. A degenerate who not only liked killing people, but torturing them and recording every moment of it to share with the sick fucks in his killing network. What if he'd already found Chloe and Sarajane in whatever this hidey-hole was

Chloe had texted him about? His frustration level was running high over that—a secret place in the house he didn't know about?

The LT and Marsh crept up the porch steps and each stood on one side of the door, which the intruder had not fully closed upon entering. The two men exchanged a look in the darkness. Kerry raised his hand to signal their pre-arranged entry method at the same instant a tremendous crash emanated from inside the house.

After that, everything seemed to happen at once. The door eased open and there stood Mary.

Too shocked to do or say anything in that instant, Marsh heard her say, "He's in the dining room," and then he understood what the crash was. Somehow, Mary had tipped over the hutch filled with Chloe's family-heirloom dishes.

"Dining room," Marsh whispered to the LT. He motioned him to go straight, then right, hoping, since they'd met there just hours earlier, that the LT remembered the way. Marsh took the other route to the dining room via the living room and through the kitchen.

"*Police!*" Kerry shouted. "Put down your weapon and come out with your hands above your head."

"*Fuck you!*" came the reply.

Kerry spoke again, drawing the intruder's attention, giving Marsh a chance to approach without being noticed. "The house is surrounded. You have no way out alive if you do not comply. *Put down your weapon* and raise your hands where I can see them!"

Marsh made the doorway and leveled his gun on the intruder, who had his weapon aimed through the other doorway, in the LT's direction. "Drop it!"

Startled, the intruder spun, discharging his gun. The shot went wild. Marsh fired a split second later. Simultaneously, another shot sounded from the living room. The killer fell backward, his gun arm raised. He got off one more shot as he landed, over Marsh's head and into the ceiling.

Marsh heard a muffled scream and his blood ran cold. Had either Chloe or Sarajane been hit by the stray bullet? Fear lodged his heart in his throat. Several more officers poured through the front door even as he opened the back door to let in the other two uniforms who had responded with them.

"Go!" Kerry ordered Marsh. "We've got him."

Marsh didn't waste a moment on where the intruder's weapon was. The others would have that under control. Two at a time, he took the stairs, screaming Chloe's name. He charged directly into the nursery, which was situated over the dining room, dismayed by the chaos, stricken with new fear for his wife and his unborn children.

"Chloe! *Chloe, where are you?*" Wild with dread and panic, Marsh flipped on the light. The damage was not as bad as it had looked in the dark, but still, no Chloe.

Mary stood by the opening of the closet door. "They're in the hidey-hole," she said.

He leaped into the closet. A string hung from a light fixture in the ceiling and he tugged it on. Once again, he shouted for his wife.

He heard a shuffling sound on the other side of the wall, listened as it moved from the center of the closet to a spot at the right end. Then a rasp and half the wall popped open. Chloe was there on her knees, her hands clutching the open door, her nightgown covered in blood. Tears streamed down her face. "Jesus," he murmured, fighting back his panic.

"Marsh, thank God. Get an ambulance! *Hurry!*"

He didn't question her, but rushed to her even as he pulled out his phone. Somehow, he managed to dial 9-1-1, give his badge number and the particulars, asking for two EMT units and the ME to respond. He didn't give a crap about the SOB downstairs, but protocol was protocol.

His heart cracked. The blood, all the goddamned blood...she must have taken the stray bullet in her belly.

*The babies!* "Where are you hit?" he asked, supporting her.

"Not me," she said.

But Marsh didn't hear her words. He only saw the blood. "Oh, God, sweetheart, I'm so sorry. I should have taken a head shot. Nailed him before he could discharge his weapon. The babies...." His voice broke and he couldn't say more.

Chloe reached up with a bloody hand and grasped his arm. "*Marsh, not me.* Sarajane. Please, she needs help."

Finally, Marsh got it. He eased past Chloe and moved in toward his old friend. Sarajane lay half-bent in a mass of bedding that was rapidly soaking up her blood.

# chapter 22

*L* uce wanted nothing more than to comply with JD's invitation to climb up into the hospital bed with him, but first things first. He had said *I love you*, but this time, from the tone of his voice, she knew he'd meant *I'm in love with you*. He had made a breakthrough and so would she. Now it was time to see where it led.

"I need to talk to you," she said. "I want you to listen without interrupting. Agreed?"

From his hospital bed, JD's expression clearly said he wasn't happy. "You did all the…talking earlier."

"I didn't say everything I had to say then. Are you going to shut up and listen, or do you want me to leave, and we'll finish this up some other time?"

His eyebrows dipped. "Like I have anything…to say about it," he muttered, still croaky.

"I'm stepping down from the bench."

JD opened his mouth and when she raised her hand, he snapped it shut.

"This has nothing to do with you. I have been think-ing about this for a long time, and not because you have been bugging me to forget about the supreme court run."

"But—"

"JD, *please*! Shut the hell up and let me finish!"

He gave her a dark look in response.

"This hasn't been an easy decision for me. Ever since I can remember, I've wanted to be a judge. I worked hard in college, I worked hard in law school. I worked my butt off so I could get a great internship in the DA's office, and I clerked for the best sitting judge at that time." She took a deep breath. "I worked hard to get elected to the circuit court, and after hundreds of days sitting in that chair, thousands of hours listening to lies, watching the guilty walk free because juries watch too much *CSI* and think they know more than law enforcement experts, I just can't take it any more."

She rubbed her hands over her face, tenting them prayer style when she was done. "I thought I could make a difference," she said quietly, then laughed sardonically. "Isn't that just the most ridiculous, egotistical thing you've ever heard? I was sure that *I* could make a fucking difference!"

"You have made...a difference, darlin'. You're a good judge. You're fair, you know the law...you treat people with respect."

"It's not enough, JD. At the end of every day, instead of feeling satisfied that I've done my best, I feel empty inside. I hate all the liars. I hate the evil. I hate the stupid people who sit on juries and let the guilty walk away because they had a tough childhood, or their daddy hit their mommy, or the devil made them do it. What have we come to as a society? Tell me that, will you?"

"I agree...but you can't give up."

"I wouldn't if I really thought I *could* go on loving the one thing I've dreamed about doing since I was a kid. Other girls wanted to grow up and be princesses and teachers and nurses, but not me. I wanted to wear a black robe and sit in a courtroom day after day, bang my gavel to bring order to the court, send bad guys to prison. Don't ask me where that came from, but it's what I wanted."

"Too much…Perry Mason," JD quipped.

She shot him a weak grin, then began to pace the length of his hospital bed. "Now, all I want to do is run away. I have nothing to stay here for! I'll finish out my term because I owe it to the voters who elected me to fulfill my obligation to them and to the state, but after that…."

"After that, what?"

She stopped, shrugged, and stared hard at him. "I don't know. I thought I'd be starting over with you, but you've made it perfectly clear that you're done with me, so that leaves my options open, doesn't it?"

JD opened his mouth to respond, but she cut him off. "Don't try and placate me. You and I both heard you say our relationship isn't working, and quite frankly, I don't want to marry a man who doesn't listen when I talk."

"I listen," he said.

She raised both eyebrows at him.

"Ah, shit!" he said, throwing his legs over the side of the bed, disconnecting something that made a monitor go crazy.

"JD, please! Stay put."

"Fuck staying put," he bit out. "The woman I love…the woman I'm…*in love with!*…is telling me she's getting…ready to take a hike…and I need…my legs to stop her. Shit, my throat is…killing me."

Luce stared at him, dumbfounded, despite her earlier suspicion that the man she loved had finally faced his commitment demons.

Two nurses pushed through the door in response to the monitoring device giving off the signal that JD's heart had stopped.

Instead of requesting a crash cart and calling a Code Blue over the PA, they backed out of the room and left the man with his bare butt hanging out, and the woman he was kissing with wild abandon, alone to carry on.

Luce didn't know how they did it, but she and JD both managed to climb back into the narrow hospital bed. With his injured chest, they had to lay sideways, but that didn't hamper them kissing or exploring the other's parts, both exposed and not exposed.

It was one of the most sensual hours Luce had ever spent with the man she loved beyond reason. She couldn't believe how the tenor of making love could change so drastically just because a man finally acknowledged that he was *in love*. She also hadn't known that two people *could* make love while one of them was fully clothed and the other wore a skimpy hospital gown, but it was not only possible, it was as erotic as hell.

"Take off your slacks," JD murmured against her mouth.

"No. We're in a public place."

"The nurses won't be back."

"They don't have to come back. They'll know and they'll spread it around the hospital and the cop outside the door will spread it around the police station and then it'll be all over the courthouse…."

She couldn't finish her response because he took her mouth again and let his tongue silence her. His hand fondled her breast beneath her sweater, as he had long since undone the clasp of her bra. Luce could hardly think for the hot desire pulsing through her veins. She grasped his bare ass and pulled him closer still, until she could feel his erection pressing against the place where she wanted him to enter her.

"JD, we can't do this here," she tried again. "It's a hospital, a public place. I've never—"

He squeezed her nipple gently at first, then with more pressure and an electric current shot from her breast to her groin. "You're killing me," she cried softly against his mouth.

In response, he guided her hand under the gown to his groin, then slid his hand between her legs and began to rub her. Thirty-five years old and Luce had no idea that a woman could climax while a man rubbed her through her blue jeans. Not only did she come, but she came twice, burying her face against his throat so her ecstatic cries would be muffled.

With her hand working on his erection, every muscle in his body tightened and convulsed as he reached his own point of no return.

They lay softly panting for a long time, then JD pulled the sheet up over them.

A long time later, a nurse came in to check on him and found them asleep in each other's arms, none the wiser as to what had gone on in the bed since the last time the patient's vitals had been recorded in his chart.

# chapter 23

*t*he light in the hidey-hole was dim, emanating from a bulb that had to be over thirty years old, but Marsh managed to get Sarajane laid out flat so he could assess her injury. The perp's bullet had torn through the ceiling, through the wood floor, and by some fluke, into Sarajane's leg. She bled so heavily, he knew an artery had been nicked, at the least.

"I need something to make a tourniquet," he told Chloe.

"Pillowcase," she said, pulling it off the pillow even as she suggested it.

"Good. Can you make your way out and let the LT know where we are?"

"Yes," she responded, her voice tremulous. She stood and wobbled, then corrected and headed for the doorway.

"Sarajane? Can you hear me?" Marsh asked as he tore a wide strip from the pillowcase. "I'm going to put a tourniquet on your leg." He fashioned the makeshift device, then withdrew a pen from his pocket and used it to tighten the tourniquet at the knot.

"Chloe…?"

"She's fine. She's gone to tell the LT and the EMTs where we are. I'd move you out into the nursery, but I think they'd better tend to you in here first, just in case." He left unsaid that if the femoral artery had been hit, she shouldn't move at all until she had medical attention.

Of course, Sarajane, being the Deputy ME, knew that as well as he did.

Moments later, he heard a commotion outside the small room and an EMT stuck his head around the corner.

"Light's not so good in here. What have we got?"

Marsh gave his assessment. Sarajane moaned.

"I've got a halogen lamp, if there's a place to plug in."

Marsh looked around the dimly lit room. "I don't see a plug."

"It's not far from there to the bedroom. Let's just get her moved and I'll plug in out here. I don't want to make any mistakes because I can't see."

Marsh agreed and he stood off in a corner while the two EMTs came in and gently moved Sarajane into the nursery. "Where's my wife?" he asked when he joined them.

"She was out on the landing, handing out directions to us," one of the EMTs said. "She was covered in blood—we thought she was the victim, but she said she wasn't hurt. The other unit coming up after us will take a look at her anyway."

"She's eight months pregnant," Marsh said.

"We noticed. They'll take care of her."

Marsh looked down at Sarajane. In the light of the halogen lamp, she looked deathly pale. Her eyes were half closed and her pulse beat so madly, it looked like her throat was alive. He knelt down and put a hand on her forehead. "I'm here, Sarie. I'm going to go check on Chloe, but I'll be with you at the hospital, okay? These guys are going to take care of you now, so don't worry.

You're going to be okay."

Sarajane's only response was her eyelids lowering all the way.

"We got her," the other EMT said. "Go see about your wife."

Marsh rose and left the room, but didn't find Chloe on the landing. He stuck his head in the bedroom, and then the bathroom, but she wasn't there, either. He looked in his office, in the spare bedroom, and the guest bath. No luck.

A frisson of dread crawled down his back.

He tore down the stairs two at a time and nearly collided with Kerry at the bottom.

With a solemn look on his face, the LT put a hand on his arm. "Marsh, the EMTs have Chloe in the ambulance. It turns out she was hit by the bullet. Apparently, she and Sarajane were huddled together for warmth and when the slug tore through Sarajane's leg, it grazed Chloe's side."

Marsh had no memory of being afraid of anything in his life, but at that moment, he tasted fear as if he had ingested it. He tried to push past Kerry, but the man held firm.

"You need to remain calm, okay? You're not going to do yourself or Chloe any good if you fall apart. I know you want to go with her in the ambulance, but we've had a fatal shooting here, and we have protocols to follow. I need your weapon. Let's get that taken care of, then you can go."

"Screw protocol!" Marsh shouted. "My wife—"

"Is not critically injured," Kerry reminded him. "The EMTs say it's just a graze, but because she's pregnant, they want her in the hospital for a complete check-up."

The rational part of Marsh recognized that every word out of Kerry's mouth made sense, but *Chloe* was in that ambulance, with a gunshot wound. Chloe, who was eight months pregnant with *his* babies. Brenden and Mary Kate. Babies he'd once thought he'd never be able to father. With more calm than he actually felt, he pulled his backup weapon from his holster and handed it over to the LT.

The second gun of the night he'd handed over because of a shooting in *his* house. What an f-ing nightmare.

"Thank you," Kerry said, dropping his grip on Marsh's arm, taking the gun. Then he moved out of the way before Marsh could mow him down.

Moments later, Marsh stood at the open door of the ambulance.

"Climb in, if you're coming," the EMT said.

Marsh didn't need to be told twice.

"Move up there and keep out of my way, okay?" the EMT said, more as an order than a request.

Marsh nodded and went to the front of the compartment.

Chloe gave him half a smile, but it didn't reassure him that she was okay. She lifted a hand in his direction. He squatted and took it, wondering if the EMT would tell him to give it back. He didn't.

"I didn't know you were hurt," Marsh said, his voice full of misery. "I didn't know, Chloe."

"I didn't know either," Chloe reassured him. "I thought…I don't know what I thought! I felt okay when I showed the EMTs where Sarajane was. The next thing I knew, I was bent over in pain and sitting on the top step, with a different EMT asking me if I was all right. My right side burned like crazy and it was obvious by then I was bleeding…. You know the rest." She offered him another weak smile.

Clasping her hand in both of his, Marsh lowered his head against his fists and prayed.

"Mary warned me," Chloe said. "We'd be dead if she hadn't warned me."

Marsh raised his head. "I saw her. I couldn't believe it. She's given us so much to be thankful for."

"I know." Chloe grimaced on a wave of pain.

"Who's Mary?" the EMT asked. "Is there someone else in the house who needs medical attention?"

"No," Marsh said simply. "What can you give my wife for the pain?"

"Nothing until we get to the ER. Being pregnant, I'd rather let the doc make the call and we're almost there. You doing okay, Chloe?"

With gritted teeth, the patient uttered a strained, "Yes."

*If she's not,* Marsh thought, *I'm gonna bust your chops when this bus stops, pal.*

Once they got to the emergency room, no amount of cajoling, threatening, or flashing a badge got Marsh into the inner sanctum of treatment rooms.

"Have a seat, sir, and I'll come and get you the moment the doctor says it's okay for you to go back."

Marsh glared at her.

The nurse did not flinch. "Tougher guys than you have threatened me in the past twenty years, Detective. I can take it."

Marsh shoved a hand through his hair, raking his fingers across his scalp, leaving his hair looking as it had never looked before. He opened his mouth to reply to the Nazi Nurse, when he heard an approaching siren peter out. He bolted for the door and ran to the ambulance bay. Sarajane was already out of the bus and the gurney had been raised. Marsh kept pace alongside the EMTs pushing her. "How is she?"

"We thought we lost her on the way, but she came back, mumbling something about finding a priest. Father Dominic?"

Marsh couldn't believe it. Even facing death, Sarajane was thinking about his brother. How deep her love must go for Dom!

"You can't come in this way."

"I know," Marsh said.

Looking as pale as if she *were* lying in a coffin, Sarajane disappeared into the bowels of the ER.

Marsh hustled back inside into the waiting room and retook his stance by the double doors, peering through the window. Of course, he could see nothing but hospital personnel walking the ER hallways and curtains pulled around each treatment room, providing privacy for those in each bed.

He turned and stalked away, pacing from one end of the waiting room to another and back. Nazi Nurse approached and asked him to complete the admittance and insurance paperwork. He did both in short order and resumed his pacing.

Finally, about ready to scream in frustration or break something, he pulled out his phone and dialed Luce. She must still be in the hospital with JD. She'd want to be here with him and he could use both the support and the company.

Her phone went to voice mail and he started to leave a message, when his phone signaled he had an incoming call.

"Sorry," Luce said when he barked a greeting, "I fell asleep."

"Listen, Luce, the shit has hit the fan." He gave the abbreviated version, saying only that both Chloe and Sarajane were in the ER being treated for gunshot wounds.

"I'm on my way," she said, disconnecting.

When she arrived, she was pushing JD in a wheel-chair. His police guard trailed behind, his eyes darting around to assess the new surroundings. JD shrugged, looking embarrassed. "Even though I'm still in the god-damned hospital, they said it was the wheelchair or I couldn't come down," he explained.

At that moment, Kerry and Blake entered through the main ER doors.

"How are they?" the LT asked.

"Don't know yet," Marsh said, his face taut with worry and restrained anger. "They won't tell me squat and they won't let me go back."

Blake put a hand on his shoulder. "This hospital is one of the best in the nation," he said. "They have rankings up the wahzoo and plenty of experience treating gunshot wounds."

Marsh gave Blake a look, but decided his friend and fellow police officer meant well, so he resisted decking him.

"How are you holding up?" Kerry asked.

"How do you think?"

"Let's move over to the corner for privacy. I want to give all of you an update." Kerry turned and walked away.

Marsh had never seen his LT so somber or so ashen. JD had been exactly right when he'd said they had a clusterfuck on their hands.

The past eighteen hours had been a *living* clusterfuck.

# chapter 24

*W*ith JD first, his wheelchair being pushed by Luce, everyone followed the LT. He moved a couple of chairs out of the way to accommodate JD, and Luce sat down beside him. Kerry sat on the other side. Marsh and Blake stood, effectively blocking the group from others in the waiting room. Behind them stood the officer assigned to guard JD.

Kerry leaned forward and dropped his head into his hands, silent for several moments. When he finally looked up, his expression looked as bleak and haggard as Marsh felt.

"This is the most convoluted, sickening case I have ever seen," the LT began, his tone grim with disbelief. "To give credit where credit is due, our IT guys are absolutely amazing, not only with their knowledge, but with their fervor. They just do *not* quit! Because of them, we have confirmed that these Paired-Up fucks are in all fifty states, DC, two provinces in Canada, Puerto Rico, and Mexico. So far, we've managed to keep this away from the media, and as of this moment, pairs have been rounded up in thirty-seven states, DC, and both Canadian provinces."

He rubbed his eyes with the heels of his hands. "I have never seen law enforcement move this fast before. Ever. If we can keep a lid on this until morning, we might have a chance of getting the other pairs in the remaining thirteen states and Puerto Rico. Mexico I don't have a hope for, but the authorities there have been notified and given names and addresses, so we'll see. Maybe they're better at catching serial killers than they are at stopping drug cartels."

"Who's the brain trust masterminding these douche bags?" JD asked.

"Every indication is that it's the bozos we rounded up at the gas station." He hesitated, frowning. "That van of theirs is a traveling IT hub with satellite wi-fi, high-tech video equipment, multiple smartphones, notebooks—you name it, they got it. Apparently, they don't commit murders themselves, they just *orchestrate* them. Isn't that just special?" he asked sarcastically. "Two little rich boys travel around the country, following their trainees, giving them how-to instructions, encouragement, and support."

"Support?" Luce asked. "What the hell does that mean?"

"Serial killer franchise opportunities," Marsh muttered. "Corporate training."

"Where does the rich part come in?" JD asked.

"They write game software. They have one called 'Murder by Night' which is enormously popular, and altogether, their games have netted them in the millions." Agitated, Kerry stood. He looked from JD to Luce and back to JD. "They also come to places like Salem, Oregon and try to intimidate judges and cops. Or worse. We have one dead cop, one who may not make it, another"—he looked at JD— "injured, and two injured civilians. What a goddamned mess!"

JD was gripping the armrests of the wheelchair so hard, his big-fisted knuckles were completely white.

Marsh wanted to punch something, but instead, he crossed his arms over his chest and fumed and burned like an underground volcano. "So the guy in the phone booth, the guy in the van, the dead guy—*both* dead guys—in my house, they're confirmed as the instigators?"

Kerry shook his head. "Not sure about the dead guys in your house. Both had Nebraska DLs. They aren't the ones we found on the list for Nebraska, so it's possible they're part of the leaders' team. Who the hell knows? They came after people in your house, so maybe they're journeymen for the organization. Maybe, maybe, maybe." He threw his hands in the air in frustration. "Shit! I just don't frickin' know!"

"Are there more?"

"We don't think so."

"Thinking isn't going to cut it here," Marsh ground out, his voice kept low to avoid garnering attention from others in the waiting room. "We have got to *know* for fucking certain. I can't have my wife or my babies at further risk. Luce and JD have got to be able to sleep at night. And what about Sarajane? She's another innocent bystander in all this!"

At the sound of Luce's choked sob, all eyes went to her. She buried her face in her hands. "This is all my fault! If I'd quit sooner, I never would have been hearing this case and none of my friends would have gotten hurt. Sarajane wouldn't be fighting for her life."

JD tugged on Luce's hand, pulling her over into his lap. He held her as she cried it out, soothing her with murmured words no one else could hear.

Beside Marsh, Blake swore softly. The outer doors to the ER opened and the few others in the waiting room grew silent. Marsh looked over his shoulder and found a wall of blue approaching. Salem PD had arrived in force. One of their own had been killed tonight. Another clung to life by a thread, his head bashed in, a Deputy ME was still in limbo, and the wife of a cop had also been shot.

Behind the twelve or so patrol officers, Marsh saw Blake's wife, who also happened to be Luce's court secretary. He nudged Blake and jerked his head left.

Blake broke away and moved quickly toward Connie, who met him with her arms open. "I couldn't stay away," she said, tears running down her cheeks. "Mom came over to stay with the kids. How are they?"

"Don't know yet," Blake said. "We're waiting."

No sooner were the words out of his mouth than a doctor came through the inner sanctum doors. "Detective Fielding?" he called.

Marsh broke away and strode toward the doctor, his heart pounding with anxiety. "How's my wife? Can I see her now? And what about Sarajane?"

It wasn't often that the waiting room was full of cops, but the doctor had apparently seen it before, because he didn't back away or show any surprise as the law enforcement group formed a half-circle around him. "I can't tell you about Ms. Nichols," he said, "except to say that she's in the OR and they are doing their damnedest to make sure she comes through. Our surgical staff here rivals any in the country. She's in good hands."

"And my wife?" Marsh pressed, his heart pounding with fear.

"Mrs. Fielding—and the babies—are doing well. Just to be on the safe side, we had an obstetrician come down to give her a look-see and he says everything is good. Her wound" —he traced a line on his right side from just above his waist to just under his armpit— "is long, but not deep. However, the bullet did lodge at the back edge of the armpit. We removed it and sutured the incision. I've cleaned the graze and dressed it, as well. With the okay of the OB, we've given her something for pain that should not affect the babies. We've also administered a mild sedative to relax her. As you can imagine, she's extremely agitated by tonight's…events."

Marsh wanted to reach out and shake the doctor, but he clenched his fists at his sides instead. "So, can I see her *now*?" he demanded.

"Yes, we're getting ready to move her up to the floor. I'll take you back and you can make the transition with her." He looked over his shoulder and motioned to the desk nurse. "Get an update from the OR for these folks, will you?" He touched Marsh's elbow. "One more thing. She gave me her OB's name and we've contacted her. She's on her way over now, just to give your wife some extra assurance. She's deeply concerned about the babies."

Marsh was concerned about Chloe *and* the babies. If the shooter was not already lying dead on his dining room floor, he'd go back and shoot the piece of shit fifty times.

"Marsh!" Luce called out.

He turned.

She waggled her cell phone at him and mouthed the words, *Call me*.

He nodded and followed the doctor through the double doors.

Chloe was pale, groggy, and teary-eyed when Marsh pushed back the curtain to her cubicle.

She tried to smile, but a sob came out instead. He moved quickly to her left side and bent to kiss her. For long moments, he stood with his face pressed against hers, his own tears trickling down his beard-stubbled cheeks, mingling with hers. "Thank God," he murmured over and over.

"Sarajane…," Chloe managed. "How is Sarajane?"

"We don't know yet."

"She's got to be all right."

"She will be, babe. She will be."

Chloe raised her left hand and cradled the back of his neck. "I should have thought sooner that half the pair was missing."

Marsh uttered a strangled laugh. Nancy Drew in the making. "I'm a cop. *I* should have figured it out, not you.

"No one…to blame…but the…bad guys…."

Her hand fell away from his neck and Marsh froze in fear. He pulled away slowly, afraid of what he would find, but the pulse in her neck beat steadily. She had fallen asleep.

He put one hand on her forehead, stroking her with his thumb, and took her left hand in his, their wedding rings touching, giving him solace and reminding him of what a lucky man he was to have found a woman like Chloe.

# chapter 25

$S$ everal more law enforcement personnel had joined the group in the ER waiting room by the time the nurse came back with an update on Sarajane.

"The femoral artery was nicked," she informed them. "Ms. Nichols lost a lot of blood, but the application of the tourniquet probably saved her life. That and fast EMT response." Her gaze swept the group. "The doctor has repaired the damage and he's getting ready to close. She'll be in recovery for awhile, but after they move her up to ICU, she can have visitors. Family only." Again, her eyes moved over the group. "Any family here?"

Luce stepped forward. "Sarajane has only an aunt who lives up near Portland. We grew up together and we're like sisters." Her voice faltered and her eyes grew moist. "I don't want her to be alone…."

"She won't be alone," the nurse assured her. "Her *sister* is here. I'll let you know when they've moved her."

Luce grasped the woman's hand. "Thank you."

The nurse, whose name tag said GABBY, gave Luce's hand a squeeze. "No problem." After another survey of the growing group, she said, "I also checked on your patrol officer, Andy Parr. He was unconscious upon arrival from a blow to the head. They've put him into a coma because his brain swelled. His parents are upstairs with him now. Just a warning—the ICU waiting room is not all that large, and I hear it's pretty full of men and women in blue already, but down the hall and around the corner from there is a much larger waiting room with vending machines."

The nurse turned away and then back again. "I know there's a lot of praying going on here right now. There's also a chapel, if anyone wants it. Aside from that, the best you can do is keep a positive attitude. I've been in this business long enough to know that there's a lot to be said for that." With a quick nod and a smile, she headed back for the double doors.

"Almost forgot!" she said, turning around one more time. "You," she said, pointing at JD, "are supposed to report back to your hospital room ASAP. The doctor wants you there when he makes his rounds so he can release you." She wagged a finger at him. "We need the bed."

JD grinned and rose out of the wheelchair.

"Sit back down," Gabby ordered sternly. "You're in *my* place now, and we have rules, you know."

In a good mood because he knew he was going to be released shortly, JD did as he was told. He winked at Gabby and made her blush. Life was getting back on track. If all went well, he'd be back in the office within the hour, working on this case like he should have been from the beginning. Or maybe not. The LT probably wouldn't okay it just yet. Which meant he could take Luce home…continue with some unfinished business.

All the uniforms took off down the hall, along with some of the plain-clothes guys. Blake and his wife rode up in the elevator with JD and Luce and the officer assigned to keep the newly reconciled couple in his sights. Connie listened, stunned, as Luce gave her an abbreviated version of what had transpired since she'd found the word BOMB! written on her windshield.

Once JD had gotten dressed, he opened the door of his room, climbed back into the wheelchair like a good little patient, and suggested they find some coffee. Luce informed the floor nurse where they were headed and they moved down the hall to the waiting room. JD sprang for hot beverages from the dispensing machine. An hour later, a nurse poked her head in and said the doctor was on the floor.

The foursome made their way back to JD's room, only to find said doctor waiting, his toe tapping on the linoleum, outside JD's door. "You cops are the *worst* patients outside of doctors," he groused.

JD grinned. "Nice to know." He shot a hot glance at Luce. "Even though I'm not fond of hospitals, I can't say my stay here was *that* bad...."

Luce's face turned a fiery shade of scarlet. JD laughed. "It'll probably make my blood pressure sky-rocket, but I need you to give me a kiss, darlin'."

"I'd prefer to give you a bop on the bean," Luce said, bending down to meet his lips.

"Save the kinky stuff for later," JD murmured, claiming her mouth.

"You'll pay for that," Luce practically gasped when she pulled away.

JD laughed. "I certainly hope so!"

"I can see you're back to your normal self," Blake commented, his tone dry, "and I'm not even a doctor."

JD laughed again. It was good to be alive.

Blake and Connie walked with Luce back to the waiting area. The patrol officer assigned to watch over her and JD had stayed behind at JD's door.

"I wonder if the doctor *will* release him," Luce said.

"He's back to being full of it, that's for sure." Blake grimaced. "Sorry, no insult intended."

Luce offered him a half-smile. "I know. He's cocky in a way that's still lovable."

"That's for sure," Connie said, garnering a considering look from her husband. "Well, he is, she said defensively. "Some people are cocky and obnoxious. JD isn't like that."

Blake's cell phone rang, and he excused himself to step away.

"I guess you don't have to worry about ruling on the dismissals and/or mistrials," Connie said.

"I guess not." Luce sighed. "I can't say I'm not relieved. This is the worst case I've ever heard."

"The court reporter is out on stress leave."

"I'm not surprised. I'd like to be out on stress leave myself!"

Her phone vibrated and she looked down at the screen. *Room 312.* "Chloe's a floor above us," she told Connie.

"Gotta go," Blake said.

"What's up?" Luce asked.

"There's a riot at the jail. Attila and Vlad have got the inmates in an uproar. Everyone is recalled. They need help over there."

"Oh, my God! What's next?" Luce asked.

Blake leaned down to kiss his wife goodbye.

"When are they going to let you sleep?" she asked him, concern wrinkling her brow.

"I'll try to catch forty winks later. I have a feeling it's going to be a long, drawn-out situation."

Luce cocked her head at him. "What makes you say that?"

"They have control of the communication center. They got the guards, they have the guns."

Luce had taken the tour when the new jail opened. The communication center was an open hub surrounded by cells on two floors. "How the hell could they overpower the guards? That's supposed to be impossible in that setting."

Blake shrugged. "I guess it was improbable, not impossible, because they did it."

Wheels started churned in Luce's head. "Did they have inside help?"

Blake's eyes widened in surprise.

"Face it," Luce said, "stranger things have happened during this case, and one of them, at least, got into the secure parking area at the courthouse to plant that fake bomb and write on my windshield."

Blake jammed his fingers through his short-cropped hair. "Jesus, this just keeps getting worse and worse. I gotta go." He turned to leave and stopped when JD came rolling in.

Dressed and ready to go, JD said, "I heard. Declared fit to work."

JD stopped in front of Luce, reached for her hands and pulled her down. He planted an extremely hot kiss on her. Then he reached into his pants pocket and pulled out the ring she had given back to him the day before. "Put this back on your finger, Luce. We're getting married. You name the date, darlin', and I'll be there." He slid the ring on, gave her another sizzling kiss, then turned and said to Blake. "You gotta push me outta here or the doc *and* the nurse promised to call security."

Blake grinned. "No problem."

JD narrowed his eyes. "Okay, then. Let's go get these fuckers."

Luce was more than mildly disappointed she wouldn't be taking JD home with her for a few hours of uninterrupted whoopee-making, but she understood the gravity of what was going on at the jail.

The last thing she thought she'd be doing instead was thinking about a wedding, let alone planning it. Certainly, it was months away. Her best friend, who would be her maid of honor, was still in surgery, and her second best friend, who would also stand up for her, was a month or less from delivering twins. Could life get any more complicated?

"Why don't we go up and see Chloe, then I'll take you home so you can shower and change." Connie suggested when the men had gone. "Then I'll bring you back so you can sit with Sarajane."

"Thanks, Connie. You're a gem, in and out of the courtroom." Luce gave her friend a hug and turned to the patrol officer who was currently her shadow. "Does the plan meet with your approval?"

"Fine by me, long as you know I'll be following you. Someone was supposed to switch with me at seven a.m., but if things are still bad out there," he said with a shrug, "you might be stuck with me."

"I'm sorry, I don't even know your name," Luce said, peering at his nametag.

"It's Kip Striker, Judge. Pleased to meet you."

"Likewise," she said. "Keep vigilant, Officer Striker. We don't want any more dead police officers around here."

He nodded, his expression somber.

The three of them took the elevator up a floor and went to Chloe's room. The door was part-way open, so Luce knocked lightly and stuck her head inside. "How is she?" she whispered.

Haggard, sitting in the chair beside his wife's bed, holding her hand, Marsh replied, "Still sleeping. I think that's the best thing for her right now. Just got off the phone with her OB. She had a call after the ER doc contacted her and had to take care of a delivery first. She's...well, she's on whatever floor the delivery room is on. I'm so freaking tired I can't even think straight."

Luce crept in and brought the other chair in the room over and told him to put his feet up on it. Then she went to the closet and pulled an extra pillow and blanket out. Once she had him settled, she put a kiss to his forehead and told him to get some sleep while he could. "I'll be back as soon as I shower and change. Sarie should be out of recovery by then and in ICU. I'll check-in with you as soon as I know anything."

At the door, she hesitated. "You okay?"

"Once I hear from our own OB's mouth that Chloe and the babies are okay, I'll be okay."

"Got'cha. Can I bring you anything?"

"A grande with an extra shot of espresso. After I take a little catnap, if I can, I'll need some extra whiz to keep me awake. It's going to be a long day."

Luce decided not to tell him what was going on at the jail. Her old friend had enough on his plate, as it was.

Instead, she decided to give him some good news. "JD and I are patched up. He gave me back the ring, told me to set a wedding date."

"Thank God! I thought I was going to have to rearrange his face or his brain, or both, if he didn't straighten up."

Luce laughed softly. "You have always been my protector, haven't you, Marsh?"

"Yeah, but I'm gladly handing over that job to JD. You," he said, with a slight lift to his lips, "apparently need fulltime care."

"Smart ass," she said on a laugh, closing the door softly behind her as she left.

# Foolish Heart

**SARAJANE NICHOLS**
**&**
**DOMINIC FIELDING**

# chapter 26

*Three weeks later*

**t**he Fielding house had been turned into something of a hotel.

Marsh, with JD's help, converted the dining room downstairs into a bedroom for Sarajane. The adjoining full bath and no stairs made it convenient for her to recover from the surgery to repair her femoral artery.

Because Mary (the former ghost of the house) had caused the destruction of pretty much everything in the dining room by overturning the hutch containing Chloe's grandmother's grandmother's dishes (achieved by the twitch of a nose to help Marsh apprehend the man who had tried to kill his wife), nothing had been salvageable and the transition to bedroom had been simple.

With the queen bed from the spare bedroom moved downstairs for Sarajane, the guest bedroom now temporarily held twin beds, which the babies would eventually grow into. Marsh's grandmother, Rose Riordan, slept in one and Margaret Steen, otherwise known as Mags to her friends, took the other one.

Chloe had met Mags when trying to figure out who had *really* killed her great-great-great aunt, Mary Mac-Fee (the ghost), in 1901. Mags had handed over a box of things to Chloe that had belonged to her late husband's great-great-great grandfather. In that box had been a journal chronicling the murder of Mary, a feat the nasty Jarvis Steen had considered the greatest accomplishment of his many ill deeds. Mary's fiancé, Jamie Conroy, had been charged, tried, and hanged for the offense three days after her death.

Because of Chloe, that wrong had been corrected.

Mary and Jamie were now happy together in the afterlife.

Occasionally, when Rose or Mags needed to be away from the house for a day or so, Genevieve Laroche, otherwise known as Sarajane's Aunt Gennie, would come and stay and take the other twin bed. When she was not at the Fielding house, she stayed at Sarajane's in the Craftsman-style house Marsh had renovated and lived in prior to marrying Chloe. They had kept the bungalow and Sarajane was now their tenant.

Rose, Mags, and Aunt Gennie hit it off instantly. Marsh's younger twin brothers dubbed them The Girls. They often stayed up late in the night playing cards or chatting about old times.

Marsh's office also had seen some hard times, but that, too, had been set right, with not a bullet hole in sight.

During her recovery, Chloe worried constantly about the state of the disrupted nursery. The birth day of the twins she carried grew ever closer, and the twins grew commensurately. Still recuperating from her own injury, she was not allowed to perform any tasks that might cause her wound not to heal properly. A physical therapist helped keep her in line, doing some exercises that would help build the strength back up in her arm. Any time Marsh spent in the nursery restoring it to it previous homey cuteness, Chloe sat in the corner "supervising" him from the rocking chair that had survived the shooter's vandalism.

Luce and JD repainted the dining room, Marsh's office, the hidey-hole, and the upstairs hallway after ServPro had completed all the blood removal.

Chloe didn't like to dwell on that aspect, because when she did, she was certain that minute traces of the shooter's evil blood remained, having seeped into anything wooden—the floors, the banister, the baseboards, the trim. That's what she got for not only writing about homicides, but for being married to a cop. She *knew* things.

Chloe also didn't like the idea of The Girls having to clean her house, but when she argued with the three older women about hiring a housekeeper, they each informed her, in their own way, that they were "old, not incapacitated." Before the shooting that had injured her and Sarajane, she had often uttered two of those same words herself, so she accepted them from The Girls with equanimity. More than once, Chloe hoped she'd be as young as they were when she reached their ages.

*Sometimes, life can be so confounding*, she thought. *And unexpected.* She sat in the rocker with the mint green-checked cushion watching Marsh put together another rocker with a mint green-striped cushion to replace the one the killer had broken during his rampage. For years her only real friend had been a ghost, or *spirit*, as Mary had preferred to be called. Then she'd met Marsh and everything had changed. He had six brothers and sisters, two parents, and a grandmother, all of whom she loved with all her heart. Then there were his friends—Sarajane, Luce, JD—whom she loved equally. She really had inherited a family when she and Marsh married. How lucky could one girl get?

She had a father of her own, but his third wife, with whom he now had four children, didn't like Chloe hanging around. Chloe thought that was because Ilene didn't want to be reminded of how old Jack Faust actually was. Chloe had a brother, too, but she rarely saw Kyle and only occasionally spoke to him on the phone. She kept in touch because his girlfriend, Ally, called often to talk.

And then, just this morning, Kyle had phoned to say he and Ally we coming for a visit. You could have knocked Chloe over with the proverbial feather. She hadn't told Ally about being shot, but now that they were coming, she didn't have much choice.

Kyle had been understandably shocked when he called back almost immediately, but what surprised Chloe most was that he had taken the news so hard. If she hadn't been mistaken, her brother was actually crying when he'd hung up the phone. Less than an hour later, Ally had sent their flight itinerary via email. They would be arriving in four days. Would Chloe mind making reservations at a nearby hotel for them, for two weeks?

*Two weeks?* Then it dawned on Chloe that her brother was hoping to be around when his niece and nephew were born. Chloe was so touched, *she* began to cry. Marsh had found her that way, sprawled like a beached whale on their bed, going through Kleenex like crazy.

Once she'd stopped blubbering, they had discussed which hotels might be closest, which were economical, and which had a pool (Kyle and Ally were from Southern California, after all). They hadn't reached any decisions yet. Then suddenly, since she had nothing else to do but think, Chloe had a brainstorm.

This was a big old house. Large rooms, plenty of space to spread out. She couldn't believe she'd rambled around in it all by herself, notwithstanding Mary-the-Friendly-Ghost, for nearly two years after her mother had died. According to family tradition, Chloe as the eldest (and only) daughter had inherited the house.

With her foot set to easy-rock and her fingers laced across her burgeoned belly, Chloe said, "We could put Kyle and Ally in the attic. Now that it's all fixed up, it would be a quaint, romantic hideaway for them. And Kyle used to beg to have that for his bedroom when he still lived at home."

Marsh looked up at her from across the room. Chloe loved the way his face crinkled up with worry. "Don't you think that'll be two too many people in the house? We're practically overflowing as it is."

"It is a lot of people," she admitted, "but I haven't seen my brother for over five years. If he stays at a hotel, we won't be able to sit around and just chat. He'll be going back-and-forth, back-and-forth."

"Chloe." He drew her name out.

"Marsh." She drew his name out. She leaned forward as much as her belly would allow. Either Brenden or Mary Kate kicked in protest. "I have never had much of a family and now that I do, I want to enjoy it, *them*, to the fullest."

"You have years ahead of you to enjoy family."

"But I might not see Kyle again for another five years."

"We can take the kids to Disneyland. You can see him then."

"As I said, five years. You can't take children under five to an amusement park. It would be a disaster."

"It wasn't five years, anyway. He came to the wedding."

"And I actually got to visit with him for all of about two hours! That's still like only seeing him every five years."

"What about the cooking?"

"I wouldn't try to cook!"

"That's not what I meant."

"We have three excellent cooks in the house—you, Rose, and Mags. Add Aunt Gennie, when she's here. We won't starve."

"Where will everyone sit when we eat?"

"The table in the kitchen easily seats six and with the leaf, it'll do eight or more. And now that you've added the bar, we could seat four there."

"In other words, 'Give it up, Marsh.'"

She leaned back and started her rocking again, pleased that her husband was so smart. "Exactly!"

"You know the doctor doesn't want you walking up and down the stairs more than once or twice a day."

"I know, but your office is practically right across the hall. There's a sofa and two easy chairs. We can visit in there. We can even have light meals in there, if someone brings up a tray."

"You have an answer for everything, don't you?" he asked, his tone wry.

Batting her eyelashes at him, affecting a coquettish innocence, she said, "I try."

Marsh laughed. He knee-walked over to Chloe, gathering her gently in his arms. "I love you so much," he whispered against her lips.

"I love you, too. All the way to Pluto and back."

"That's a long way." He kissed her, lingering, laughing again when he felt a soft thump against his chest. "One of them wants me to stop."

"Don't stop, he or she is only saying 'hi.' I like kissing you, and since this is the only sex I get these days...."

He laughed. "I wouldn't call this *sex*."

"I wouldn't either, but since we won't be able to *have* sex for probably another seven or eight weeks, I take what I can get." She pulled his hand up to her breast. "Pardon the pun," she said, "but feel free to cop a feel."

And he did.

# chapter 27

**S**arajane lay in bed, bored not just to tears, but beyond, all the way to desperation.

She had everything she needed to entertain her close-by: a small high-def TV, a radio, stacks of paperback books, several hardbound forensic texts she'd owned for years but never had time to read, a Sudoku puzzle book, and an ereader on which she had downloaded game apps, along with several ebooks by new authors and a couple by some old favorites.

A stack of several days' worth of various newspapers, in which she had absolutely no interest, occupied the space beneath the bedside table. If she wanted to know more about the crimes of the century that had involved Luce and JD being threatened and her, Chloe, and JD being shot, she would pick up the phone and call any of the dozens of people she knew at Salem PD.

Also on the bedside table, perched on the tower of hardbound books, she had a cup of coffee, still warm enough that steam rose from it, as Mags had just delivered it on a small plate that also contained two *biscotti*.

At Chloe's house, there was never a shortage of the

Italian cookies, which she special-ordered by the gallon-size container from a company in Arizona.

Sarajane wanted to get up and walk around, but she was allowed only to move from the bed to the easy chair in her bedroom, or from her bed to the bathroom, and if she had supervision, she could walk from the bedroom into the kitchen to join the others for a meal, instead of taking a tray in her room.

*For crying out loud!* She'd been shot three weeks ago. She shouldn't be watched like a toddler taking her first steps. She should be up and moving around like old times already!

But she wasn't.

Sarajane knew it was because they all loved and worried about her. Everyone was so kind, so solicitous. Rose read to her, Mags tried to teach her needlework, Aunt Gennie worked diligently to draw forth her psychic abilities. Sarajane had resisted. "Prowess in the world of mysticism will come to the end in the Nichols family when you're gone, Aunt Gennie," she had informed her father's sister just that morning.

But Aunt Gennie was having none of it. "I didn't know I was a medium until I was in my twenties," her aunt had retorted. "Once I realized I was…well, *different*, I embraced my gift. Cultivated it."

Sarajane wouldn't have called being able to see the future a *gift*, but to each her own.

She also wouldn't have admitted that ever since she'd come out of the anesthetic, she *had* been feeling different, and not because of her leg wound.

No, *feeling* didn't quite describe it. She had been *seeing* differently.

Aunt Gennie described her own ability as a second sight. Sarajane wouldn't go that far, but she had definitely begun experiencing *something*. Not a fugue or dream state, certainly, but perhaps a trance, or even a day-dream.

The last thing she still did *not* want to be able to do

was foresee the future! And yet, the first day she'd taken up residence in the Fielding house, the sun had been shining in the window as she napped and when she awoke, still feeling hazy but relaxed, into her psyche had popped the...the...*whatever* it was that informed her Kyle, Chloe's brother, was coming for a visit with his girlfriend. He had called just hours later.

Later in the day, *whatever* had given her something about Chloe's dad, whom she'd met once, quite by chance, at a crime scene years ago. Jack Faust, a former Oregon State Police officer, according to *whatever*, was going to show up at Chloe's door one of these days and apologize for being an asshole father. Now *that* would be a vision worth having come true!

Sarajane smiled, thinking fondly of Chloe. They'd been acquaintances first, had met because of Chloe's writing. Then Chloe had met Marsh, a friend since Sarajane's childhood, when he'd substitute-taught a criminal investigation class. She and Chloe and Luce were now the *tre migliori amiche*, the three best friends. She supposed she had Marsh to thank for that, but she had Chloe to thank for making Marsh the happiest guy around.

If only Marsh's brother, Dominic, *Father* Dominic, were that personable and available.

Thinking about Dom depressed Sarajane all over again. She'd been *whatevering* about him, too. He been walking around in ordinary street clothes, no white collar around his neck. Like *that* would ever happen. Dom was married to the Church. He'd taken his vows. He'd taken them so seriously that he'd gone to war with that collar on, served as a spiritual counsel and confidant to soldiers in Iraq and Afghanistan.

And now, no one in his family had heard from him for over three years. It was like he'd dropped off the face of the earth, but how could he? Neither Dom, the man she knew, nor Dom, the priest she didn't, would simply vanish without a word to his family! Marsh and his brother Kieran, now a prosecuting U.S. attorney, had been unable to find out anything about Dom's whereabouts, not even from the military. Kieran had gone so far as to engage the assistance of Oregon's two senators, to no avail.

Something wasn't right with Father Dominic.

She both cursed and blessed the memory of kissing him. Such an impetuous but delicious kiss, nineteen long years ago!

And, he'd kissed her back. If he hadn't done that, she might have been able to forget him. But he had, and she couldn't.

That kiss had been amazing. So amazing, that no other man could live up to it. So amazing that just the thought of it kept her burning inside for him, even knowing she could never have him.

Did that make her stupid, delusional, sick, hopeless? All of the above?

And now there was another *whatever*, of him walking up....

Cursing herself, Sarajane ran a string of profanities together that had no meaning. She rolled over in bed so she could sit up, the effort laborious but not quite as painful as it had been three weeks ago.

In the latest *whatever*—she decided right then she had to find another name for the phenomenon that had overtaken her and settled on *vision*—Dom strode up the winding sidewalk with the beautiful dwarf zinnia borders to Marsh and Chloe's house. Impossible!

Dom wouldn't even know Marsh and Chloe had gotten married, that he was about to be an uncle for the first time. How could he? If no one knew where Dom was, how would Dom know anything about them in return? He wasn't some kind of spy, for heaven's sake.

Still....

"Ready for a refill on your coffee?" Aunt Gennie asked, breezing in unannounced. She shot a glance at the still-full cup. "Guess not. Had any good dreams lately?"

Struggling up off the bed so she could move to the chair, Sarajane said, just to bug her aunt, "I *dreamed* I won the lottery."

Aunt Gennie, bent over the bed to straighten it, froze. "Really? A big one?"

"A big one what?"

"Lottery."

Belatedly, Sarajane realized she really *had* envisioned winning the lottery, and should have kept her mouth shut about it. Too late. It was a big one, too, or at least big enough that she'd be happy about it, even after taxes. She thought about lying, telling her aunt she'd just made it up, but what if, some day, that vision bore fruit and she *did* win the lottery? Then Aunt Gennie would probably throw a huge party to celebrate the assured continuation of the mystic Nichols clan *juju*. "Big enough."

Aunt Gennie finished making the bed. "I didn't know you played the lottery."

"I don't. Never bought Megabucks or Powerball tickets and never played scratch-offs."

Her aunt frowned. "Then why...?" She screwed up her face thoughtfully. "You pulling your old Aunt Gennie's leg, Sarie?"

She had an out. Should she take it? Tongue-tied, Sarajane finally said, "Of course not!"

"Then soon as you're able to get out, you better hightail it to the nearest convenience store and buy yourself some lottery tickets, young lady."

Other than being shot, nothing else exciting was going on in her life. Why not? "Maybe I will."

"Want me to turn on the TV for you?"

"No, thanks. My brain is atrophying enough as it is."

"The radio then?"

"No, but maybe one of the easy listening CDs? Something calming." *As if I'm not calm enough,* she thought. *I'm so calm, I can actually sit still long enough to watch grass grow. I need to work!*

As if the thought itself had given her a light-bulb

moment, Sarajane twitched. "Can you hand me my phone, Aunt Gennie?"

"Sure." Her aunt retrieved the smartphone from the bedside table and handed it over. "Anything else I can do for you, sweetie? That coffee must be cold by now. Can I refresh if for you?"

"No, thanks, it's fine."

"Well, if you're sure…." Aunt Gennie put the coffee cup and cookies on the table beside Sarajane's chair, gave a last look around and left the room.

The phone rang twice before someone picked up at the ME's office. "Cameron, hi! It's me." She added, in case her boss had forgotten about her, "Sarajane."

He chuckled. "It sure is! How's it going, kid? We miss you around here."

"I'm doing well, thank you, but I'm getting ready to start pulling the hair out of my head one strand at a time, I'm so freaking bored sitting here doing nothing every day. I was wondering, is there any backlogged paperwork I can do here? Any case notes to be scanned? Autopsy particulars to be inputted?"

Dr. Cameron Swift, the Chief Medical Examiner, inhaled on a breath of surprise. "Are you *sure* you're really Sarajane Nichols, the biggest complainer on the planet when it comes to doing paperwork, asking me if I have any *paperwork* that needs doing?" He laughed again, obviously pleased. "Well, slap my butt and call me Judy!"

"Okay, Judy, is there some paperwork I can do at home? I'm begging you! *Please!*"

He chortled again. "Miss having you around SJ. No one can make me laugh like you do."

"Is that a yes?"

"Yes, my dear, it's a yes. I'll have Freddy bring some stuff over to you. You sure your doctor is okay with this?"

"I haven't asked him, but since I'm allowed to sit in a chair, all I need is a card table and I'll be good to go.

You have saved me from daytime TV, Cam. I owe you big time!"

"You'll owe me paperwork without complaint when you come back, Ms. Nichols." He tried to affect a stern tone, but failed.

"Sure," she said meekly, knowing she'd never be able to make that kind of commitment and that Cam wouldn't be expecting it. She thought he rather enjoyed sparring with her about the amount of paperwork the ME's office generated and her suggestions for how they could streamline the office processes.

Being from different generations had something to do with his reticence to move into the twenty-first century where electronics were king, but mostly, he still maintained that most people learned more by actually reading a report in their hands than by looking at it with glazed eyes on a computer screen. Sarajane couldn't find fault with that aspect of his argument.

All in all, he was a peach of a boss, a diligent ME, and a crack medical doctor who left no human cell unturned when it came to performing autopsies.

"I'm going to try and make it over to see you on the weekend," he said. "This place has been hopping lately, and without you here…."

She could almost see him lifting his shoulders in that sad-dog manner of his.

"Anyway, it's been so busy, I've been checking every night to see if the moon forgot to wane."

Sarajane's nights had been restless and lacking in sleep, so she felt safe in telling him, "No such anomaly has occurred, Cam."

"Well, whatever's causing it, we're goddamned busy down here and I want it to slack off. Anna's beginning to think I ran away with another woman."

"Like she would!" Sarajane said, chuckling. Cam and Anna had been married thirty years, which she knew because she'd been invited to a party thrown by his adult children to celebrate the event. The Swifts were still as happy and in love as Marsh and Chloe, the newlyweds. "Ask Freddy to bring me a large strawberry shake from DQ, would you? I've been craving one like crazy. Tell him to skip the whipped cream."

"Done. Take care, SJ. Anna sends her love, too."

"Back at her. Thanks, Cam."

Sarajane disconnected with a sigh of satisfaction. She got herself out of the chair and limped and hobbled to the bathroom, using the crutches the doctor had insisted upon. Next week, if the doc gave her a thumbs up, she was starting physical therapy. If all went well with that, maybe she could be back in her own home soon.

Had she been completely honest, being in the converted dining room/bedroom was a helluva lot better than remaining in the hospital or going to a convalescent facility. She loved Marsh and Chloe to death, but she already felt like she'd out-stayed her welcome and she really did miss the little bungalow she rented from them.

Besides, how many people and how much turmoil could a pregnant woman and an expectant father take, anyway? Some days the Fielding house was like Grand Central Station.

# chapter 28

*F*reddy Nelson knocked on the front door around three p.m. Mags, with Aunt Gennie right behind her, gave him a once-over before allowing him admittance. "I've brought SJ a milkshake and some busywork," he explained.

"Busywork!" Mags exclaimed. "She's—"

"Perfectly capable of doing busywork while she sits in a chair," Sarajane cut in, crutching in from the bedroom. "Hi, Freddy."

He showed visible signs of relief. "Hey, SJ. How's it going?"

Aunt Gennie circled him, looking him up and down. Sarajane knew exactly what her only relative had in mind.

"Aunt Gennie, Mags, this is Freddy Nelson, from my office. He's the other Deputy ME I work with. He's not married, because I know that's exactly what you're wondering, and he swings the other way, so you don't have to go into match-making mode, okay?"

"Well!" Aunt Gennie said, her arms suddenly akimbo. "Now you've gone and embarrassed the poor boy."

"Not in the least," Freddy said, grinning. "Here's your shake, SJ." He started to hand it to her, realized her hands were full of crutches, and gave it to Mags instead. "Gotta get the rest of the stuff out of the car. Back in a flash."

He made two trips and under Sarajane's direction, put the boxes next to her chair in the bedroom and set up the card table. "This is cool," she said. "I've never seen a rectangular-shaped card table before, and it slides right over the arms of the chair so I can still put my leg up on the ottoman *and* reach the table to work."

"When I started loading up your stuff—the laptop and the portable scanner, included—I figured I'd better find you a table that would accommodate everything and still be accessible."

"You did good, Freddy," Sarajane said, pleased.

"Thanks. The house has wi-fi, right?" he asked.

"Yep."

"Good, then you can log into the database from here. I'll get everything plugged in and hooked up. Oh, yeah, here's a thumb drive, too. If you need to print something, I thought maybe you could do it on Chloe's printer, so I wouldn't have to cart one of the inkjets over."

"Good thinking."

"Cam says, if you need more to do after this, just call. He's got twenty boxes, at least, stacking up."

"And he says *I* complain about doing paperwork."

"He's the worst," Freddy agreed as he set up the peripherals.

Sarajane sat on the bed, sipping her strawberry shake, watching him. "Thanks for this. I know DQ was out of your way."

"No problem. I thought it was such a good idea, I ordered one for myself, except mine was chocolate." He checked the scanner to verify its functionality. "Okay, everything is good to go. If you have any questions, call me. I like getting out of the office for reasons other than dead people."

"I will, and if I can ever return the favor, just let me know."

Freddy grimaced. "God forbid I have to ever go through what you did, SJ. Let's just call us even, all right?"

"You're the best."

"We're *both* the best," he said, "and I want you back to work sooner rather than later. Cam's a good boss, but he's crabbier when you're not there to make him laugh."

Sarajane grinned. "Cam crabby? Hard to believe."

Freddy laughed. "Take care." He kissed her cheek, then was out the door."

The hours flew by as Sarajane sat at her makeshift desk, entering reports into the database, scanning copies of Cam's hand-written autopsy reports for emailing to requesting agencies. She shifted periodically, trying to ease the pain in her left thigh without much success. Before she knew it, she was half-way through a box.

"Knock, knock," Marsh's grandmother said from the doorway.

Sarajane looked up with a smile. "Hi, Rose."

"You look happy."

"I am. Not quite the same as being at work, but at least it *is* work."

"Just don't let yourself get too tired out." Rose entered the room and sat on the bed. "I've thought of something else you and Chloe might be interested in. I've just been upstairs talking to her about it."

"Oh, yeah, what?" Sarajane leaned back in her chair, reaching for a pill bottle. She extracted one tablet, then downed it with ice water from the insulated glass on the side table.

"I know that you girls were going to take the infant care class with Marsh, but with all the…commotion, you've had to skip it. I was thinking, would you be interested in having the instructor come and give the classes here, at the house?"

Sarajane took another swallow, then put the glass back. "I think that's a fantastic idea, Rose! What did Chloe say?"

"She likes it, and I'd already talked to Marsh before I brought it up to Chloe." Rose folded her hands in her lap. "The thing is, the babies could come at any time, and none of you even knows how to change a diaper, or get a bottle ready, or dress a baby or bathe it."

"When you put it like that," Sarajane said, suddenly feeling incompetent, "we sound like total bunglers." She chuckled, trying to make a joke out of it.

Rose shook her head emphatically. "That's not what I meant at all. I just know that you would've already learned all this weeks ago, if not for the…for the…."

"Shooting," Sarajane filled in.

"Yes, the shooting." Rose's eyes filled with tears and her voice grew hoarse. "I don't know why I have such a hard time saying it." She swiped at her eyes. "I just know I thank God many times a day that you and Chloe and the babies are alive, and I ask Him to see that you heal completely."

Humbled, Sarajane said, "Thank you, Rose."

"You and Chloe and Luce are like my very own granddaughters," she said. "I couldn't bear it if…." She trailed off, unable to voice her worst fears.

"I'd get up and hug you, if I could," Sarajane said sincerely.

"So, that's a yes?" Rose asked, rising.

"Definitely. I'm bored out of my gourd with this recuperative crap. I'm dying to learn how to change diapers. Bring it on!"

Rose bent over and gave Sarajane the hug instead.

Later, as she turned off the light and tried to get comfortable in bed so she could sleep, Sarajane wondered if she hadn't overdone it by sitting up so much during the afternoon, then compounded things by insisting she was fully able to make it to the table to join the rest of them for dinner.

The stew, which had been made by Mags and simmered in the large Crockpot Marsh had bought to facilitate group meals, had been delicious. Rose's homemade bread had been phenomenal and the half-glass of red wine Aunt Gennie had allowed her (because of her medication) had been exquisite.

But now…. God, how her leg ached. Actually, it was worse than an ache. The part of her that wanted to get on with her physical therapy next week resisted asking the doctor for pain meds that would offer more relief than she got from ibuprofen. Another part of her, the practical side that recognized she had a pretty high tolerance for pain, knew she had no choice but to contact the doc and let him know that it felt like someone was sticking hot knife blades in her wound.

Sarajane made the call first thing the next morning. The doctor had a full schedule, but his receptionist said if she could come right away, they'd work her in. Knowing Marsh was up because she'd heard him come down the stairs, Sarajane used speed dial to call him on her smart-phone. He picked up on the second ring.

"Hi, it's your friendly downstairs tenant," she quipped. "I need a favor."

"Sure, what's up?"

"I have to see the doctor and they said if I come right now, they'll squeeze me in. I need a big, tough guy to get me there."

Marsh laughed. "That's me! Are you okay?"

"I guess I'll find out once I get there," she answered evasively. "Since I can't really get dressed, I'm just going to brush my teeth, comb my hair, and put on my robe. Can you give me five?"

"I can give you as long as you like, Sarie. Do you need some help? The Girls are up already."

Sarajane thought about asking for Mags, as she was a little younger than Rose, but then decided she could help herself. "No, thanks. I can do it."

No sooner had she disconnected than a knock sounded at the door. "Come in," she said to whomever it was, thinking it would either be Mags or Rose. Instead it was Aunt Gennie.

"I knew you'd be needing me this morning," her aunt said.

"Don't tell me you had a dream," Sarajane teased, reaching for her crutches.

Aunt Gennie frowned. "All right, I won't. You use the bathroom and I'll get your robe and slippers ready. Do you want to wear socks?"

"Yes, I think so."

In about triple the time it usually took her uninjured self to use the bathroom, wash her hands and face, and brush both her teeth and her hair, she was back in the bedroom, where she rested her crutches against the dresser so she could slip into her robe. She sat while Aunt Gennie maneuvered her feet into the socks and slippers. "I don't like going out in my nightwear," she groused. "I feel like one of those people you see who are too lazy to get out of their pajamas before going to McDonald's for breakfast."

"I doubt they have a bullet hole in them anywhere," Aunt Gennie chided.

"I know you're right…."

"Ready?" Marsh asked from the doorway.

"As I'll ever be," Sarajane said. "I hope this isn't making you late for work."

"You know the cop's life, Sarie. Hours are pretty flexible, but even so, the LT understands that I'm at your disposal until you're back on your feet. And if I can't come when you need me, JD will."

"My heroes," she said wryly, but she knew that he knew that she was really saying *Thank you.*

# chapter 29

Marsh insisted on waiting while Sarajane went in for her appointment. When the physician had finished his exam, he called Marsh into the exam room.

Sarajane offered him a wobbly smile, and he could tell she was in pain. "How's she doing?" he asked the doctor.

"Our girl has an infection. I've prescribed an antibiotic that should take care of it, as well as an ointment I want her to massage in twice a day. I'm also giving her a scrip for Oxycontin for pain. There's a lot of nerve damage going on at both the incision and initial wound sites," the doctor explained. "I think it'll work better than Oxycodone because it's time-released and has a longer pain-relief life, and as we found out right off, Hydrocodone doesn't seem to work for her."

Sarajane waved her hand at the doctor. "I'm here."

"Sorry." He redirected his gaze toward her and put his hand on her shoulder. "If it doesn't work, or it's not giving you at least twelve hours of relief, call me and I'll work out something else, but under *no* circumstances are you to take more than two of the Oxy a day. Understood?"

Sarajane nodded.

"Good." He turned back to Marsh. "My nurse emailed all the scrips over to the pharmacy, which Sarajane says is near your house, so they should be ready by the time you get there. If things really get bad, of course, you need to call me immediately."

Once again, he addressed Sarajane. "If you still have pain but it's not debilitating, take a couple of ibuprofen to tide you over until your next dose of Oxy. If you have to do that for more than two days, again, you need to call me."

Sarajane blinked at him. She was hurting badly, but he'd given her the drug a few minutes earlier and it was already starting to take the edge off her pain.

"Sarajane," the doctor said, "do you understand what I'm saying about the medication?"

She nodded, but between not sleeping well the night before and the potency of the drug, she wasn't feeling talkative. She had to force herself to say, "Yes."

"I got it, doc," Marsh said. "We'll be watching her, make sure she doesn't overmedicate."

"Good, good. I'll see you next week at your scheduled appointment time, Sarajane. I think we may put off physical therapy for another week after that, make sure the infection is gone."

"Okay," she said.

The doctor and Marsh helped her off the exam table, and Marsh grabbed her crutches and eased them under her armpits.

"Hate these," she mumbled.

"I know," Marsh commiserated, "but you gotta use 'em. It's either that or I carry you."

"You will not!"

He raised an eyebrow at her. "Bet me."

Sarajane had known Marsh too long and too well to doubt him. She thanked the doctor and made her way out of the office at a snail's pace, toward the van Marsh had driven for her convenience, rather than his truck. On second thought, snails probably traveled faster. She'd moved so slowly back at his house, he'd insisted on carrying her down the stairs at his front porch. Now he'd have to carry her back up again when they got home.

This getting shot business really sucked!

God, was she feeling good and sorry for herself today.

On the way back home, a groggy Sarajane asked, "What's the status of the Paired-Ups?"

Marsh spared a glance for her while he drove. "You sure you'll remember what I say later?"

"I would've asked last night at the dinner table, but I didn't want to upset—"

"You think Chloe's some kind of wuss, that she can't take hearing about these assholes?"

"I wasn't worried about your wife," Sarajane murmured. "I don't want The Girls worrying about those whack jobs coming around again."

Marsh put on his signal and made a turn. "I hear you. Gran is hiding her anxiety well, but I know she was really thrown by everything that's happened. She loves Chloe and those babies like crazy already.

"I know. So give."

"They've located and arrested all the Killzone freaks except for the Montana and Texas pairs. Both are big, wide-open states and the respective agencies don't think they've left, but are hiding out somewhere, maybe still committing murders they don't know about yet."

"Montana's so close."

"It is, and we've got someone on Luce and JD constantly."

"Bet they love that."

"Luce is sort of used to it because she's had a bailiff in the courtroom, but JD's throwing a shit fit."

Sarajane laughed softly. "Mr. Macho."

Marsh nodded. "Exactly. Now that he's moved into Luce's place, they can not only look out for each other, but we only need to have one officer on them at a time, instead of two separately."

An image of Pat O'Hara, sitting dead in his patrol car outside the Fielding house the night he'd been assigned to watch over Chloe and Sarajane, flitted through Marsh's mind. He knew that a lone officer outside Luce's house might be at equal risk, but the men assigned to that duty had been well-briefed ahead of time. God willing, those preparations would be enough to save not only their own lives, but Luce and JD's, as well, if it came to that.

"Have they set a date for the new trial to start?"

"Not yet. I talked to Luce while I was waiting for you and she said Judge Calvin is going to hear it. Word is, he's not going to let them proceed together. I think that's the best way to go." He blew out a frustrated breath. "After they caused that riot at the jail, the Sheriff decided they shouldn't even be in the same building, even though they're both in solitary. Took a while, but they've split them up."

"How did they do that?"

"One is still at the Marion County jail and the other is being housed in the Linn County facility. It's less than thirty away so it's not too bad of a commute to get his ass to the courthouse, if need be. If the judge denies a joint hearing, by the time the second trial comes up, they can bring the a-hole back to Marion County because his sidekick will have gone on to death row by then."

"Fat chance of him being executed with the governor's moratorium still in force."

"Maybe we'll have a new governor by then."

Beside him, Sarajane sighed, rubbing gently at her thigh.

"Does it hurt bad?"

"Not so much since I took the Oxy. It's taking the edge off a little. I'm going to take some ibuprofen when we get back to the house, though, since he said I could."

"He said after ten hours, not one. Give it some time to

work."

Sarajane stuck out her bottom lip in a gesture he recognized from childhood. It meant she'd damned well do what she pleased.

Marsh's fingers clenched around the steering wheel. Chloe and Sarajane being shot was so senseless.

If he'd only realized while he'd been sitting in that conference room down at the station that half the killing pair was still unaccounted for—all of this pain and anguish might have been avoided. Chloe shouldn't have been the next thing to an invalid when she should have been enjoying the last month of her pregnancy and getting the final touches ready for the twins' arrival.

Sarajane wouldn't be facing a nasty infection, either, or months of physical therapy, and perhaps never walking again without a limp. Luce and JD would still be under armed surveillance, regardless, because two pairs of killers still had not been arrested.

"You think Dominic will ever show up?" Sarajane asked out of the blue.

"What brought that up?" Marsh responded, startled.

She lifted her shoulder. "Just wondering."

Marsh considered that an evasive reply and remained silent for a minute while he considered what was really behind the query. Finally, he said, "You were mumbling about Dom when they transported you in the ambulance."

"I was not!"

"You were. You think the EMTs just pulled my brother's name out of the air?"

She remained stubbornly silent, closing her eyes, probably hoping to forestall further conversation.

"You been having a *juju* moment of your own, Sarie?"

Her eyes flew open and she jerked her head toward him. "What makes you ask that?"

"I guess I've been around your Aunt Gennie too much lately," he said. "She tells anyone who will listen that she's certain the *juju* will strike you any day now." He grunted. "You know, this *juju* stuff both intrigues and bothers me. I looked it up on the Internet and it was originally a gypsy word for 'luck,' but now it's mostly used to mean '*bad* luck.' There was even one definition that says it's a premonition of the future."

""That would be Aunt Gennie's version," Sarajane said dryly. "She says she gets her second sight when she kinda goes into a dream state, not for a long period of time, but long enough to see events or things and to remember them." Sarajane rearranged herself, apparently trying to get more comfortable. "She mostly sees things that *symbolize* events or people, but she often finds it difficult to decipher the *meaning*. Except...."

"Except what?"

"Well, she says she always knows *who* is involved, even if she can't tell *what* is going to happen."

Marsh eased his foot against the brake pedal for a red light. He tapped both his index fingers against the steering wheel and looked at her. "And you, Sarie—do you go into a dream state, too?"

Sarajane straightened in her seat as if someone had put a live wire to her. Perhaps if she hadn't been drugged up, she might have been able to keep it to herself. Instead, the Oxycontin seemed to work like truth serum on her. "You won't tell anyone, will you?" she whispered.

"Chloe and I don't keep secrets from each other."

Sarajane shrugged. "I wouldn't expect you not to tell Chloe. She lived with a ghost, for Pete's sake. If anyone would understand precognitive visions, she would."

Satisfied that he wasn't being asked to deceive his wife, Marsh said, "When Aunt Gennie told me she'd had a vision of white collars tumbling around in the air like they were being swept up in a twister, who do you think I thought of? And now you're asking me if I think Dom will ever turn up again?" Marsh glanced at the signal and eased away at the green. He briefly looked back at her, a look of compassion on his face. "Aunt Gennie said she wasn't going to tell you about her most recent *juju*."

"About Dom? She didn't!" Stunned into momentary silence, Sarajane finally asked, "How could she keep that from me?"

"Take it easy. She didn't do it to be mean. You've endured a lot of crap lately. She's worried about you and didn't want to add to the load."

"Still...."

"I can only deduce that you had a precognition of your own," Marsh said, trying not to sound skeptical. "Did it involve white collars?"

"No," Sarajane admitted. From the expression on her face and the tone of her voice, misery and hope warred evenly within her. "It *was* Dom I saw, though. He was walking right up to your front door and he wasn't wearing a white collar at all."

# chapter 30

Contrary to the doctor's advice and Marsh's warning, Sarajane took the two ibuprofen, removed her robe, used the bathroom, then immediately crawled into bed and slept soundly until well after the noon hour.

She woke feeling slightly better, without the searing pain in her thigh. She was also hungry and remembered that she had missed breakfast. She got out of bed, slid her feet into her slippers, and pulled on her robe. When she reached for her crutches, one fell forward to the floor and the other fell sideways, hitting the stack of paperbacks and catching the lamp cord on it's way down.

The racket brought a trio of elderly women scurrying to her room. They didn't bother to knock.

"Are you okay?"

"Did you fall?"

"What happened?"

She answered them all at once. "I'm fine, I didn't fall, I'm just clumsy and knocked over my crutches when I reached for them."

Aunt Gennie, the youngest of them, came around and offered her shoulder for Sarajane to lean on as she hobbled away from the mess on the floor and around to the end of the bed. Rose ran off to get the broom because the light bulb had broken. Mags picked up the crutches and handed them to Gennie, put the lamp back on the table, then started gathering the paperbacks, careful to avoid broken glass.

Rose returned with a whisk broom and dustpan and handed them over to Mags who made short order of the shards. Rose unplugged the lamp, removed the shade and unscrewed what remained of the bulb. She read the label on the base and left the room again, returning several minutes later with a new three-way bulb.

"You three are amazing," Sarajane said.

"We are," Aunt Gennie agreed, drawing chuckles from her elder friends.

"You hungry?" asked Rose. "Mags made some delicious cream of mushroom soup for lunch and there's some homemade bread left from dinner."

"Actually, I'm starved. Any chance I can eat in the kitchen?"

"You can eat anywhere except upstairs, sweetheart," Aunt Gennie said.

"And Chloe's down having her lunch, as well, so you two can visit," said Rose.

"I'll go set a place," Mags contributed. "And there's banana cream pie for dessert."

Sarajane groaned, but she wasn't sure whether it was from delight or despair. She was in danger of having a muffin top by the time she left the Fielding house!

She excused herself to go to the bathroom, then took the door that adjoined her room to the kitchen a while later. Her soup had already been dished up and several slices of bread had been put on a small plate for her.

"Water or iced tea?" her aunt asked once she was seated.

"The tea sounds good. How are you doing, Chloe?"

"Okay, except for trying to master the art of eating soup left-handed. It didn't turn out so well for me," she said ruefully. "Mags put mine in a cup so I can drink it. I can't believe it still hurts to lift my arm!"

"I know *exactly* how you feel," Sarajane said with vehemence. She eased her leg up on the chair that Rose had padded with a small pillow from the living room sofa. "Ahh," she said.

"The Girls told me about the infection. Still having pain?" Chloe asked.

"Not so much right now. The new meds the doc gave me are apparently working, but aside from that, the wound is starting to feel itchy and tight as it heals and everything pulls." She picked up her soup spoon, frowning. "I'm starting to sound like a chronic complainer!"

"If you are, then I am, too," Chloe commiserated. "I'm so worried I won't be able to hold my babies...."

"Speaking of babies," Rose said, apparently trying to lift their spirits, "I lined up Colleen Fitzgerald, the infant care teacher, to come to the house. She says since it's just the three of you, she can do everything in one night. She'll be here tomorrow evening at six. We'll eat early."

"So soon?" Chloe asked. "That was fast."

"I explained the situation to her," Rose said, "and she was more than happy to accommodate."

"Can we actually learn it all in one night?" Sarajane asked, spooning up her soup.

"She'll cover how to hold them and change their diapers, and also bathing, burping, and feeding." Rose looked fondly at Chloe. "The rest, she says, will come naturally."

Chloe actually laughed. "I doubt that, but I appreciate her confidence." She looked at Sarajane. "You sure you're up for it?"

"Absolutely. Maybe we should go buy a couple of baby-size dolls to practice on after she leaves."

"As you know," said Mags, arriving at the tail-end of the discussion, "I never had children, so I've never changed a diaper. If I want to help out, maybe I'd better sit in on this class."

"I don't think one more would hurt," said Rose. "I intend to sit on the sidelines and listen myself. Been a long time since I took care of any babies!"

Aunt Gennie said, "All of us are going to do fine. Whether we've had any of our own or not, each one of us has an inherent ability to do it right, and Marsh, bless his heart, will take to it like hummingbirds take to bright red flowers."

Sarajane grinned. Her aunt did have a way with words. She wondered how Marsh would like being compared to a hummingbird.

"Is Luce coming?" Chloe asked. "She did tell us she might like to attend the class with us."

Rose pushed away from the counter. "I didn't know that. I'll call and ask and if she says yes, I guess I'd better call Colleen back and tell her to be prepared for a small crowd."

"The more the merrier," Chloe said as she polished off the soup in her mug. "I'll welcome all the help I can get with two babies in the house!"

"What time does your brother arrive on Thursday?" Sarajane asked.

"They're landing at PDX at 9:05 in the morning. Marsh was going to drive up and get them, but they wanted to rent a car so they don't have to borrow one to get around down here. They should be here by noon, I'd think."

"Do they know they're coming to Recuperation Central?"

"Yeah, and they're fine with it. Kyle was actually excited about staying in the attic." She finished off the last bite of bread. "Boys will be boys, you know. He used to sneak up there to play, even though Mom forbid it."

"Why would she do that?" Sarajane asked, surprised.

"I'm guessing it had a little something to do with Mary scaring the crap out of her up there a couple of times when she was younger."

"Ah," Sarajane said on a laugh.

"Who's Mary?" Mags asked.

"I'll tell you later," Rose said. She looked at Chloe. "That is, if it's all right with you?"

Chloe nodded.

Aunt Gennie chimed in. "Let's leave these girls in peace for a while. We were going to change the linens on Sarajane's bed, remember? And while it's nice, and the girls are visiting, we should take a walk around the block."

As soon as the older ladies left the kitchen, Sarajane turned an amused glance toward Chloe. "Doesn't take Rose long to deflect questions about Mary."

"No, and I'm sure she'll have a blast giving Mags the scoop."

"Has she been back since that that night?"

"No." Chloe rearranged her butt in the chair and reached for another piece of bread. "I've never been much of a churchgoer until recently, but I do pray and I thank God every day that Mary warned me there was an intruder." She visibly shuddered. "You and I probably wouldn't be here talking to each other right now if she hadn't."

"I'd like to thank her for saving our lives," Sarajane said, "so if she ever comes back, you be sure and tell her for me, will you?"

"Definitely."

"I haven't done much praying since…well, since Dom took off, but I also thank God every night, not only for Mary warning you, but for Marsh having the where-withal to put that tourniquet on my leg. Even though the artery was only nicked, I might have bled to death before the EMTs got to us."

"We were both lucky, in so many ways," Chloe murmured. She picked up her spoon and put it in the cup, then placed the cup on her empty bread plate. "Has any-thing changed for you since the…the shooting?"

Sarajane thought she might play dumb and say, *What*

*do you mean?* Instead, she asked, "Have you talked to Marsh today?"

"No, I was still sleeping when he brought you back. I had kind of an uncomfortable night, and he doesn't like to wake me when I finally fall asleep." Chloe put her elbow on the table and rested her chin in the palm of her hand. "So, what gives?"

Sarajane blew out a breath. Chloe was her friend and friends share things. "I suppose I have a finer appreciation for life," she said, "and I…." She broke off, staring down at her soup bowl, as if she could read the mushrooms, or something. When she finally looked up, she knew from Chloe's expression that she didn't look happy. "I got the *juju*," she finished on a whisper.

Chloe's good arm fell to the table and her mouth dropped open. "The *juju*? Like Aunt Gennie's second-sight *juju*?"

"Not exactly, but close."

Chloe leaned forward on her elbow, her expression now eager. "How so?"

"I knew your brother was going to come, before he called you."

"No!"

Sarajane nodded. "I'm going to win a sizable lottery."

"You're kidding!"

"Nope." She decided not to mention Chloe's dad to her. "And I saw Dom walk up your sidewalk, pretty as you please, and knock on your front door."

"Dominic? Marsh's *brother*?"

"Yep."

"When? When is he coming?"

"I don't know, but perhaps the better question, since no one's heard from him in almost three years, is how does he know where Marsh lives now?"

Chloe waved away the query. "He's been in the military as a chaplain. He'll have connections. The military can find anybody."

"Marsh couldn't find *Dom* through the military."

"True." Chloe chewed on her bottom lip. "Well, maybe Dom's been in touch with their folks."

"If he's been in contact with Maureen and Quinn, surely they would have called and said so." Her eyebrows dipped in a frown. "*Why* would he come *here?*"

"To see his brother?"

Sarajane supposed it could be just that simple. Although, really, had anything ever been simple where Dominic Fielding, the love of her life, was concerned?

"Ohmygod!" Chloe cried.

"What?" Sarajane cried back.

"You've got the *juju*, but unlike Aunt Gennie, you see both the who *and* the what."

Sarajane stared at her friend in stunned silence. Until that moment, it hadn't hit her that her *juju* surpassed Aunt Gennie's. *Ohmygod* was right....

# chapter 31

Sarajane worked through the second half of the box she'd begun to tackle the day before. With her leg aching badly, she took another Oxy at eight, along with another dose of antibiotic, rubbed in the cream the doc had prescribed, and called it an early night.

After ten hours in bed under the influence of the new pain med, she didn't toss and turn during the night and woke up, for the first time in a long time, feeling refreshed.

She made her way to the bathroom and managed to get a shower and a shampoo without much trouble. She left her honey-colored hair to air dry because it had a natural wave to it that she actually liked. Then she applied moisturizer to her face and skin, at least where she could reach.

Her doctor had told her before leaving the hospital that he favored the moist wound care approach and gave her a full sheet of instructions to follow. "Moist wound care," he had said, "results in up to fifty percent faster healing, lowers the chance of infection, doesn't destroy newly formed tissue, and leaves less scaring." So much for avoiding the infection!

Other than minor scrapes and cuts as a kid, Sarajane had never had a major wound, so she entrusted her care to his capable hands. So far, she'd seen her wound each time the dressing had to be changed. Though always appalled at the sight of it, because it was healing from the inside out, as opposed to dry healing, which went the other way, she had to admit it was less gruesome with each new bandage. Except for now, of course, it was an angrier red than usual from the infection, and warm to the touch.

The doctor had also warned her that leg wounds were slower to heal and that even with physical therapy, she could take up to a year, or even longer, to get full strength back in that appendage.

Every time she thought about it, Sarajane found herself getting a little depressed. Not only would she probably have an ugly scar on her thigh, she might never be fully back to where she was before that homicidal maniac had fired his weapon.

And then, when she started feeling good and sorry for herself, she'd think about how Chloe had also been shot, and how, if the bullet had gone just one or two inches to the left, Chloe might have lost one or both of the babies. At that point, she'd promptly tell herself to shut the hell up and be grateful everyone had survived the ordeal alive.

She also counted herself lucky to have such good friends. Really, how many women had a house rearranged for them, with sudden built-in caregivers (The Girls) no less, who also knew how to cook and hold you when you cried?

Once she was dressed in a fresh nightgown, and had taken all her meds, Sarajane headed to the kitchen for breakfast, which she'd been able to smell since waking. Someone had made cinnamon rolls and her mouth watered in anticipation. She might even have two, if there were two left and everyone else had eaten.

When she maneuvered her way into the kitchen, it was empty. A plate of cinnamon rolls sat in the center of the table and a place had been set for her, with a carafe of coffee left within easy-reaching distance. Just the thought of how considerate everyone in this house was brought tears to her eyes. God, how she loved them all!

She poured herself a coffee first, then helped herself to a roll, savoring several bites before she picked up the newspaper someone had left on the table. For the first time in over three weeks, she decided to have a look at what was happening in the world. The news was the same-old, same-old—monetary crises, tornadoes tearing up neighborhoods, terrorists at work in the Middle East. North Korea and Iran still playing with nuclear weapons, both wanting to blow up the United States. What the new pope was doing.

A vague sound, almost like knocking, caused her to pause from her reading. She cocked her head, listening, but whatever it was had stopped.

She went back to the paper. Locally, Judge Calvin had denied the Paired-Ups' request to be tried together. So, Marsh had heard right. The two killers in Texas had been arrested late the day before, found at a ranch in the panhandle, where they'd tried to take two residents hostage and planned to torture and murder them. Fortunately for the homeowners, they'd been ready for any eventuality and two more Paired-Ups had been stopped.

Sarajane heaved a sigh of relief, but still worried about the two remaining psychos in Montana. The state just wasn't that far from Oregon. She hoped they hadn't gotten any bright ideas about springing the pilots of their psycho spaceship, who were being held in isolation in separate jails, or for that matter.... Good lord! What if they *did* still plan to come after Luce and JD?

She thought she heard the knocking sound again, but when she concentrated, trying to hear, there was nothing.

She went back to ruminating about The Pair-Ups' masterminds. Other states, including the masterminds' home state of California, were clamoring for them to be extradited, but Oregon had first dibs, possession being nine-tenths of the law. They had been indicted on numerous charges, including aggravated murder, which had been compounded when they killed a police officer and would result in a death sentence, if convicted. The indictment also had listed multiple counts of attempted murder, kidnapping, assault, solicitation to commit murder, use of interstate communication to solicit murder, and menacing. The list of charges was so long it almost made Sarajane's head spin, and the reporter hadn't even listed all of them.

For relief, she turned to the funnies. She was laughing over Ziggy when the doorbell rang.

It wasn't until then that it finally dawned on her how quiet the house was. Why hadn't she noticed when she'd been listening and trying to pinpoint the knocking sounds? Even so, she expected one or more of the lively but elderly trio, who had assumed nursing, cooking, and housekeeping duties in the Fielding house, to rush to the door to see who had arrived.

Not a footstep could be heard all through the house. Belatedly, as she rose, Sarajane happened to glance at the fridge and saw a note.

The doorbell sounded again.

She went over to read the missive penned in Aunt Gennie's perfect handwriting, using the counter for support instead of her crutches.

> Sarie dear,
> Everyone's sleeping, so we're going out to run errands. Picking up Mags on the way home. Back by noon. Call if you need us—or anything—sooner.
> Love, Aunt G and Rose

The doorbell rang again.

Sarajane hobbled back to the table where she'd

propped her crutches up in the corner of the alcove.

She made her way to the swinging door that lead to the living room, sidling through sideways, and slowly, with as much care as possible so she wouldn't lose her balance.

The doorbell rang for a fourth time. Whoever it was, he or she was damned persistent.

No sooner had the thought passed through her mind than she heard Chloe calling from upstairs. Actually, screaming from upstairs, though from here, the scream just wasn't that loud and she realized Chloe's bedroom door must be shut. She barely made out, "Is anyone here? I *need* you!"

The doorbell chimed once more.

Sarajane looked up the stairs, knew she couldn't climb them, and decided that whomever was at the door might be of some use. She shouted back at Chloe, "Hold on!"

"Hurry!" Chloe screamed. *"The babies are coming."*

Sarajane couldn't believe she'd heard right, but Chloe screamed again.

"Ohmygod, *ohmygod!"* Sarajane cried, hurrying as fast as she could to the door. Was that what all the knocking was about? She simply hadn't heard Chloe screaming with a floor and two closed doors between them, so maybe Chloe had been pounding against the floor to get attention? Did that mean Chloe was *on* the floor?

"*Ohmygod, ohmygod!"* she repeated, frantic. Caution urged her to ask who was at the door, or even to use the peephole first, but worry about Chloe caused her to throw caution to the wind. She unlocked door, then tried to step aside gracefully so she could open it.

Suddenly, the person on the other side of the door began to pound against the wood and shout, startling Sarajane. She faltered, trying to regain her balance. She didn't count on the tip of her crutch snagging on the leg of the small table that stood beside the door to catch keys and whatnot. She also didn't count on the other crutch to go flying out from under her other arm, hitting the door as it flew open and crashed against the wall.

Sarajane lost her balance, cartwheeling backward, hitting her head first on the table and then with a solid thunk against the wood floor.

"Upstairs. Chloe. Help," she managed to utter before she passed out—and in that moment she was absolutely certain she had died and gone to heaven.

There could have been no other explanation for why she saw Dominick Fielding looming in the doorway.

# chapter 32

*C*hloe's voice was hoarse from screaming. Tears of pain and frustration streamed down her face. Brenden and Mary Kate had decided to arrive with a bang on a day when everything was upside down, including Chloe.

Her smartphone was dead and she belatedly cursed her stupidity for not having a landline installed in the house. She made a mental note to get one so this never happened again.

She'd slept little during the night because the babies were putting up such a fuss inside her and she couldn't get comfortable, no matter what. Marsh must have told his grandmother and Aunt Gennie to let her sleep if they found her snoozing, because she'd found a note on the bedside table saying they'd gone out on a few errands and would pick up Mags on the way back.

Upon wakening less than an hour ago, she'd lain in bed not wanting to move because she'd finally found a comfortable position and the babies weren't poking and kicking her every which way, expressing their displeasure at being so cramped inside her.

However, nature eventually called, so she'd contorted herself out of the bed. No sooner had she stood than her water broke. It had so startled her that when she'd grabbed her phone, she'd slipped in the wetness and gone down with a major *thunk* on her ass, one leg bent under her.

*Please, God,* she prayed, *it hurts, but don't let me have a broken leg. Please, please, please!*

And then she'd started screaming for help, but no one had answered. Sarajane's bedroom was not directly below the master bedroom, but Chloe screamed as loud as she could and hoped Sarie would hear her cries anyway. Of course, the old house was solid and her door had been closed, but still. Several times, she tried pounding the floor with her fist. It didn't occur to her that Sarajane might not be in her room.

As the contractions grew harder and closer together, she did her breathing techniques and tried to count just how close each one was to the one before. And then she started to get scared. She had to get some help!

A tipped jar of molasses would have looked like it was competing in the Indy 500 compared to the speed with which she unfurled herself. She didn't actually think her leg was broken, but it hurt like the dickens. She worked herself around so she could get up on the knee of her uninjured leg and pull herself up. The problem was that the bed had no footboard, so the only thing to grab was the bedcovers, and all they did was slide her way when she got a grip on them.

She sank back down against the floor as a contraction wracked her body. She tried to count, to see how long it lasted.

At that moment, she heard the doorbell.

She started screaming again.

Several moments later, the doorbell rang again.

She screamed again. "Is anyone here? I *need* you!"

Another contraction took her.

She didn't know how many times the doorbell had

rung, or how many times she'd called out *I need you*, when she heard Sarajane shout up the stairs, "*Hold on!*"

Thank God! She screamed back, "Hurry! *The babies are coming!*"

Chloe scanned the room, wild-eyed. There had to be something....

Her eyes lighted on the bedside table and the Rosewood Apple Blossom vase that had belonged to a great-somebody in the family tree. Before she could readjust herself to scoot over and grab the vase, Mary appeared in front of her.

"Oh, my darling girl," Mary said. "You've hurt yourself and the babies are coming."

"The vase," Chloe ground out. "Can you throw it through the window? Someone's at the door. Might be able to help."

Before Chloe had even finished speaking, the vase rose off the table and hurled through the window, shattering the glass.

Whoever was ringing the doorbell began to pound wildly on the door, shouting.

"He's going to help you," Mary assured her. "Don't worry. Your babies will be fine."

Chloe doubled over with another contraction, wondering who Mary was talking about, but before she could ask, Mary disappeared.

She prayed through a haze of pain for God to send her a miracle so her babies would be born alive.

The man at the door stared down in disbelief at the woman lying on the floor in a flowered nightgown.

Sarajane? What was she doing here? Why was she using crutches? Was she dead or alive?

He knelt quickly to assess her condition, feeling for the pulse at her throat. Strong and steady. She opened her eyes briefly, though it was obvious her gaze was unfocused. "Upstairs. Chloe. Help," she said, and then she lost consciousness.

"*Hurry!*" came a voice from across the room. "*Up-stairs!*"

Dom blinked, wondering who the redhead in the long dress was. He blinked again and opened his mouth to ask, but she was no longer there.

He stood and bolted up the stairs. He'd heard screaming and then something had come flying out the upstairs window. Someone was trying to get his attention, he had no doubt of that.

At the closed door, he considered knocking but he wasn't the kind of guy who announced his arrival in a time of need. He threw open the door and came to a screeching halt when he saw the woman curled up against the side of the bed. She clutched her massive abdomen, obviously in the throes of labor.

"Jesus and Mary," he muttered.

She looked up at him through strands of long hair. "Marsh, help me," she whispered, so low he barely heard her.

"Not Marsh, Chloe. I'm Dominic, but I'll help you, love. Have no fear of that. I'll help you."

"Dominic?" she murmured. "So Sarie was right...." She convulsed with another contraction.

He pulled a cell phone from his pocket and dialed 9-1-1. He knew the address because he'd memorized it the day before, and he gave it to the dispatcher. "I need two ambulances," he said. "One woman in labor, one unconscious from a fall. I also need you to contact Detective Marsh Fielding at Salem PD. Tell him this is an emergency. His wife is in labor at home." He rattled off his cell number and asked her to tell Marsh to call him. "I'll give him an update on whether she's made it to the hospital, or if the baby is coming at home."

"You're not going to deliver it yourself, are you?" the dispatcher cried, sounding startled and amazed at the same time.

"Wouldn't be the first time, might not be the last

time. Do it. Please." And he disconnected.

"Babies," Chloe rasped.

"What?" he asked. What else hadn't his parents bothered to tell him the day before?

"Babies. Two of them. Twins."

Dominic hadn't done a lot praying in recent years, but he closed his eyes momentarily and said simply, silently, *Please*....

"Okay, love, let's get you up off the floor and onto the bed. You can't be very comfortable down there."

"Water broke when I got up. Slipped in it. Fell and hurt my leg. Phone's dead."

"When it rains, it pours, doesn't it? Well, don't worry Chloe Fielding, I'm going to take care of you, okay? Trust me."

Marsh got the call from dispatch, but all he heard was, "Your wife's in labor at home...."

Already on his way home for lunch, he slapped the blue flashing light onto the roof of his car and turned on the siren.

Within two minutes, he was in his driveway behind a vehicle he didn't recognize.

The front door stood wide open and he found Sarajane inside on the floor, her crutches helter-skelter beside her. He knelt to check her pulse and she opened her eyes.

"I'm okay. Chloe...."

Upstairs, he heard Chloe scream. Without even thinking, he pulled his weapon from the holster and bolted up the stairs. At his bedroom door he shouted, "Police! Freeze!"

The man bending over his wife turned his head in Marsh's direction. "Dominic?"

"Put your damned gun away, brother. We've got some babies to deliver."

Marsh did as he was told.

"Take off your jacket and wash your hands, then find

me two clean pillowcases and a clean sheet and sterilize
a pair of scissors. And if Chloe has any kind of small
hair clips, sterilize those, too, then get your butt back
here. Your babies are coming."

Marsh had heard of cops delivering babies in the back
seats of patrol cars, and cabbies delivering babies in
taxis, but he never, not in a million fucking years,
thought he'd be delivering his own babies in his own
bedroom.

He didn't even think to ask his brother if he actually
knew what he was doing. He simply trusted Dom and
rushed off to follow his instructions exactly.

Chloe was an organized woman. He knew exactly
where to find the linens and exactly where to find the
hair clips in the second drawer of the bathroom vanity.
For all that, he needn't have even wondered if he'd be
able to pull everything together, because Mary stood in
the bathroom doorway, motioning him toward her. She
had everything Dominic had asked for already laid out
on the countertop.

"You just need to sterilize the hair clips and the
scissors with the alcohol," she said, before she and the
linens floated off into the bedroom. He returned to
Chloe's bedside in under sixty seconds.

"Sheet first," said Dom.

Mary handed it over. Dom reached for it, faltered for
a moment when he realized it wasn't Marsh doing the
holding.

"Who…?"

Not *how*, Marsh noticed, but *who*. Damn, Dom could
see Mary! "Dom, meet Mary. Mary, this is my brother,
Dominic."

"I know," she said sweetly, then added with some
urgency, "Here are the pillow cases, and now I'm going
to step back out of the way. It's nice to finally meet you,
Dominic."

In the time it took him to take a breath, Dom stared at
the transparency that was Mary MacFee, then looked at

Marsh, a huge question mark in his eyes.

"I'll explain later," Marsh promised, and Dom went back to work.

Once he put aside the pillow cases and had the sheet situated under Chloe, Dom uttered words meant to soothe her. "It's going to be okay, love. Your babies are in good hands. You're in good hands."

"I know," Chloe said through clenched teeth. "Mary told me."

Marsh cast a grateful glance toward the ghostly apparition. "Our daughter will bear your name," he told her.

She smiled. "I know. I'm so pleased."

"Mary," Chloe said through gritted teeth, "Sarajane asked me to thank you for saving her life."

"Tell her it was my pleasure. She has a lot to live for...."

"I will," Chloe gasped. "Thank you from me and Marsh, too."

"I'll always be watching out for the two of you," Mary promised. "Now, you focus on getting those Plan B babies born."

Marsh let out a bark of laughter then looked back at his brother, still shocked to see him there. "It's good to see you, Dom."

"Likewise, brother. Just didn't expect it to be like this."

"Gotta...pussshh," Chloe gritted out, her face red with effort.

"I got this, Marsh. I want you to get behind Chloe and support her while she pushes. Hold it just a second, love, 'til your husband gets up there."

Again, Marsh did exactly what he was told. He and Chloe had taken a birthing class and some of this they had practiced. He lifted her up, removed the pillows, and slid in behind her. He had to wonder, though, if he would have been quite so calm if not for Mary's reassurances and his brother's quietly calm demeanor.

Chloe raised the hand of her uninjured arm to grasp

his and began to push. The guttural sounds coming from her throat sounded nothing like his wife, but then he'd never heard her pushing a baby out before. He'd never loved her more than he did in that moment.

"Okay," Dom said. "That's good. This little one has crowned. Another couple of pushes like that and he or she will be out."

In the distance, they heard sirens approaching. Marsh thought his neighbors would probably like the residents of the Fielding house a lot better if they moved to another neighborhood. They'd certainly had more than their fair share of activity over here during the past month.

Three things then happened simultaneously. Chloe had to push again and announced it with a scream this time. The sirens stopped out front. And a herd of old ladies came in the front door shrieking like banshees.

Marsh heard the EMTs telling people to get out of the way as they bounded up the stairs. He focused only on Chloe, his love, his life, his reason for living, speechless and awestruck as he watched his son be born.

# chapter 33

*i*f the dictionary had contained an illustration of the word *havoc*, a split-view of the Fielding house would have been the ultimate example.

Marsh thought back over the afternoon as he held his beautiful, tiny, perfect daughter in his arms. Her equally beautiful, tiny, perfect brother lay contentedly in Chloe's arms.

Brenden and Mary Kate had arrived.

Chloe was content, but exhausted.

Dom was a hero, but exhausted.

Marsh was just plain exhausted. It was stressful watching your wife push out babies, while the brother you hadn't seen in years delivered them with no problems, like he'd been born to it.

Dom sat in the corner, one foot on his knee, his elbows resting on the arms of the chair, his fingers templed in front of him.

"Thank God you were there," Chloe said to him again.

"Thank God you threw something through the window," he countered, "or I might have turned around and walked away after I hit that doorbell for the fifth time."

Chloe exchanged a look with Marsh. "I, uh, didn't exactly throw the vase."

"You didn't?"

Chloe shook her head. "No. Mary did."

Marsh stared at his wife in amazement. "*Mary?*"

Chloe nodded. "With the nose-twitching thing?"

"That's the redhead's name?" Dom asked. "Mary? There was something strange—"

"I'll tell you later," Marsh cut in.

"Did someone think to call Colleen and tell her the class is cancelled?" Chloe asked Marsh.

"Gran did. At least I think she did. I pretty sure that's what she told me when she and her buddies were peering in the nursery window."

The babies were small but healthy at five pounds for Mary Kate and five pounds, two ounces for Brenden. Having been born at home, they were being monitored in the nursery overnight, then they and Chloe would spend one additional night and go home just in time for her brother to arrive.

Marsh's head was spinning.

Dom stood. "I'm going to go check on Sarajane."

"Call and let us know how she is, will you?"

Dom pulled out his phone. "Give me your cell number." He input it as Marsh rattled off the digits, then shoved the device back into his pocket. "Sorry we had to meet like this, Chloe, but I have to tell you, I couldn't have asked for a stronger, better woman for my brother to marry." He flashed her a smile and said to Marsh. "And she's pretty, too."

A tired Chloe grinned back at him. "You Fielding men sure have a way with words."

Dom laughed and bent down to give her a kiss on the forehead. He took the opportunity to stroke Brenden's tiny, perfect little head, then did the same to Mary Kate. "I'd give you a hug, brother, but I don't want to squash the little one." He substituted with fond squeeze to his brother's shoulder.

"Come back to the house later, will you?" Marsh asked.

At the door, Dom nodded. "See you tomorrow, Chloe."

"Good. And give Sarie a hug for me, will you?"

An indefinable expression crossed Dom's face. If Marsh could have put a name to it, he might have called it fear.

Dom closed the door softly behind him and turned right, following the hall to the stairwell. He walked half-way down the steps and stopped on the landing. He leaned against the wall and released several deep breaths, had a little—okay, a *long*—talk with himself, then continued on to the floor where Sarajane Nichols lay as a patient.

He knew the room number, but he stopped and inquired about her at the nurses' station.

"She's sleeping, but you can peek in, if you like."

Dom wanted nothing more and he did just that. He actually did more than peek. He stepped quietly inside and took a chair in the corner, where it was dark. He sat and folded his hands in his lap. Some might have thought he was praying, but Dominic Fielding had not uttered a prayer in more than two years.

Try as he might now, as much as he wanted to say a prayer of recovery for Sarajane, his mind was blank. Just as earlier, all he'd been able to come up with before he began the task of delivering his brother's babies was a fervent *Please….*

So, Dom sat there, watching Sarajane sleep. When they were kids, he'd had a soft spot for her. By the time they were teens, he knew damned good and well she had a crush on him. As a grown woman, did she still have feelings for him?

He didn't understand why she would. Yes, she'd been brazen enough to steal a kiss from him once, and he'd been emboldened enough to give it right back to her—even though he'd known better—but he'd told her then, and he'd tell her now, he was not the man for her.

He no longer had his life pledged to God, but he'd seen things…he'd *done* things…things that made him less of the man that he wanted, *needed*, to be. And he couldn't be the man for Sarajane. Not now, not ever.

She moaned softly in her sleep and he froze when his name passed her lips.

She was not awake, but a tear slipped from her eye and slid down the side of her face.

Dom was not given to superstition, but in that moment, he wondered if Sarajane had heard every thought tumbling through his head.

"Dom," she murmured again, still asleep.

He had half a notion to shake her, wake her up, tell her to stop calling for him. That notion never fully blossomed, for Dom knew himself well enough to know that if he did, in this darkened room, he'd take Sarajane in his arms and kiss her like the starving man he was.

He eased up out of the chair and opened the door, sliding back out into the hallway like a fugitive or worse, a man afraid of his own shadow.

For in truth, he was both.

# chapter 34

ose fixed sandwiches for herself and Dom. They sat at the kitchen table, discussing the day's events. Finally, she got around to asking him where he'd been for the last two years.

Dom almost told her he didn't want to talk about it. That's what he'd said to his parents yesterday, when he'd stopped there first. But like his brother, he had a special relationship with their grandmother and didn't want to disrespect her. He said simply, "Wandering."

"Without your collar."

"Yes."

"And why is that?"

"That part, I don't want to go into right now."

"Hmph."

He remained silent.

"Is the collar gone permanently?"

"Yes."

"I see."

Dom was glad someone did, because he sure as hell didn't.

Rose polished off the last of her ham sandwich and

stood. "Too much excitement for an old lady," she said. "I'm going to bed. Guess you'd better sleep in Sarajane's room, for tonight at least. We just changed the sheets on the bed yesterday, but if you want clean ones—"

"Don't bother. I can sleep on the sofa."

"Dominic, you are well over six feet tall. There's not a sofa in this house you'll fit on lying down. I'll change the sheets."

He stayed her with a gentle hand. This wasn't an argument he wanted to have or needed to win. One night on Sarajane's sheets was not going to kill him. At least not physically. "I'll take her bed and you *won't* change the sheets."

Rose smiled at him, then leaned down and gave him a hug.

Dom slid his arms around his grandmother. It had been so long since he'd had any loving human contact, he'd forgotten how it felt. Yesterday his parents, today it was Gran. He almost choked with emotion.

"It's so damned good to have you home, Dominic. I've prayed for you every night."

"Thanks, Gran. I love you."

She pulled away and planted a kiss on his stubbly cheek. "I love you, too. We've been incomplete without you."

She gave him a quick overview of where things were in the kitchen, gave him directions to Sarajane's room, told him where to find clean towels in the adjoining bathroom.

Dominic was sitting on the front porch when Marsh pulled into the driveway just after ten p.m. Nursing a icy-cold microbrew, he pondered just how much he had missed American beer.

His gaze swung from the bottle in his hand to watching his brother approach. Although eighteen months apart in age, they were as close as their twin siblings. He and Marsh had always told each other everything. If there was anyone he could talk to now, it would be him.

The question was, how much *could* he talk about right now, even if his spirit was willing?

"Get'cha a beer?" Dom asked as Marsh climbed the porch steps.

"Get me two," his brother replied, his tone wry. "I think I need 'em and it may be a while before I can indulge again."

"Gran made some sandwiches, too. Want to sit out here?"

"Yeah. I need some fresh air and it's a nice evening. I'll wash up if you want to get the suds and grub."

Dominic was back in a couple of minutes carrying the remainder of the six-pack he'd started, a plate of wrapped sandwiches, a bag of chips, and some napkins. He put everything, including the bottle opener he'd stuck in his shirt pocket, on the little table between the two resin wicker chairs on the porch and turned them so he and Marsh would be facing each other.

He grabbed his half-full bottle of Drifter and took a seat.

Marsh came out, sat, and gratefully accepted a beer from the six-pack.

"Haven't had one of these for almost seven years," Dom said. "I missed it."

"Where you been?" Marsh asked after he took a long swallow from his bottle.

"Around."

"That's pretty goddamned ambiguous."

"Yep."

"Shit."

Dom drained his bottle and reached for a fresh one. "Can we talk about you first? Last I heard you were a dedicated bachelor and now, here you are with a gorgeous wife and two beautiful babies."

Marsh, who had been scowling at his older brother, smiled. "I'm the luckiest guy on the planet," he admitted.

Dom listened and sipped as Marsh told him how he'd met his wife in a class he'd taught at the JC. "If the Cap hadn't had that heart attack and needed someone to fill in for him, Chloe and I might never have met." He pulled the cellophane off the sandwich plate and helped himself to one. "Funny how things work out, huh? Karma? Fate? Whatever."

Dom studied his brother with brooding eyes. Of the two of them, Marsh had always been more personable, more of a go-getter. Dom had decided in high school that if his own name meant "belonging to the Lord," he should be a priest. To this day, he wasn't sure where he'd got that notion, or why he'd believed and pursued it, but he had. His parents hadn't discouraged him in any way, and he had taken that for their approval. He didn't envy Marsh his outgoing, motivated approach to life. He was happy for his brother, for his success at work, his happiness at home.

Sometimes he just wished he'd led a similar life, been a little more like his younger brother. Experienced a similar happiness, that's all. But he did not envy him. Envy was a cardinal sin and Heaven knew, he did not want to break any more of God's laws than he already had.

Marsh finished one sandwich, washed it down with what remained of his beer, and reached for another. "I haven't eaten since breakfast," he said by way of explanation.

Dom silently handed him another brewsky.

Marsh went on to tell him about Chloe's spirit, Mary MacFee, and how Chloe had discovered who really murdered her.

Dom, for the first time in his life, stared open-mouthed. "You mean to tell me that woman was a ghost? That's just not possible."

"She was and it is. Trust me on this one."

Stunned, Dom stared at him. How had he forgotten one important thing about the redhead? *She was transparent!* "A spirit…."

"That is a conversation we should have in more depth

with Chloe and Gran," Marsh said, "but you can take it as truth."

Marsh continued with news about Luce Maguire and his partner, JD Kemp. He listened to the story of the serial killers who'd gone after Luce and JD, and in the process had killed a cop and wounded another one, along with JD, Chloe, and Sarajane.

"So that's why your wife's arm is bandaged and Sarajane is on crutches?"

Marsh ground his teeth together, his emotions obviously still running high on the topic. "Yes."

"What happened to the bastards who shot them?

"The guy who shot JD was hit by bullets from four guns—mine, JD's, Luce's, and Sarajane's."

"Deader than a doornail," Dom noted with satisfaction.

"That's not very priestly of you."

Dom ignored the comment. "And the one who shot Sarajane and Chloe?"

"Also dead. My LT and I both got him."

Dom nodded. "And this *spirit* came to warn Chloe to hide, and then she hung around and tipped over a huge piece of furniture to help you get the killer?"

"Sounds fantastical, doesn't it?"

"Yes…and call me crazy, but I do believe it."

"I didn't, at first. When I met Mary, I could see her, so I thought Chloe was pulling some kind of prank on me."

"What changed your mind?"

Marsh laughed. "She floated."

"Chloe floated?"

"No, Mary did. Instead of walking, she kind of floated."

Dom shook his head amused. "I'd have liked to have seen that."

"She floated today. You were just too busy to notice."

Dom grunted.

"She's come back three times now since she moved

on," Marsh said. "The first time was to tell us we were going to have twins. That time, Jamie was with her. You stay in this house long enough, you *might* see her if she comes back again."

"A haunted house," Dom said, bemused. "I never thought I'd see the day that you'd be living in one."

Marsh laughed. "Me, either!" He finished his second sandwich and pulled some chips out of the bag. "So, where the hell have you been, Dom? Have you seen Mom and Dad? They've been crazy with worry about you."

"I stopped there first. They told me how to find you."

"And?"

"And they neglected to mention everything that's been going on down here in Salem! I asked, but they both kind of looked at each other with a smile on their faces and said, 'Ask Marsh.'"

"So now you have." Marsh downed a swig. "Your turn to tell me what the hell's been going on with you."

Dom leaned forward on his elbows, the beer bottle clutched in his fingers, staring intently at his brother across the darkness. "I *want* to tell you, Marsh. All of it, but I may not be able to get it all out at once." He slammed his bottle down on the table and lowered his head into his hands. "I may not be able to get it out at all." His shoulders started to heave.

Not for the first time in his adult life, Dominic began to sob.

# chapter 35

**S**arajane opened her eyes, trying to focus, wondering where she was. After several confused blinks, she registered the blood pressure cuff on her arm, the pulse monitor on her finger, the ache in her head, and the steady sounds coming from the monitoring devices beside her bed.

Back in the hospital.

*Crap!*

It took her aching brain several moments to remember what had happened. Kitchen table. The doorbell. Hearing Chloe call for help. Answering the doorbell because she couldn't climb the stairs to help her friend.

Stumbling with the crutches. The door flying open. Her flailing every which way.

Dominic Fielding standing in the doorway.

Sarajane bolted upright in the bed, much to the protest of her head. *That couldn't be right!* Dominic was …was…well, no one knew *where* the hell he was, but he certainly hadn't been standing at Marsh and Chloe's front door in Salem, Oregon!

*But you had a vision, Dom striding up the side-*

*walk....*

As the fog in her brain cleared, even as her headache persisted, she blinked rapidly. Had he actually been sitting in the corner of this very room, watching her?

Good grief, she was in trouble if her visions seemed like reality. Either that, or she had a doozy of a head injury and she was hallucinating, big time.

The nurse hurried in. "Are you okay?"

Belatedly, Sarajane realized she'd pulled something loose, registering some kind of distress on the monitoring device at the nurse's station. "Sorry, I guess I sat up wrong and dislodged something."

The nurse checked everything over and reattached the pulse monitor to the machine.

"Why am I in ICU?" Sarajane asked, even as she put a hand to the back of her head.

"Head injury," the nurse confirmed. "They did a CT scan soon as you came in. I guess you hit really hard and they were afraid you had a fractured skull. Your pupils were slightly irregular."

"Great!" Sarajane muttered. "What was the verdict?" Sarajane asked, thinking that would explain her vision of Dom.

"No fracture, but you do have a concussion and a nice egg on the back of your head and a smaller one on the side. You were out quite a while."

"That explains a headache the size of Jupiter," Sarajane mumbled. And perhaps, it also explained imagining Dom in the doorway. Concussions were serious and nothing to mess around with. "But ICU? For a bump on the head?"

"You're pretty popular around here," the nurse said, "having spent almost three weeks with us recently."

Sarajane realized in that moment that the nurse looked familiar. "Georgia, right?"

The nurse nodded, raising up Sarajane's bed and fluffing the pillow behind her. "I'm surprised you remember me. You were pretty out of it when I was assigned to you."

"I have a good memory for names and faces," Sarajane said. "It kind of goes with the territory for me. I guess my job is so dehumanizing, to a certain extent, that I want to make sure I never forget the…people I meet along the way."

"I pegged you for a compassionate person," Georgia said, offering Sarajane a cup of ice water. "When you were in before, you never stopped asking how everyone else was when we weren't even sure we weren't going to lose…." She trailed off, obviously shocked by what she'd almost said.

"Me?" Sarajane finished for her. She clasped the woman's hand, trying to reassure her. "I see so much bad stuff on a daily basis, you can't scare or shock me that easily. I know it was serious. Knew it from the moment that bullet went through me. I suppose I just had faith that I'd be all right, and as soon as my friend put that tourniquet on my leg" —she shrugged— "I felt it deep down inside me. And speaking of Marsh, would you mind dialing a number for me? I want to see how his wife, Chloe, is doing."

The nurse slapped her head, as if she were trying out for a V8 juice commercial. "How could I have forgotten to tell you that right off! Hold on, I'll be right back."

For agonizing seconds, Sarajane lay frozen in her bed, wondering what horrible thing had occurred that the nurse had to leave the room. Was she getting someone to help her break bad news? Had Chloe also been hurt? What?

Georgia came back in, a piece of paper in her hand. "Sorry, the information was written down and I didn't want to make any mistakes or forget anything. Your friend, Chloe Fielding, is in maternity. She delivered twins this afternoon, a boy and a girl. The little girl weighed in at five pounds and her brother, born first, was two ounces heavier. Their names are—"

"Mary Kate and Brenden," Sarajane said, smiling

with relief. "And they're all okay?"

Georgia nodded. "The babies are being monitored and all of them will stay tonight and tomorrow night, and if all's well, they can go home the following morning."

"Oh, thank God! When can I go see them?"

"Tell you what. If you're a good girl and eat a little something of the food I ordered for your evening meal, I'll check and see if I can wheel you over to the other building for a quick look-see on my lunch break."

"What time is it?" Sarajane asked, worried she might not get to see Chloe, too.

"Just a little after nine. Do you need to use the bathroom before I go get your chow?"

Sarajane thought about it for a moment. "Yes."

Georgia recorded all the readings in Sarajane's chart, then unhooked everything and helped her push back the covers before she eased her legs over the side of the bed. "Easy does it, kiddo."

Feeling slightly wobbly, Sarajane stood. A wave of dizziness washed over her and she was grateful for Georgia's support.

"Just let it pass," the nurse advised. "I'll get you into the bathroom and wait outside the door to give you privacy. You know the routine, if you need help—just pull the cord and I'll be there, like that." She snapped her fingers.

Fifteen minutes later, Sarajane was allowed to sit in a chair and eat from the lowered bed tray. Georgia had ordered her a plain turkey sandwich with a light coating of mayo, a cup of blueberry yogurt, and a 7UP. Sarajane was surprised to discover she was actually hungry and ate everything the nurse put in front of her. Of course, she'd spent so much time browsing through the paper, she hadn't taken more than a few bites from those cinnamon rolls at breakfast. *I need to get my priorities straight*, she thought ruefully.

"Ready?" Georgia asked around ten.

"Yes."

"Okay, here's the deal. Patients in ICU don't get to go out of the building, but the ER doc who sent you up says it's okay to take you over to Building D. The caveat is, we have to be back in thirty minutes."

"Thirty minutes?" Sarajane squeaked out.

"Yes, or you can't go. Remember, you'll be discharged in the morning, so you'll have more time to visit and see the babies then."

Sarajane decided not to argue. The nurse had gone the extra mile for her as it was. She nodded her assent. "You don't think it'll be too late, do you?"

"No," Georgia replied with a smile. "I called over— your friend Chloe is sitting in a wheelchair in the nursery, staring at her babies."

Sarajane tapped lightly on the glass between her and the nursery. Chloe looked up and grinned, motioning her in.

Sarajane looked over her shoulder at Georgia. "Can we?"

"Special dispensation," Georgia said. "Mask up and hit the sanitizer as we pass it."

Sarajane eagerly did as she was told while the nurse maneuvered the chair into the nursery.

Only two other babies besides the Fielding twins were in the nursery at the moment. "The other babies are in with their moms," the maternity nurse said. "The four in here are all being monitored."

"They're okay, though, right?"

"Fit as little fiddles."

The two bassinettes containing Mary Kate and Brenden had been situated near the window. "I understand that we not only have a large family here, but that every cop in the city might be coming by to see the little ones, so the twins got the front row," the nurse explained as Georgia pushed Sarajane up next to Chloe.

The two of them managed to exchange a hug despite

Chloe with her recovering arm and Sarajane with her recovering thigh, and now her head. "They said you were going to be fine," Chloe said, "but I'm glad to see you with my own two eyes, just to be sure."

"Back at'cha," Sarajane said. "Was it a hard delivery?"

Before Chloe could answer, Dee, the maternity nurse, invited Georgia to join her for a "cup'a joe while the girls visit."

Back to their conversation, Chloe said, "I don't have anything to compare it to, but I'd say I got off lightly. A few easy contractions, then my water broke." She described slipping in the liquid and falling, the dead battery in her phone, calling endlessly for help, pounding on the floor with her hand, Mary "throwing" her heirloom Rosewood vase out the window to get the attention of whomever was ringing the door bell.

"I heard something that sounded like knocking, but every time I tried to pinpoint it, I couldn't hear anything. I thought it was coming from outside or something. I never dreamed it was you!" Sarajane's voice clogged with emotion. "I'm so sorry, Chloe. I went into the kitchen from the door that adjoins my room, so I couldn't hear you. I barely heard you when I pushed through the swinging door into the living room to go answer the doorbell."

One of the babies squeaked. Sarajane identified Brenden by the blue card in the slot of his bassinette. "They are so beautiful," she whispered, almost reverently.

"They are, aren't they? When I first dreamed of having Marsh's baby, I never in my wildest imaginings thought it would be this amazing. Every moment of discomfort and pain was worth it."

Sarajane experienced a stab of regret and maybe a small pinch of envy. She, too, wanted a baby, and she wanted it with Marsh's older brother, but Dominic was long gone and long lost to her. For a moment, she didn't realize Chloe was speaking again. "What?"

"You've heard about the miraculous delivery, right?"

Sarajane tore her eyes away from the babies and met Chloe's gaze. "Miraculous delivery?"

Chloe laughed softly and grabbed her hand. "Ohmy-god, Sarajane, are you in for a story!"

# chapter 36

"Three years ago," Dominic began, his voice heavy with emotion, "when I was sent to Afghanistan, I thought life might grow a bit calmer for me. In many ways it was, but the shit hit the fan in that country pretty quickly, as I'm sure you know."

His gaze focused beyond Marsh's shoulder. Physically, he was there with his brother, but his thoughts, his memories, were not. "In May of 2009, the President announced escalated war in Afghanistan. A little over a year later, Congress ratified it. Over two thousand American troops have been killed and over eighteen thousand injured. Sixty percent of the deaths occurred after 2009."

"I hadn't realized that," Marsh said.

"I didn't want to see anyone die," Dom said. "On either side. You know I'm not opposed to war, it's simply a necessary evil on our planet, but the whole escalation thing...." He got up and stood at the porch rail, looking up into the starry night sky. He'd gotten his voice under control but nothing could lessen his emotional turmoil.

"They sent me back to Iraq in less than a year. I didn't want to go—I thought those troops in Afghanistan needed me more—but they had other priests there, so I left."

He said nothing for several minutes and blessed his brother for not forcing him to speak.

Finally, he said, "I'd been back less than a week when it happened." He kept his back to Marsh. "You know, people over here think the war is over in Iraq. Hussein is gone, most of his relatives are either dead or out of the picture. People are getting on with their lives." He bit out an epithet. "Don't you believe it! The Iraqi people are struggling every damned day. There was this little kid who used to come around to our camp. His name was Rahim. He was seven."

Dom shook his head, trying to clear it. "The guys would give him candy and gum, sometimes home-baked cookies their moms had sent. I taught him English and how to play chess and Uno—that kid was such a quick learner! One of the other guys used to tie balloons into animal shapes for him and the other kids."

Dom began to pace in the confined space, bumped into the railing, stopped. "He loved helping us out, liked it when we gave him small chores." He uttered a nostalgic laugh, remembering. "That kid would do anything for a piece of chocolate. The morning it happened, we'd eaten chow already, and the company was getting ready to go out into the field. We weren't too far from the village market and a couple of the guys wanted fresh fruit. I volunteered to go get it. Father Shattuck, an Episcopal priest at the camp, offered to give me a lift. He was transporting four soldiers into town to relieve four others on patrol."

He slammed his fist against the support post. Three times.

Marsh joined him where he stood, stayed his brother's hand. "You don't have to tell me, Dom."

"I do!" Dom shouted. "I've been running away from

this for almost three years. Haven't talked about it to anyone, even when they said I had to talk to the Army shrink. I went every day for two weeks and I never spoke one word to him." He hit the post one more time. "You know what I did? Week three, I ripped off my collar and threw it in the dirt. I told them to get fucked, packed my bag, and left. Never looked back, except in my head, and my head still can't get itself around what happened."

"You'd better tell me then. You need another beer to get through it?"

Dom thought about it, decided he didn't have to drink it, decided he might get some relief from throwing it against something instead. "We no sooner left camp than we came upon Rahim and his little sisters, Farrah and Leyla. They were a few years younger, always trailing after him."

"Shat— Father Shattuck—stopped to see if they wanted a lift anywhere. Even though we had four armed soldiers in the back, and a journalist who hopped on board just before we drove off, three little kids wouldn't take up much room. The girls scrambled in, but Rahim came aboard slowly, looking more serious than I'd ever seen him. He sat behind me and I kept looking over my shoulder, trying to make conversation with him. He looked like he was ready to cry. Those dark eyes of his were big as saucers. I invited him and his sisters for a game of Uno when we got back and he said, 'Not this time, Faddah Dom. Not this time.'"

Dom drained half his bottle of beer, then went back to his chair. Marsh followed. Dom sank down, wishing he could actually crawl into the seat and disappear as if it were some kind of magical rabbit hole. Instead, he clutched his bottle until his knuckles went white and continued.

"No sooner had Shat pulled up outside the market than Rahim jumped out. He yelled at his sisters to stay in the Humvee, but they wanted to get out with him. They idolized their big brother. 'Make them to stay!' he screamed at me, then turn and ran into the market. The girls weren't having any of it, and I didn't see why they should. It was damned hot that day, already in the nineties. They ran after him, excited, like they thought he was playing a game with them. Rahim turned and looked at me just as he got to the entrance to the market. He screamed, '*Ana asif!*' over and over again. I didn't know until later what it meant."

"What *does* it mean?" Marsh asked.

"It means *I'm sorry.* Tears were streaming down the kid's cheeks like rivers."

"Ohmygod."

Dom guessed his brother knew what was coming next. He almost couldn't even say it."Those two little girls were out of the vehicle and at their brother's side before I realized what was going to happen."

He tried to put the beer back on the table, but it fell over, spilling brew everywhere. Neither he nor Marsh moved to clean it up. Dom dropped his head in his hands and began to weep again. "I couldn't get to them fast enough. *Dead.* All of them *dead.* So many *dead.* Body parts everywhere, heat, flames, smoke...."

"Jesus. *Jesus!* Were you injured?" Marsh said, his voice hoarse.

"Yes, but it didn't matter. I *knew* Rahim. I should've *known* that something wasn't right. He had on a jacket and it was so freaking hot that day. I should have *known.*"

Marsh rose from his chair and went around the small table and knelt down to comfort his brother. "God, I'm sorry, Dom. I had no idea, but you can't blame yourself for what happened."

"I sure as hell can," Dom snarled.

"Okay, you can, but you shouldn't. Someone once said war is hell, and even though I've never experienced it, I believe that. I also believe that you can't control what others around you choose to do, nor can you stop them from doing it, if they're determined. You know that kid didn't strap that bomb to himself. Who did it?"

"In the U.S. we call them hoodlums, homeys, maybe gangsta' wannabes. Over there, they call themselves loyalists. A group of teenage boys who thought the U.S. should get the hell out and leave Iraq the way it was. One of them was Rahim's cousin. Their way of sending their message was to strap a bomb on an innocent seven-year-old boy instead of to one of their own bodies. The little cowards had been egged on by one of their uncles."

"The little girls…were they killed, too?"

Dom nodded. "And over fifty others, including Shat, the journalist, the four soldiers. It was morning. People were doing their shopping. Another seventy-five or so injured."

"Including you. How long were you laid up?"

"A few days." He picked up a napkin and wiped his face. "I caught a piece of shrapnel in my shoulder, nothing serious. I was on the right side of the Humvee when it went off. I'd been trying to coax Farrah and Leyla to come out on my side, but they jumped out the other door." He shuddered violently.

"It was the worst thing I've ever seen," Dom said, his voice shaking. "There was nothing left of poor little Rahim, pieces everywhere, and his sisters…. Leyla was younger, she couldn't keep up with Farrah, so she was further away from the blast. Who knew a dead child could look so peaceful after being partially obliterated by a bomb?"

"I can't even comprehend it, let alone imagine it," Marsh admitted. "Now that I have kids of my own, I can already feel my perspective changing."

"Even before I left the hospital, I started paperwork for discharge. I'd given the Army ten years. That was enough."

"None of us knew you were injured."

"No, I requested that my family not be notified. It wasn't a serious injury, physically, and I didn't see the need to worry anyone."

"You think we weren't worrying when we didn't know where you were or even if you were alive?" Marsh asked, incredulous.

"You have a point," Dom conceded. "For that, I'm sorry."

"You said you threw down your collar—did you mean that figuratively or literally?"

"Literally," Dom said, his voice suddenly hard. "I promised God I'd dedicate my life to him and I did. No matter what I saw, or how many questions I had about what I saw, day in and day out, I was still committed to him. Until that day. Everything blew up *and* caved in on me that day. I'm done with the Church for good."

"What did the Church have to say about that?" Marsh asked.

"They tried to talk me out of it, of course, but I'm done being a priest. Hell, I may never set foot in a church, *any* church, again."

Marsh sank down on the porch and settled against the wall, his knees bent in front of him. "So, where have you been since then?"

"I've been wandering. I went to Jerusalem, thinking what I needed was a dose of enlightenment from the Holy City, but none came. From there I went to Rome, got a room across from the Vatican and spent a lot of days in St. Peter's Basilica praying for edification, guidance, clarification, something, *anything*!"

"You didn't find what you were looking for."

"No. All I was saw was the opulence, the grandeur, the grandiose. I prayed and prayed, hoping God would talk to me, but I heard nothing."

"Were you actually listening?"

Dom opened his mouth, then snapped it shut. When he finally spoke, his tone was weary. "I believed I was listening, but it's possible I wasn't. I'd been in the war for ten years, but I'd never been *in* the war. I ministered to wounded soldiers in the infirmary every day, heard the confessions of some, gave the last rites to others, but I was never up close and bomb personal. One moment people I knew and cared about where there, the next moment they weren't." He heaved a laborious sigh. "I didn't...I *don't* know how to deal with it."

"I'll help you," Marsh promised.

"I know you will, brother. And if I still believed in God, I'd thank him for that." Dom reached out and clasped his hands tightly over Marsh's where they rested on his knees. In a voice shaky with grief and guilt, if not remorse, he said, "I left out one thing."

"What's that?" Marsh asked.

"Before I left that camp, before my discharge came through, I found that kid's uncle and I killed him."

# chapter 37

"Miraculous delivery?" Sarajane said again. "Is this going to be related to your Immaculate Conception."

"Far from immaculate," Chloe said with a grin.

"There you go, getting that gooey look on your face again."

Chloe laughed. "Gooey? I'm just in love with my husband."

"I never noticed," Sarajane said, her tone dry. "So tell me about this miraculous delivery."

"I'm assuming you don't know who was at the door."

"No, but while I was unconscious and in spite of being concussed, I know who I *thought* I saw at the door, then I realized it had to be an illusion."

Chloe shook her head, her eyes dancing with mirth. "Wasn't Dominic by any chance, was it?"

Sarajane narrowed her eyes on her friend. "Just because I told you about my vision doesn't mean you get to tease me about it. Some friend you are," she said, but her words held no heat.

"I'm not teasing you, Sarie. It *was* Dominic at the

door. Dominic has come home!"

If she hadn't been sitting, Sarajane knew her legs would have given out beneath her. "Dom *was* at the door?"

Chloe nodded.

"Pinch me," Sarajane instructed. "Hard."

Chloe reached over and pinched her on the forearm.

"Ouch!" Sarajane cried.

"You told me to do it hard."

"Yeah, but I didn't think...Dominic has really come home?"

Again, Chloe nodded. "When that vase went sailing through the window, he said he knew something was wrong. He was getting ready to break down the door when you unlocked and opened it."

"Funny you should mention that," Sarajane said, remembering more of the incident. "I didn't actually touch the doorknob, but the door flew open."

"Mary," Chloe said simply.

Sarajane's eyes got wide. "She's really your guardian angel, isn't she?"

"It seems so. Dom said your crutches got tangled up when the door opened and you went flying every which way. You were conscious long enough to send him upstairs."

Stunned, Sarajane listened to the details of how the miraculous delivery had occurred. "I'm getting sick of riding in ambulances," she muttered. "Plus, I keep missing all the good stuff!"

"I doubt you even remember *being* in either ambulance," Chloe said. "And I'm not sure me grunting and screaming my head off delivering two babies was 'good stuff.'"

"Let me be the judge of that, will ya?" Sarajane's head went back and forth in disbelief. "Dom *was* at the door and he delivered Mary Kate and Brenden. Next, that talking pig in the commercials will be real."

Chloe, who didn't watch much TV, said, "A talking

pig?"

"He's a spokespig for some insurance company."

Chloe giggled.

"Get on with the story. Please."

"Marsh got there just in time to assist. Well, with Mary's help. And Rose and Aunt Gennie drove up with Mags just as the EMTs got there. The rest of us were still upstairs and" —she laughed— "I have to say, I guess it became somewhat of a zoo at that point."

Sarajane grinned. "I can imagine."

"I don't know," Chloe said. "I'm not sure I could imagine it if I hadn't witnessed it for myself. Everyone who had a phone had it out and pressed to his or her ear, including my husband, who called to let JD and Luce know we were on the way to the hospital. Rose was calling family, Aunt Gennie was calling someone, though I have no idea who, and even Mags had her phone out." She laughed softly. "Mags told me this evening when she stopped by that since everyone was calling someone, she felt she should, too, so she called her home phone and left herself a message about the miraculous delivery."

"Ah, so she's responsible for the naming of it."

"Yep, and appropriately so, I think. I'm so grateful Dom knew what to do, because I'm here to tell you my husband would not have."

"I still can't believe he's here. Dom, I mean. Why is he, did he say?"

"Marsh told me about your vision and Dom not wearing a collar, and also about Aunt Gennie's vision of collars being sucked into a tornado thingy." She hesitated a moment. "I don't want to give you hope if it's not warranted, but Dom wasn't wearing the Roman collar when he delivered my babies."

"Not?"

"Not."

Sarajane felt a frisson of excitement course through her body. Her voice came out a whisper. "What do you think that means?"

"I don't know," Chloe admitted. "I really don't know anything about priests or the Catholic church except what I've learned from Marsh and me going to Sunday services recently. I would imagine priests are supposed to wear their collars all the time, but maybe there are times when they don't."

"Gee, that's nailing it right down," Sarajane said a bit crossly.

"Hey, don't kill the interpreter. I'm just speculating."

Sarajane said, "When can I hold them?"

"Probably tomorrow."

"Dominic is back."

"He went to your room for a while before he headed back to our house."

"I thought I *dreamed* that I saw him sitting in the corner."

Chloe studied her for the space of several breaths. "You definitely have the *juju*."

"I know," Sarajane said, her tone miserable. "Damn."

"Maybe not so bad," Chloe said. "During all the commotion today, Mary was right in the middle of it."

"You're kidding?"

"I'm going to backtrack a bit. It was a circus and I was in pain, so at first, I thought it was probably just wishful thinking. Then Marsh got there, and Dom started spouting instructions to him to get this and that, only Mary beat him to it."

"Wow!"

"Dominic saw her, too."

"Double wow!" Sarajane frowned. "That's not fair he can see her and I can't!"

Chloe reached over and patted her hand. "I wish I could do something about that."

With a shrug of resignation, Sarajane asked, "What did he say?"

"Nothing. He was busy delivering babies, but he had this brief, kind of shocked expression on his face when he got handed the sheet and it wasn't Marsh doing the handing."

"That must have thrown him for a loop. So, he's at your house now?"

"He's going to stay with us."

"Where, exactly? You're pretty much full up."

"I'm not sure, and I'm too tired to think about it, but I'm sure someone there will figure it out."

"I should go back to my own house tomorrow, after I'm released. He can have the downstairs bedroom."

"No, you need to be where there's someone around all the time and that'll be too much for everyone to try to juggle schedules to be at your place. Maybe Dom can take your room at your house."

The thought of Dominic Fielding sleeping in her bed, sleeping on her sheets, even if she wasn't there with him, sent a delicious shiver to all of Sarajane's feminine regions. She put a clamp on her thoughts before they could wander to what she and Dom could do together in that bed.... "That would work," she finally said. "Does your brother know that you delivered?"

"No, we decided he'll find out soon enough when he gets here tomorrow."

"What a thrill he's going to have when he sees these kidlets." She studied the babies. "How will you tell them apart when they're dressed?" she asked, frowning slightly.

"I won't have any problem. They look different to me already." Chloe chuckled. "Even if, for some reason they're dressed the same, which they might be at the start, they're different genders and that'll be pretty obvious at diaper-changing time."

Sarajane grinned and continued to examine their little faces. "Brenden has a little more hair and it's slightly darker. Poor Mary Kate," she said with a mischievous grin in Chloe's direction.

"Stop it!" Chloe grinned back. "She's going to have plenty of long dark hair and her daddy is going to be scaring the boys away from her at an alarming rate."

"Speaking of dads, are you going to tell yours he's a grandfather?"

Chloe's sad expression made Sarajane wish she'd never asked the question.

"No," her friend said on a whisper, then in a stronger voice added, "Dad knows where I live if he ever has a desire to take up our relationship again."

"No offense, Chloe, but your dad is a sorry SOB."

"None taken. Too bad, though, that my half-siblings will not know my children. Counting the four of them, from the moment they were born, Mary Kate and Brenden have eleven aunts and uncles, two honorary aunts, one honorary uncle, two grandparents, one honorary great-aunt, one great-grandmother, and one honorary great-grandmother."

"You should add your dad to that list."

Chloe sighed wistfully. "Maybe someday I'll be able to do just that."

Sarajane wanted to reassure her, but didn't know exactly what to say.

Chloe readjusted herself in her wheelchair. "I never had family growing up and now look what I've given my children, all because of Marsh—not just a family, but a *huge* family."

"All because of *you*," Sarajane corrected. "You were a magic potion for Marsh."

Chloe looked at her. "You need to sprinkle some magic of your own on Dominic. I think maybe he's ready for it."

"I can't compete with his chosen profession," Sarajane said.

"This isn't going to be a competition," Chloe said. "This is going to be a rescue. Dom is lost because of something he saw or experienced. He isn't wearing the collar anymore, so I take that to mean he's lost his faith. You can help him find it again."

Sarajane studied her friend with disbelief. "You think

Dom's lost his way, given up God, the Church, every-thing he's worked for and believed in for the past twenty years and I'm going to help him get back? What makes you think so?"

"Because," Chloe said, her tone gentle but firm, "you love him. Maybe he's destined to finish his life as a priest. Then again, maybe he's not."

Sarajane might have argued on either side of that coin, especially since she had strong doubts that she could be any kind of savior to a man who had dedicated his life to the *real* Savior.

*chapter 38*

*b*oth babies were in the room with Chloe when Marsh arrived the next morning. He strode in and kissed her first, then went to the bassinettes and put the back of his index finger against each baby's cheek, rubbing gently. Compared to his big hands, their tiny heads looked like they belonged to porcelain dolls.

He looked at Chloe, smiling. She was smiling back. "Did you get any sleep last night?"

"Actually, I did," she said. "I went to the nursery after you left and Sarajane came up for a while."

"They let her come clear over here from ICU?"

"Yeah, the nurse got permission from the ER doc."

"How's she doing? When I stopped by her room, she was sleeping and I didn't want to wake her."

"She's okay. The doctor is going to release her today. She wants to go home, but I told her it'll be a lot easier on The Girls if she just stays with us. Everyone will be in the same house."

"How's your leg?"

"Aches a little, but it's not incapacitating."

To prove her point, Marsh watched his gorgeous,

stubborn wife throw her gorgeous legs over the side of the bed, barely limping as she joined him at the bassinettes. He leaned down and kissed her again, longer this time. "I love you."

"I love you, too." She snuggled close to him, and continued. "Sarie thought she'd imagined Dominic at the door."

"She must have been completely freaked out when she found out one of her *visions* came true."

"She doesn't like to talk about it, that's for sure. Plus, her aunt hasn't had an easy life, seeing things."

"You didn't have an easy life living in a house with a ghost, but you managed. She will, too." He turned and slid his arms around her. "She's got all of us for a built-in support group. She'll be fine."

Chloe laid her head against his chest, sliding her arms around him. "I hope so. She's going to need it with your brother back. She's really worried about him, and she's so in love with him…."

"I know. I already told my brother I'll kick his ass if he hurts her."

"And he said?"

Marsh gave her the gist of his conversation with Dom, for now, omitting his brother's retribution.

"Wow," Chloe said. "He quit the priesthood?"

"Looks like it."

She pulled back, nibbling at her lip with worry. "Do you think…?"

He knew what she was going to say, had thought it himself, but unlike Sarajane or Aunt Gennie, he had no second sight to give him the answer. "I wish to hell I knew," he said.

At that moment, Mary Kate screwed up her little face and mewled. "Ahhh, what is it, sweet baby?" Chloe crooned, scooping up her daughter in her arms. Brenden slept on, his tiny brow slightly wrinkled, his lips puckered up.

"How's your arm?" Marsh asked, concerned.

"Not bad. The babies are so tiny, it hardly feels like I'm holding anything." She looked up at him, her big green eyes full of emotion. "Thank God! I don't know what I would have done if I couldn't hold them."

Marsh watched his wife nuzzle Mary Kate with her lips, speaking soft soothing words to his newborn daughter. He was so overcome with his own emotion, he felt his eyes well with tears. "I love you so much, Chloe. Thank you for these beautiful babies."

Chloe's gaze lifted to him again. Holding Mary Kate with one arm, she extended her free hand to clasp his. "You had just as much to do with it as I did." She flashed him a cheeky, suggestive grin. "And I can hardly wait to get practicing again…."

Marsh felt his other head begin to swell with antici-pation.

Chloe noticed. "Good thing we're going to have a house full of people for the next two weeks," she said. "It will help us keep our minds off of…other things."

Marsh grinned. "I doubt that, but the sentiment is well-intended." He leaned in for another kiss just as Brenden made his awakening known to the entire floor.

Sarajane asked the orderly to wheel her to Chloe's room. She promised that she would not leave the hospital on her own two legs, but reverted to the old childhood trick of crossing her fingers as she made the promise, just in case she decided not to keep it.

The orderly knocked on the door then pushed it open all the way so Sarajane could pass through. Chloe had one chair, Marsh the other. Each had a baby and a bottle. "I thought you were going to nurse," Sarajane said after *hello*s and *how-are-you*s were exchanged.

"I am, but they want me to try and get them used to a small nipple and sucking first. My milk is just starting to come in, so I'll get some breast-feeding lessons later from the lactation specialist."

Marsh laughed. "They have specialists for everything these days."

"We didn't get to take our infant care class," Sarajane said. "I was really looking forward to it."

"Rose rescheduled her for tomorrow night," Chloe said. "Seems we'll have a nice big audience for the event."

"I can hardly wait," Marsh said, his tone dry. "Maybe we should invite JD and Luce over, too. Make it a *really* full house."

"They're already coming," Chloe informed him.

"There must be somebody down at the station who wants to come…."

"You're lucky I love you even though you're such a smart ass," Chloe said, arching an eyebrow at him.

Marsh laughed.

"Is, uh, is Dom at your house?" Sarajane asked.

"Yes, and before you go getting stubborn about going back to your own place, he's coming to pick you up." He finagled his wrist in a way that didn't disturb Brenden's sucking and checked his watch. "He should be here any minute. I told him to come straight to Chloe's room, because I figured that's where you'd be."

Sarajane scowled at him.

Chloe chuckled.

"What?" Marsh said.

"I guess Chloe already filled you in on our talk last night."

"Yes, and she said she'd convinced you to come back to the Fielding palace, so what's the problem?"

"Palace?" Sarajane said, laughing.

Marsh shrugged. "What can I say? I'm feeling kingly."

"You are so full of it," Chloe said, giggling.

Marsh shot her a knowing grin.

Sarajane frowned, worrying her lower lip. "Um, is Dom staying at the palace?"

"Relax, Sarie, Dom is going to stay at your place.

Chloe suggested it, and I think it's a great idea."

"You would." She opened her mouth, but before she could say more a tap sounded on the door and Dominic Fielding entered the room.

Whatever she'd been about to say suddenly escaped her. In fact, her tongue was so tied, she could have marketed it as a pretzel.

# chapter 39

*h*is eyes on the new parents, and with Sarajane parked out of the way in the opposite corner, Dom didn't see her at first. "The little ones are awake," he said, delighted. "What beautiful babies they are!"

Sarajane wondered why he didn't have on his traditional priest's garb. Was it at the cleaners? Had the Church relaxed the dress code? Had he left it in some foreign country? Was Chloe right, and something had happened to test his faith? *What?*

She studied Dom while he talked to Chloe and his brother. He looked a lot like Marsh, which meant he had dark hair and green eyes and a jaw that leaned toward squarish. He was taller than his brother at about six-three and he'd always been a little fuller in build, but now he looked like he'd lost at least twenty pounds. He didn't look unhealthy or ill...he looked *haunted*.

She wondered where he'd been for the past three years, what he'd seen, what he'd done—or what had been done to him. Always the most serious of all the Fielding boys, he almost seemed downright somber now. She wanted to make him laugh again, like he had when discovering the babies were awake. She loved the sound of his laugh. It was so infrequent, it was a joy to behold.

She sat quietly, watching him fawn over the twins, thinking what a great dad he'd make, sad beyond belief that he'd never have the chance to have what his brother had. *Admit it*, she thought, *you also feel a little bit—okay,* more *than a little bit—disappointed for yourself.*

Since she was eight years old, she'd dreamed of walking down the aisle in a beautiful white dress, Dominic waiting for her at the altar, handsome in his black tux, both of them together making babies, at least five of them....

The day he'd entered the seminary, her dream had begun to fade and by the time he'd taken his vows, it had been completely obliterated. Well, maybe not completely. Over the years, she released it from hiding periodically, re-examined it, dwelled on how or what or when she might have done things differently, made him change his mind about becoming a priest.

Sometimes when she did that, she cursed herself for caving in to her desire to kiss him that once. It seemed so long ago now, but she remembered it, felt it, *experienced* it as if it had just been yesterday.

She'd met other men along her path through life, dated and kissed them, but never shared the ultimate intimacy with any of them. She knew she had somewhat of a reputation for being a prude, but that didn't bother her. Her life, she understood, was destined to be lived as an old maid. A *virgin* old maid, at that. *Imagine,* she thought with irony, *in this day and age!*

She wasn't even conscious of having uttered a half-sob until Dom swung around and faced her where she sat in the wheelchair.

"Sarajane!"

"Hello, Dominic."

"I didn't know you were here already."

"Yep," she said, trying to force some perkiness into her voice. "And raring to get out of this place. I understand you're my ride."

"Yes. Yes, I am." He moved toward her, never taking his eyes off her face. "Despite your ordeal, you look...."

Sarajane wondered why he couldn't complete his thought. She decided to give him some help filling in the blank. Her tone flip, she furnished, "Amazing, wonderful, beautiful?" She forced herself to laugh, so he'd know she was joking.

Instead, his expression remained serious. "Yes," he said. "All of those."

Momentarily discombobulated, Sarajane sat staring at him, hoping she wasn't gaping up at him like a beached fish. Finally, she gave her head a little shake to clear the fog and said, "You're looking well, too."

She could have said more, but imagine telling a priest he looked sexy, hot, good enough to eat—in triplicate! First of all, she didn't want to embarrass herself in front of her friends, and second of all, she didn't want Dominic Fielding to know that she still pined for him after all these years. Talk about how pitiful that would look!

His gaze wandered over her, and then *she* got hot. *God, forgive me for my lustful thoughts!*

"Are you ready to go?" he asked.

"Uh, actually, I just got here myself, and I was hoping to hold one or both babies before I leave." She tore her gaze away from his and looked toward Chloe and Marsh. "Any chance?"

Despite the fact that she had not wanted to make herself look the fool in front of them, both Chloe and Marsh shared almost identical expressions of compassion.

Sarajane forced a smile to her face.

Marsh stood and brought Brenden over to her.

Sarajane used the sanitizer, then took the baby, almost with reverence. She'd never *held* one before. He was so tiny, so fragile, so amazing. Her heart overflowed almost to bursting with emotion for the little guy. Marsh was like a brother to her and Chloe had become one of her two best friends.

Sarajane didn't even realize she was weeping until Dom handed her a tissue from the dispenser. She took it without using it, then looked up at Marsh, who still stood beside her, and then across the room at Chloe, still holding Mary Kate. "He's so beautiful. I feel…." She struggled for words. "I feel overwhelmed with love for him. For both of them."

Marsh put a hand on her shoulder and squeezed. His eyes were wet. Chloe nodded, her own tears flowing.

Sarajane looked up at Dom last. His cheeks were wet with his own tears. She finally wiped her face as she looked back down at Brenden. Her voice warbly, she tried to lighten the mood. "I'm sorry—I never intended to start a sobfest."

After a heartbeat of silence, they all chuckled. Brenden blew some bubbles between his tiny little lips. She decided the best course of action would be to focus on the baby, which wasn't difficult. She stroked his soft cheek with her finger, smoothed his baby hair tenderly with the palm of her hand, unwrapped his swaddling and inserted her finger into his teeny little fist. He grasped it tightly, then began to make sucking noises with his mouth.

"Want to feed him?" Marsh asked.

Sarajane hoped she didn't have that deer-in-the-headlights look on her face. "I've never fed a baby before."

"Neither have I," Marsh said, "but it's easier than I thought it would be. He knelt beside her and inserted the nipple of the bottle into Brenden's mouth. The infant began to suck, his effort greedy.

Sarajane laughed, delighted. She eased her hand under Marsh's and took over. Amazed with her newfound ability, she glanced up at Dom. He had an expression of such tenderness on his face, it almost undid her. She felt bad about hogging the baby, when his uncle stood looming over him, obviously wanting his turn. "Do you want to hold him?" she asked.

Chloe spoke up. "Dominic, you can take Mary Kate. I

need to use the bathroom and Marsh can help me get there.

Dom tore his eyes away from Sarajane and Brenden, cleaned his hands, and moved over to take the chair Marsh had vacated.

Chloe stood and handed over Mary Kate. Marsh reached her a moment later. "I might like a stroll down the hallway while Auntie Sarie and Uncle Dom watch the kids," Chloe said to Marsh.

"But—" said Sarajane.

"But—" said Dominic.

Marsh grinned. "Hey, you two, if I can hold a baby and give it a bottle for a few minutes, you can do it. We're not completely hopeless here."

"You mean helpless," Chloe teased.

Marsh laughed. "That, too!"

Dominic felt awkward. He always felt that way when he was in the same room with Sarajane, especially when he was *alone* with her. Having two babies who were not even twenty-four hours old for company did not consti-tute, to him, having two more people in the room.

To avoid having a conversation with Sarajane, he kept his gaze on Mary Kate. She stared back at him with dark eyes, giving him a start. Just a moment ago, her eyes had been closed. "She's looking at me," he said in wonder.

"Brenden's looking at me, too," Sarajane said, the same wonder in her voice. "He seems to be studying me."

"Likewise."

"I read that newborns can't really see anything clearly right away. That we're still fuzzy to them."

"Couldn't prove it by me," Dominic said. "Mary Kate looks highly intelligent to me and she's really got a soul-deep gaze going on."

Sarajane chuckled. Brenden began to fuss. "Uh-oh."

She raised the bottle to check it. "Empty."

"He wants to be burped. Probably has air in his little tummy."

"How do you—never mind. Any man who knows how to deliver a baby knows if it needs to be burped. How did you come to be an obstetrician, anyway?"

Dom shrugged. "When you're in a war zone, you do what they tell you, go where they want you to. Sometimes, we helped out the villagers. Medics liked me along because I was a priest. Turns out Muslims prefer an all-female delivery team, but they don't turn male care away if that's all there is. Babies are as precious to them as they are to us and they want them to make it out alive. I assisted on over a half-dozen deliveries."

"That must have been an amazing experience."

"Sometimes. Other times, I was a little freaked out by the sanitary conditions, or lack thereof, but then I'd remember that those people have been living in conditions like that since forever, so it was more or less expected of them to carry on, regardless."

"How sad," Sarajane said.

"It is, in a way, but the other side of the coin is, they don't know it any other way." He watched Sarajane set the bottle on the counter, then gently rewrap the baby's torso the way she'd found it before she'd gone exploring for his little fingers. "Put the palm of your hand on the back of his head and neck to keep him supported, then put him on your shoulder and just pat him gently on his back with the other hand." He grinned. "You may get some upchuck on your shoulder."

"My clothes wash," she said, and began alternately patting Brenden and rubbing him.

He rewarded her with a healthy burp.

"Goodness!" she said, "That was a big one."

She eased him back down, cradling him in her arms, and began to murmur softly. Dominic couldn't understand the words, but he understood the love that flowed not only from her mouth, but from her heart.

His own heart clenched in response. So much time had passed. What could he say to her? How would he say it? *Should* he even say it?

If only he still believed in God. He would pray for an answer to his prayers and his dilemma.

# chapter 40

$b$y the time Dominic got his rental car around to the front exit of the birthing center, Sarajane had been wheeled down by an orderly and was waiting under the portico.

Surprisingly, at least to him, she still sat in the wheelchair. Sarajane was stubborn and she had never been a conformer. She liked to break rules, not follow them. He had expected to find her standing impatiently beside the chair, toe-tapping.

Dom thought she looked beautiful sitting there. Her lustrous honey-blonde hair hung waves just past her shoulders and she wore not an ounce of makeup because she simply didn't need it. Sarajane Nichols was a natural beauty.

Her aunt had brought over loose fitting sweats to accommodate the dressing on her leg and she also wore a simple white cotton blouse beneath a light-weight jacket. Slightly dark half-moons beneath her intelligent blue eyes testified to her exhaustion, and no wonder. Recovering from a serious gunshot wound, undergoing surgery, worrying, weeks in the hospital, falling and having a concussion, back to the hospital. That would take it out of anyone.

Not that Sarajane was just anyone. From childhood, she had always been a live wire. If the Fielding boys engaged in a sport in their oversized backyard, Sarajane, living on one side of them, and Luce, on the other, were out there almost before he and his brothers. The Fielding girls sure did not enjoy playing baseball or tag football or soccer, or even badminton, but Sarajane and Luce did. Both his sisters insisted that the neighbor girls only did it to impress the Fielding sons, but really, did eight-year-old girls actually think that way? Dom thought not, but what did he know?

He pulled up to the curb and got out. Sarajane tried to stand and almost tripped on the foot rests. He folded them back and extended his hand to her. "If you feel the least bit dizzy," he instructed her, "tell me. And lean on me, okay? I'm big and strong. I can take it."

Sarajane stood stock still and blinked her big blue eyes up at him. Dom felt something purely sexual course through him. He swallowed hard, then again. Finally, he found his voice. "I'll get you settled in, then take the chair back inside."

She nodded, staying silent.

He maneuvered her crutches into the rear seat first, then her into the front. Within minutes he was back in the car and pulling away from the hospital.

"Thank God," she murmured, putting her head back. "I fucking hate that place." She started upright, sending him a shocked look. "I'm so sorry! I shouldn't—"

"Have fucking said that?" Dom finished for her, amused. He knew Sarajane wasn't the type of woman who regularly peppered her conversations with profanity. "Please, don't apologize. You've been through hell over the last month. If you want to cuss, you should." He offered a grin to confirm his words.

Sarajane gave him a lopsided smile. "Still, I shouldn't swear in front of a priest," she said, primly readjusting herself in the seat so her head was back against the headrest again. "I'm starving. I hope there's some food in the fridge at Chloe's, not that there wouldn't be, but with all the commotion...."

"Do you feel up to stopping somewhere along the way?"

"What did you have in mind?"

"Whatever. Fast food, drive-thru, sit-down. You name it."

Sarajane bit her lower lip for several moments. "I'd kill for pizza and beer." She looked over at him. "You think the beer will hurt me? All I've had today for meds is Tylenol and one dose of antibiotic."

"I think it would be okay. You're not driving. If you pass out, I'll catch you."

"Gee, thanks."

Dom laughed. That made twice in one day. It came out a little rusty, but he felt a whole lot better for having done it. "What's the antibiotic for?"

"Infection in my wound. Just started taking it day before yesterday."

He frowned. "Is it helping?"

She quirked her lips as she considered his question. "I think so. I guess the doc will tell me if it's not when I go for my checkup next week."

"I'll give you a ride to the appointment."

"You will?"

"Why not?"

"I, uh, just thought you might not be here next week."

He grunted, but decided on no further explanation. Yet. "You pick the spot."

"Spot?"

"To eat?"

"Oh, yeah." Sarajane directed him to her neighborhood, to Gino's Pizzeria. "I heard you're going to be staying at my place. After we eat, we'll go by my house, so you'll know how to get there. It's actually Marsh's house. Well, Marsh and Chloe's now. You never saw it when he lived there, did you?"

Dom shook his head. "Marsh used to write me about it, then...." He trailed off. What more could he say? *Then, I broke the fifth commandment, deserted life and my family, and ran off to hide from the world, and oh, yeah, spent a lot of time alternately begging God to forgive me, to help me, then cursing Him when he seemed to abandon me?* That explanation would be fairly accurate, though by no means complete, but regardless, he kept it to himself. He wasn't ready to give Sarajane any particulars about the last few years of his life just yet. Maybe he never would be. It had taken a lot out of him just to tell it to Marsh.

"He did a fabulous job renovating the bungalow," Sarajane went on, unenlightened to his inner turmoil. "I wanted to buy it, but then Chloe got pregnant and Marsh said he had to start building the kids' college funds."

"My little brother has really taken to married life and fatherhood."

"He has."

He pulled into the parking lot of a new strip mall. "This place any good?" he asked. He hadn't eaten any breakfast and his stomach announced that by rumbling.

Sarajane looked at him askance. "Would I suggest a place that wasn't any good after I just got out of the hospital?"

"I guess not." Dom had the good grace to try and look chastened. By her smug nod, he guessed he'd succeeded.

He instructed Sarajane to remain in the car until he got around to help her out. He retrieved her crutches from the back seat.

"I'm not an invalid," she groused when he opened her door.

He raised an eyebrow. "Oh, really?"

She took his proffered hand. "One thing you Fielding men have in common is smartassness."

Dominic really laughed that time, right from the belly.

He decided in that moment that he was glad, after all, to be alive.

At the counter, they grabbed a menu. Dom thought Sarajane might be more comfortable if she could lean against the wall and put her leg up. She agreed. They had their pick of booths, since they had beat the lunch crowd.

"This place sure smells good," he said.

"Trust me," Sarajane said, sliding slowly across the leather bench, "there is no place in the world that makes pizza like this. New York style or Chicago deep dish. Take your pick. Both are great."

Dom slid in across from her. "What's your favorite?"

"Either way, with plain old pepperoni, sausage, black olives, and extra cheese. Keep the artichokes and sun-dried tomatoes and goat cheese away from me, please! I do *not* like gourmet pizza."

He tore his gaze away from Sarajane, where it could have lingered for far too long and far too noticeably. While he perused the menu, a server in a Gino's T-shirt and tight blue jeans with a frayed knee showed up.

"Hi! Can I get you started on some beer while you're deciding?"

Sarajane opened her mouth, then looked at Dom. "What kind do you like?"

Dom glanced up at the server. "What kinds of micro-brew have you got on draft?"

"Heffie, Stella, Mac and Jack—"

"Go no further," Dom said. "Mac and Jack okay with you?" he asked Sarajane.

"Perfect."

"A pitcher," Dom told the server.

"Full-size or half?"

Again Dom looked at Sarajane. "Half." When the server had left, she said, "My leg is hurting and a glass of beer will probably dull the pain as well as, or better than, an Oxy."

"You're on Oxycodone?"

"No, Oxycontin. Time-released, the doc said, which

he thought it would work better for me." She added, her tone droll, "Course my prescription is back at the house. Aunt Gennie brought me everything I needed this morning except the pain pills."

Dom frowned. "Is the pain bad?"

She shrugged. "The infection kind of exacerbated things."

"Marsh told me about the…I was going to say episodes, but that seems too peaceful to describe two shootouts."

Sarajane nodded. "As long as I've been a Deputy ME, I've never attended a crime scene until after all the damage was done. I never dreamed I'd be part of an incident involving guns in my off hours, let alone two."

Dom put his elbows on the table and folded his hands together.

"Praying for me, Father?"

Her tone held some amusement, but he wasn't amused. "Things could have been so much worse. For all of you."

"Yes, but thank God, they weren't."

"Yes," he said, his tone slightly acerbic, "thank God they weren't."

Sarajane tilted her head at him. "What gives, Dom? I don't remember you ever being cynical or irreverent or…or…."

"Godless?" he provided helpfully.

Her blue, blue eyes widened. "Whoa…."

He was saved from having to respond because at that moment, the server arrived with a tray containing a pitcher and two chilled mugs. She took their order and walked away, swaying her behind at him, like he might be interested.

Dom had one of those irreverent thoughts Sarajane had just accused him of: He could think of only one behind that he had ever been, or would ever be interested in and it was currently sitting on the seat across from him. He picked up the pitcher and poured a mug for her.

Sarajane accepted it from him and took a long, appreciative sip.

He followed suit. And waited. She didn't hesitate long.

"I repeat, Dominic. What gives?"

Dominic slid his phone across the table toward her. "You'd better call Aunt Gennie, or she'll think the worst of why we're not back at the house yet."

Sarajane stared at him for several long moments, then picked up the cell and dialed her aunt's number. Once she had filled Aunt Gennie in on their location and their plans before heading back to the Fielding house, she said to Dominic, "Aunt Gennie wants to know if you're still planning on staying at my place?"

He nodded.

"He is." She listened, her eyes on the finger she was using to rub up and down in the condensation on her beer mug. "*What!*" she squawked, obviously startled. Her blue gaze flew to him in apparent shock. "Uh, no, no. Just leave them." She blinked rapidly. "Look, I'll see you, soon, okay? Don't worry about me. If Dom can deliver two babies by himself, I know I'm in good hands." A few seconds of silence ensued while she listened to her aunt. "Sure. Bye."

She disconnected the call and handed his phone back to him. "You must be the only man in America who doesn't have a smartphone," she said inanely.

Dom shrugged. "Don't need one. Everything okay?"

Sarajane nodded, but didn't speak. Instead, she picked up her glass and drained half of it.

"Sarie? What's wrong."

"Nothing," she said, her voice sounding strangled. "Nothing's wrong."

He reached a hand across the table and captured hers. "Tell me."

For long agonizing seconds, she stared at him, evidently fighting some sort of internal battle. Finally, she choked out, "You slept in my bed, on my sheets." Her face bloomed crimson.

At first, Dom thought she was angry or embarrassed. Sleeping in a woman's bed, whether she was in it or not, did present a set of issues with which he was not entirely familiar. "I did," he admitted. "Does it bother you?"

Her head began to go from side to side, almost imperceptibly at first, then with more determination. She picked up her mug, drained it, and slammed it down on the table. "Dominic Fielding, either you are the most obtuse man I have ever met, or you are the male version of a prick tease!"

Struck dumb by her outburst, Dominic could do nothing more than stare at her.

"Priest or no priest, you're going to hear this," she barreled on, temporarily fortified, perhaps by the beer, "so just shut up and listen, okay?"

To save himself, he simply nodded.

"You slept in *my* bed, on *my* sheets, and I wasn't there to enjoy the pleasure of your company."

Disconcerted, Dom felt his face grow hot and his manhood grow in size. What was she saying?

"Do you know how many times I've dreamed of us being in the same bed, Dom? And I'm not talking about sleeping!" She reached for the pitcher and refilled both their glasses halfway, emptying it. "You're a smart guy, so I'm not elaborating further, and I don't care if you're a man of God or not. This has been festering in my brain for a long time and you might as well know it." She pulled a napkin from the dispenser and used it to wipe her eyes. "I'm in love with you, Dominic Fielding. I have been since I was eight years old, and I will be until the day I die. If I can't have you, I'm thinking about becoming a nun."

*A nun?* He almost laughed, but caught himself in time. "Sarie—"

"Shut up," she almost shouted, looking around to make sure no one was near by. "I can't help the way I feel. I have a foolish heart. I know it. But it is what it is."

She took a deep, shaky breath. "I promise you that I will not mention this again, except to say, if I can't have you for my husband and lover, I still want you for my friend."

She gave a quick nod as if to say, *There. I did it.*

Stupefied and humbled, Dom kept his mouth shut. His brain, however, processed her outburst in overdrive.

For several minutes, neither of them spoke. Her blue gaze never faltered from his green one. She wasn't exactly daring him...or was she? He thought she might be waging another inner battle: Run or stand your ground. Her chin went up just a notch and he noticed it trembled.

He'd never loved her more than he did in that moment. What courage it took for her to reveal her deepest, most heartfelt secrets to him.

So, while they waited in silence for divine intervention, or their pizza to arrive, whichever happened first, Dom did exactly what he'd thought he wouldn't do on this day, or perhaps on *any* day in the future.

Much to his surprise, he opened his mouth and poured out his own heart and soul to Sarajane about the past three years.

He might not be ready to profess his own intimate yearnings as he'd lain in her bed all night long, on her sheets, inhaling the intoxicating scent that was hers alone. But, as the God he'd forsaken was his witness, he could reveal the horrors he'd experienced that had changed him and made such an monumental impact on his life.

# chapter 41

Sarajane listened as the man she loved spilled out his anguish. His torment was her torment. She cried more than once as he talked. To give him credit, he did not, though his jaw flexed, his eyes watered, and his fists clenched, whitening his knuckles.

She asked the occasional question, but mostly, she simply let him talk.

The pizzas arrived—one New York style, just the way she liked it, one Chicago-style deep-dish the way Dom liked it, with salami, green peppers, mushrooms, and linguicia. Both with extra cheese and fresh tomato slices on the side. The server brought plates, silverware, hot sauce, and grated parmesan and asked if they wanted a refill on their beer.

Surprised, Sarajane looked down and realized both of them had drained their glasses.

"What do you say?" Dom asked her.

"I say fill it up!" came a familiar voice.

"Luce!" Sarajane said.

Dominic rose to greet his old friend. Luce hugged him and began to cry. "I didn't even know you were back," she said. "We went to the hospital to see Sarajane and Chloe, but Sarie was already gone and Marsh told us you were home. Then we drove over to his place, but you weren't there either. Aunt Gennie said you were here, so here we are." She smacked him on the shoulder, just like old times. "You big lug! What did you think you were doing, falling off the radar for three years? Everyone's been worried sick about you."

Dominic finally got a chance to speak. "It's good to see you, Luce." He looked over her shoulder. "You must be JD." He extended his hand to JD and they shook. "You're going to have your hands full with this one, buddy."

JD laughed. "Don't I know it?" He grinned. "Still, I can't think of anyone I'd rather have my hands on...."

Luce elbowed him lightly in the gut. "JD! You're talking to a priest! Watch your mouth."

"You guys are hungry, I hope. We ordered two pizzas, so we've got plenty to share." Dominic motioned for the server, who had walked away upon Luce and JD's arrival. He asked for a refill on beer and plates and utensils for two more.

"I'm famished," Luce admitted.

"Me, too," JD said. "This place has the best pizza around."

JD sat next to Dom. Luce slid in next to Sarajane, who eased her bad leg off the seat. "Are you okay with your leg down?" she asked Sarajane.

"Yeah, it's fine."

"How are you feeling?"

Sarajane gave her a lopsided smile. "A little tipsy, to tell you the truth."

The server arrived at the table with more beer and two each of mugs, plates, and forks.

"We've already polished off one pitcher," Sarajane said, "so if you don't mind, let's dig in. I need some food in me."

They stuffed their faces with pizza and washed it

down with beer.

"Don't you have to get back to the courtroom?" Dom asked Luce.

She exchanged a look with JD. "I'm taking some time off. Between this fiasco with the Paired-Up Serials and my disenchantment with the whole law enforcement thing…."

Dom nodded. "Marsh told me. Does that mean you're giving up the law for good?"

"Yes." Just a simple answer.

"You'll find something else you love," Dom said.

Luce shot him a wry smile. "When God closes a door, he opens a window, huh?"

"Something like that," Dom replied, his tone non-committal.

"How are you doing?" Dom asked JD. "I heard you took a bullet in your vest."

"No ill effects. I thank God and department policy every day that I was wearing that Kevlar."

"I didn't get a chance to ask Marsh—is it all resolved now?"

JD reached for a slice of deep dish and said, "Still haven't caught the pair from Montana. Every damned law enforcement agency in the country is looking for them, but we got nothin'."

"Montana's a big state," Dom observed. He looked at Sarajane, then Luce. "Are you under some kind of protection?"

Luce reached over and patted JD's forearm. "This big guy is with me all the time. I can't even go the bathroom without him standing outside the door."

JD wiggled his eyebrows at her.

"We also have a shadow sitting in that cruiser in the parking lot." She inclined her head toward the window. Dom and Sarajane followed the direction of her gaze.

Despite the nature of the conversation, Sarajane experienced a sense of joy for her friends. Luce and JD had finally resolved their issues. Almost two years ago,

Chloe and Marsh managed to do the same, and now look—married and two beautiful babies.

An incredible sadness overcame her. She would never have that opportunity with Dominic unless penguins took to flying and the Catholic church changed their rules and allowed priests to marry. She sighed. Maybe the new pontiff, Pope Francis, would lead the Church in a new direction. One could always hope.

Dom began to dance the bottom of his mug against the table top. "Don't you have to work, JD? Who's with Luce then?"

"She has round-the-clock police protection, so someone's watching her all the time."

"I also have my friend Walther in my purse. He's loaded and ready to go."

Sarajane frowned this time. That hadn't worked out so well on the two previous occasions that had erupted in gunfire. She didn't need to remind Luce of that, however, since Luce had been there for the first shootout.

"What about Sarie?" Dom asked, as if she wasn't sitting right across from him. "Who's watching her?"

"We don't feel she's a target any longer. We put something up on the Killzone blog—that's their means of communication—to the effect that Judge Luce Maguire remains in her own home, not in a friend's home, or a safe house. We learned our lesson the hard way not to do that again."

"I don't like it," Dom said.

"They thought Luce was still in the house the night Chloe and I got shot," Sarajane said. "Now they won't. Unfortunately, Chloe and I were collateral damage to those ass—, um, buttheads. SPD offered me protection when I got out of the hospital, but I declined."

Dom's forehead creased into a scowl. "I repeat. I don't like it."

After what he'd just told her about the seven-year-old boy forced to walk into a market with a bomb strapped to his body, Sarajane wasn't surprised to hear Dominic express his concern. Life had too many variables to account for them all. Insert the will of crazed maniac killers and the ante upped considerably.

"To be honest," JD said, "We *want* them to make a move. Catching them is the only way any of us will ever feel safe again."

"So, Sarie gets *no* protection and Luce has only one cop outside her house, watching."

"In essence."

Dom blew out a frustrated breath. "Just give it to me straight."

JD and Luce exchanged glances. His was stubborn. Hers said, *Well?*

"We have extra security on the place now, including cameras in about six locations. Everything's monitored." He glanced at Luce again. "There's also less obvious security on us."

"To lull them in. But still not on Sarajane."

JD picked up his mug and took a long draw.

Sarajane could almost hear Dom's wheels turning.

"I guess I was in the war zone too long. I know that when there's a will there's a way, and it doesn't make a tinker's damn how prepared you think you are. Cracks exist." He looked from Luce to JD and back. "You two have been in law enforcement long enough to know that. When a killer wants to kill, nothing stops him."

Sarajane was with Dom on this one. Logically, she knew they had to bring in the last of the Paired-Ups, but emotionally, she feared a repeat of the other two incidents, only on the third try someone she loved might end up dead. Her worries had grown exponentially with the birth of the twins.

"I'm up for suggestions," JD said, his voice tight.

"As soon as I have any," Dom shot back, "I'll let you know." He exchanged glances with each of the three of them. "Just so you know, Aunt Gennie says it's not over. For any of you."

"She didn't tell me that," Sarajane said, stunned and

miffed at the same time. She hadn't really given her safety too much thought in recent days since she'd left the hospital, but now that the discussion was back in the open again, she felt a prickle of unease. "She's not telling me a lot of things lately."

"Can we talk about something a little more pleasant, just for a while?" Luce inquired, seemingly unconcerned as she reached for another slice of pizza.

JD responded and Dom chimed in, but Sarajane was still thinking about Aunt Gennie and what she'd told Dom. It wasn't like any of them were witnesses to anything, because they weren't. But they were survivors of attempted murder and according to everything she knew about the way these whack-job Paired-Ups operated, they didn't care about anything except torture, murder, and retribution. And apparently they enjoyed each equally. And immensely.

Hoping she concealed the shiver of dread she felt, Sarajane zoned back into the conversation.

"I've never had a baby," Luce was saying, "but if I were Chloe, I think I might like having an empty house, with just me and the baby."

"Babies," Sarajane corrected. "And you are so FOS, Luce. You'd be begging The Girls to come help you."

"The Girls?" Dom asked.

Sarajane explained how Owen and Niall had dubbed their grandmother and her two friends The Girls because they just kept going, like gray-haired Energizer bunnies. Dom laughed.

"You're probably right," Luce admitted, "but I think I want my kids one at a time. Honestly, I don't know how Marsh and Chloe will deal with twins. It seems so overwhelming!"

"You'd manage, just like everyone else does," Dom said. "Remember, Mom had two sets of twins, and not only is she normal, but she didn't turn into a raving lunatic along the way."

"Your mother is a peach," Sarajane confirmed, "and

man, can she cook!"

"Remember those oatmeal cranberry cookies she used to make?" Luce said to Sarajane.

"They were yummy! I wonder if she'd give me the recipe. I haven't had cookies like that in years."

"You cook?" Dom asked.

Sarajane assumed an affronted air. "Don't look so shocked, Father Fielding. I can do a lot of things that might surprise you."

Dom sent her a searing glance. "I'm sure you can."

Sarajane felt that glance spear right into her and spread like warm honey throughout her body, leaving her all tingly inside.

And then he dropped his bomb. "And you can stop calling me Father. I've left the priesthood."

# chapter 42

*L*uce gasped.

JD choked on his beer.

Sarajane sat like a stone-cold pillar of salt, wondering if she'd heard right.

Dom looked from one to the other of them. "I suppose I could have eased into that a little differently."

"You think?" Luce asked, her tone dry. "I wondered where your collar was. What happened?"

"I'd rather not talk about it right now," he said.

Luce opened her mouth, but shut it when JD shot her a warning glance.

Sarajane's gaze dropped to Dominic's throat. Why hadn't she just asked him outright where the collar was? She might have kept her big mouth shut about how she loved him, how she'd dreamed about jumping his bones. For God's sake, she'd told a man who had suddenly become available, if not attainable, everything he might want to know about how she felt about him, plus some!

Shouldn't there be some secrets if there was to be any chance of a courting relationship? Shouldn't you find out first how the male part of the equation felt about *you*?

*Really, Sarajane*, she began to chastise herself, *you should have dated more men, slept with a couple or three or four of them, gotten some experience, learned how to play both the dating and the mating game* before *you started to mix it up with, of all people,* Dominic Fielding!

Why did it have to take hindsight to learn?

If she'd gotten red in the face before, she was burning to a crisp right now.

If she could have slipped under the table to hide, she would have.

If she could have slunk out the door to ride out the rest of the afternoon in a bar down the street, she would have.

Instead, she had to go to the bathroom, and she had to do it awkwardly clunking along on crutches.

Unfortunately, Luce decided to accompany her. "Don't you dare stand outside the door," she warned JD. "You can keep a watch from here."

JD laughed, but he didn't sound amused and he couldn't hide the worry in his eyes.

Luce went ahead of her so she could hold the door open for Sarajane. The bathroom was a three-staller, but it had a lock on the main door. Luce checked that no one else occupied the room, then flipped the bolt. "What the hell?" she cried out. "He's left the priesthood?"

Still stunned by the news, Sarajane leaned weakly against the middle of three sinks.

"Did you have any idea?" Luce asked.

"None. Well, actually Chloe and I talked about the possibility, but I never imagined...." Dom had told her what happened three years earlier, explained why he'd been incommunicado, but he had not mentioned he'd given up being a priest? *Why?*

And then it hit her. He hadn't had a chance to tell her one-on-one because Luce and JD had arrived, effectively putting an end to her private conversation with Dom.

Luce broke into her thoughts. "Do you know what this means?"

"He doesn't believe in God anymore."

Luce blew out an exasperated huff. "Don't play dense, Sarie."

"I'm not. He doesn't believe in God anymore."

Luce frowned. "That doesn't make any sense!"

"It would if you knew his story."

"So, tell me."

"Not now," Sarajane said, feeling more weary than she had in weeks. "Come by the house later, after Dom's gone. If he says it's okay, I'll tell you then."

Luce crossed her arms and tapped her toes, obviously miffed, but they were friends, so she didn't pursue it. Instead, she said, "This is the man you love. You've loved him since you were in diapers."

"Not that long," Sarajane corrected.

"Practically." Luce began pace. "Wow! I can't believe it. He's been a priest for what, almost twenty years?"

"Not quite."

She stopped in front of Sarajane, grasping her hands. The crutches went crashing to the wall between the sinks. "How do you feel about this?"

"How do you think I feel? I made a complete ass of myself a while ago. When I found out he'd slept in my bed at Marsh and Chloe's last night, that he'd slept on the very sheets *I'd* slept on the night before, I told him exactly how I feel about him and pretty much what I would have wanted to do if I'd been in that bed with him."

"Wow!" Luce said again, her eyes wide.

"Exactly."

"And what did he say?"

"Nothing! You'd think, since he had this big revelation up his sleeve, he could have at least stopped me before I brayed out my deepest feelings for him."

"He's hot for you."

"Where do you get that from?"

"You kissed him once. He kissed you back."

"I wish I'd never told you about that! It doesn't mean anything. We were teenagers. Probably, neither one of us had ever kissed anyone before. At least, I know I hadn't."

"I'm sure Dom hadn't either." Luce started to chew on her bottom lip, cleaning off what remained of her lipstick. "I've been watching him watch you. A man doesn't look at a woman like that unless he has feelings for her."

"So now you're some kind of romance guru?"

"Listen, Sarie, I know how JD looks at me. I've seen the way Marsh looks at Chloe. You know I'm right, admit it."

Sarajane shook her head. "I'm in a fog right now. I don't know anything." She began to cry. "I need time to think."

"But—"

She put up her hand. "I mean it, Luce. I have to think! Just because I've been dreaming about being married to Dom since I was a kid doesn't mean he is miraculously going to ask me to be his bride. I mean, how does a guy who devoted his life to God since he was an altar boy just suddenly go from wearing a collar to wearing a condom and crawling into bed with me? It's just not going to happen! There has to be a transition of some sort, and even then, it may not happen." She gulped a breath of air, tears overflowing her eyes. "At least not with me."

Startled by her own outburst, Sarajane didn't argue when Luce hugged her. "Don't give up, Sarie. He's worth waiting for and fighting for. You know that. Hell, you've been doing that for years already!"

Sarajane hiccoughed. "I know. Oh, God, why do I love him so much? Why does this *hurt* so much?" she asked, miserable.

"Look, friend, love doesn't always feel good. If any-one knows that, I do, and if anyone tells you different, he or she is lying! You don't go run screaming in the other direction—"

"You were going to run from JD, even if you weren't screaming," Sarajane pointed out, sniffling.

"Well, yes, but I came to my senses, didn't I?"

Sarajane pulled away, tears still dripping down her cheeks. "I think it's more like JD came to his senses."

Luce frowned at her. "Let's say we *both* came to our senses. Love is a two-way street, you know."

"You should write a love column for the local paper after you leave the bench," Sarajane said with another hiccough.

Luce grinned and pulled several paper towels out of the dispenser. "Dry your eyes, Little Miss Lovelorn."

"I drank too much beer," Sarajane said, wiping at her cheeks. "It's making me weepy and I have to pee."

Luce retrieved the crutches from between the sinks and Sarajane slid them under her armpits.

A knock sounded at the door. "Everything okay in there?" JD yelled through the wood.

"Just peachy," Luce shouted back. "Give us girls some privacy, will you?"

JD grumbled back something they couldn't understand. Luce grinned. "Men."

*Men, indeed,* thought Sarajane. *You can't live with 'em and you can't live without 'em.* And in her case, it was much worse. She didn't have options when it came to either.

Before Luce unlocked the door, she turned to Sarajane and said, "Just remember, we've only had two miracles this week, and doesn't Aunt Gennie always say good luck and bad luck both come in threes?"

Sarajane didn't dispute the number of miracles, but she mentally calculated all the recent bad luck. If you counted the initial BOMB! written on Luce's windshield and the two shootouts at Marsh and Chloe's house, then the bad luck had passed. Unfortunately, Aunt Gennie had told Dom that more trouble was coming, so either the BOMB! hadn't counted as bad luck or they were about to start the next triple round.

She said as much to Luce, who stared at her, eyes wide with denial. "No way."

"Yes, way. Don't forget about the Montana pair—the reason you have security around you twenty-four/seven these days."

And if that was correct, maybe in addition to the twins there *was* one more piece of good luck hovering in the air.

Luce and JD headed in one direction. Sarajane and Dom went to her house.

He had infinite patience, Sarajane decided, as he walked slowly beside her. She inched up the sidewalk, still clumsy on her crutches despite her best efforts not to be. She thought she might throw a party the day the doc said she could start walking without them. Have a bonfire. Use the crutches for kindling. She absolutely, positively frigging *hated* them!

At the porch steps, Dom removed the cursed walking implements from under her arms and put them up against the front porch. Then he went back and scooped her up in his arms and carried her into the house.

Once inside, he went back for her crutches, obviously oblivious to the sound of Sarajane's heart pounding out of her chest. Even when sharing a life-altering kiss after prom, she had not been that close to him. The time they played tag football and he tackled and flattened her, instead of pulling the kerchief out of her back pocket, didn't count. At the age of ten, she hadn't been old enough to have rampaging hormones, even though she still nurtured the memory.

Today, at thirty-five. she had plenty of rampaging hormones.

Sarajane hop-crutched to the sofa and invited Dom to have a self-guided tour through the house. She propped her leg up on the coffee table.

He arrived back in the living room ten minutes later and said, "Marsh did an amazing job on this place. The house, the yard, everything! I guess all the stuff Dad taught us paid off."

"If he ever decides to give up his badge, he can make a living from carpentry," she said. "You ever put your skills to use?"

He shrugged his wide shoulders as his gaze wandered over the living room. "I've done a bit," he said, but didn't elaborate further.

He walked over to the fireplace and studied a framed photo of Marsh, Sarajane, Luce, and himself at his senior prom. Sarajane wondered if he remembered the kiss they'd shared that night.

"I was thinking I'd take the guest room, but it looks like Aunt Gennie is occupying it."

Her heart started galloping again. She'd completely spaced that he'd be sleeping in *her* bed. "You'll have to take my room." She gnawed on her lower lip in hopes of stilling the trembling. Why was she feeling so weepy? "I'd offer to change the sheets, but...." She trailed off, waving a hand over her left thigh.

If she hadn't been staring at him, she might have missed the scorching look he speared her with, a look so hot it almost blistered her.

"No need," he said.

"I changed them the day...the day before I got shot."

"They'll be fine." He looked away, his jaw flexing madly. When he looked back, he still seemed to be having some private struggle underway. When he spoke, his voice was low, almost hoarse. "I like that I'll be able to smell you when I go to sleep."

Shocked and excited at the same time, Sarajane said stupidly, "You do?"

He nodded. "It's...comforting."

*Comforting?* she thought, not certain if she should feel affronted or complimented. It sure was a long way from tantalizing, or arousing, or sexy. Nonetheless, she decided to accept it as a compliment.

He went on as if she weren't experiencing some sort of dilemma within herself. "Thoughts of you over the past twelve years, in the war zones and out, have given me a lot of comfort."

Good grief. How many bombshells could one guy drop in a day? "I would have thought praying to God would give you comfort," she said, hoping no rancor came across in her tone, for none was meant.

"It used to. It doesn't anymore."

"I'm sorry."

"Me, too. Talking to God was the one constant I had in my life." He shoved his hands into the pockets of his blue jeans, leaving big bulges because they were formed into fists. "Now I just feel at a loss...about everything." He threw back his head. His gaze would have been aimed at the ceiling, but his eyes were squeezed tightly shut, his face in a grimace.

In a way, Sarajane could relate to his predicament. She'd never been a staunch Catholic, but she had been baptized, confirmed, and taken her First Communion in the Church. Because Dom had been an altar boy, that pretty much guaranteed her attendance at Sunday mass.

Once he'd entered the college seminary, though, she'd stopped going. He was far away by then, and rarely came home. She probably hadn't been to mass more than ten times in the last eighteen years. Still, once a Catholic, always a Catholic.

Her job took her out on deaths that were heinous— murder, suicide, or accidental, she had to deal with them, but she would never understand the *why* of them. In that, she didn't know whether she felt God had failed her or she had failed God. "Want to talk about it?" she asked Dom.

"Shit, I don't know. Does talk really solve anything?"

"Sometimes it does. Sometimes it doesn't."

He opened his eyes and turned that penetrating green gaze on her. "When I was in your bed last night," he said on a gravelly whisper, "I was wishing you were there beside me."

Sarajane knew her eyes must have gone wide as quarters. She couldn't do anything but be honest right back. "If only I could have been."

Dominic pulled his hands out of his pockets and moved over to the sofa in two long strides. He gently moved Sarajane's leg so that she had both feet on the floor, then circled her arms with his long, strong fingers, raising her up. "I need something real right now. I don't know why, and I don't know where this is coming from, but I'm going to hold you against me and I'm going to kiss you, Sarie."

Sarajane slid her arms around his neck, nestling her body against him. She stood as much on tiptoe as her injured leg would allow. Dom lowered his head and their lips met.

His kiss wasn't hungry and it wasn't simple, but it was everything a kiss should be as far as Sarajane was concerned. He worked her lips, then the inside of her mouth. She briefly wondered where he'd learned to kiss like that, felt a momentary flare of jealousy, but then succumbed to the feelings, both emotional and physical, coursing through her body.

Dom pressed himself against her, his big hands somehow cupping her bottom, raising her up until she cradled his hardness, and still the kiss went on. They came up for air once—he taking a moment to kiss her forehead, she to kiss his throat—then they went back to it again.

They might have gone on like that all day if someone hadn't started banging on the door.

# chapter 43

*l* ike guilty children, they released each other in a panic.

Like concerned adults, their gazes locked on the front door. "Who in the world…?" Sarajane wondered aloud. She bent and reached for her crutches.

Dom stayed her with a hand. "I'll see who it is. The knocking seems too urgent to be someone selling Girl Scout cookies."

"Ask who's there," Sarajane cautioned. All she could think of were the two serial killers from Montana, still on the loose. Dom was a big man, but he wasn't made of steel, or Kevlar.

Instead of asking, he peered through the glass across the top of the Craftsman door, then opened it without a word. A uniformed police officer stood on the porch. Sarajane didn't recognize him, but then she didn't know half the officers on the force.

"What can we do for you?" Dom asked.

"We had a call of a suspicious vehicle parked at this address."

Sarajane hobbled over to join the conversation. She

introduced herself, gave her work title, and said, "The car belongs to my friend, Dominic Fielding. He's Detective Marsh Fielding's brother. He was just giving me a lift home from the hospital."

"Do you have some identification?" the officer asked Dom, stepping across the threshold uninvited.

Startled by his boldness and more than a little irritated, Sarajane said, "You do know what hap—"

The officer pulled his gun, pointing it directly at Dom's chest, and snarled, "Shut the fuck up and both of you move back. Put your hands up."

"Crutches," she said.

The intruder glared at her. "Back up on your stupid crutches *and* shut the fuck up!"

Sarajane complied awkwardly, glaring back.

She could have kicked herself to hell and back. She had the *juju*—when she intuited something, she needed to damned well start paying attention to it. But wait, *she* hadn't had the *juju*, Aunt Gennie had! Dom had mentioned it at lunch, and still they'd opened the door....

This had to be one of the Montana killers. They'd pulled this ploy before, impersonating a police officer, and again, it looked like a legitimate Salem PD uniform. Had they killed or severely injured another cop to get it? And where *was* the other half of the team? And why were they after *her*?

Almost before the thought had formed, she knew what was going on. JD had made sure the Killzone blog had the info that Luce was secure in her own home. These guys must have scoped things out, confirmed Luce was guarded, and devised an alternate strategy.

They planned to use her to get Luce and JD. They probably *had* killed another cop, and the other guy was most likely close-by, waiting for only God knew what reason or signal before he showed up at the door, too.

As the presiding judge over the first trial of the media-dubbed Paired-Up Serials, a moniker that had stuck with law enforcement, Luce had been targeted with a bomb that hadn't really been a bomb. The resulting investigation had inadvertently led to the downfall of the entire Paired-Ups, one of the most notorious killing organizations in history.

The final two apparently planned to carry on and fulfill the retribution that had begun almost four weeks before. Sarajane had no doubt they also would enjoy torturing and killing her and Dom once they got Luce and JD through the door. Psycho number two would no doubt be arriving with the video camera.

Not good. Not good at all.

Sarajane snugged the top of a crutch into her armpit and put a hand on Dom's forearm, urging him back toward her. Without actually looking at her, he took several steps back, placing himself in front of her. His gesture warmed her, but frightened her at the same time. She didn't want him taking a bullet playing hero, trying to protect her.

"Where's the kitchen?" the pseudo cop demanded.

"That way," Sarajane said, peeking around Dom's broad form, nodding toward her left.

"Get moving," he ordered, "and if either one of you so much as twitches, I'll kill you right here and now. *Got it?*"

Sarajane said, "Yes," but Dom stared defiantly at the intruder, his jaw working furiously.

The killer jammed his weapon into Dom's ribs. "*Got it?*" he demanded again.

"I got it. Now get that damned gun out of my side."

"Don't tell me what to do, motherfucker. Understand? I don't even know you and I don't like you, so I don't care if I have to blow your fucking head off right now." He jerked his head, pointing his chin in Sarajane's direction. "I'm not interested in you at all, asshole. It's the bitch I need, and I only need her for one thing."

They reached the kitchen and he moved around in front of them. He conducted a visibly insulting perusal up and down Sarajane's body. "Or maybe I need her for two things, and you can watch while I help myself to some pussy."

Sarajane had never been subjected to the threat of rape before. A cold chill ran down her spine. She began to perspire and her pulse pounded rapidly through her veins.

The gunman swung his weapon wide, toward the kitchen table. "Pull out two chairs, side-by-side and you" —he pointed to Sarajane— "sit down! You" —he pointed to Dominic— "tie her up, hands behind her back and looped through the chair rails." He withdrew a coil of quarter-inch cotton cording from inside his shirt.

Sarajane knew he must have more tucked in there, because he looked padded, which she'd initially attributed to him wearing a Kevlar vest. She sat down in the chair, her leg aching like crazy.

Dom took her crutches and leaned them up in the corner near the cabinets. He took his time following the killer's instructions.

Sarajane thought to put her hands into fists and pull them apart as hard as she could. Dom must have noticed, because he took a moment to rub her arm. Then he began to loosely wind and tie the cording. *Please, God, make the restraint easy to slip out of at some point.*

Another knock sounded at the door.

"Okay, asshole," he said, his weapon trained on Dom, "you're going back with me to get the door. I'm expecting company, and if you are, too, get rid of whoever it is, pronto, or you, your girlfriend, and whoever it is at the door are done living. Understood?"

This time Dom answered. "Understood."

Sarajane found Dom's tone mocking, but the killer apparently missed the inflection.

Once they'd left the room, she immediately began to work her way out of the rope. It was obvious the killer wasn't accustomed to trussing people up or he would have supervised the process or checked the binding himself when Dom had finished.

Her Smith and Wesson had been returned and was back at Marsh and Chloe's house, safely tucked into the drawer in the nightstand beside her bed, but she had a second gun, a small Glock, in the drawer under the portable phone. The first thing she did was grab the phone.

Turning an ear toward the living room, she heard voices and recognized her neighbor, Mrs. Trout, talking to Dominic. The widow had most likely come to inquire after Sarajane's well-being. Dom was polite and pleasant, but he firmly told her she'd have to come back later, Sarajane was sleeping. Thank goodness, the chatty Mrs. Trout did not give up that easily.

Quickly, Sarajane dialed, not 9-1-1, but JD Kemp. He answered on the second ring. She whispered into the phone, hoping he heard everything she said after her initial, "Just listen, JD."

Dom closed the front door, and he and the psycho headed back to the kitchen. Before they came into view, another knock sounded. This time, by the sound of the voices, she ascertained that the second half of the serial killer team had finally arrived.

Sarajane said a few more words, then hung up and dug into the drawer. She sat down in the chair, the Glock concealed at the back waistband of her sweats, beneath the elastic of her briefs to ensure it stayed put. As fast as she could, she put her hands behind her back and did her best to jerry-rig the rope, hoping it still looked secure if either of the lunatics bothered to look.

Not a moment too soon. She drew a deep breath, trying to still her pulse rate.

The first killer pushed Dom through the doorway into the kitchen and instructed him to sit. He withdrew another coil of cording and tossed it to his partner, who looked at Sarajane and said, "Well, well, we're gonna have us some fucking dessert, huh?"

Something resembling a growl erupted from Dom. He rose halfway out of his chair.

"Sit!" the second half of the team screamed at him.

Sarajane didn't take her eyes off the first killer. "It'll be a cold day in hell before either one of you lays your filthy hands on me."

"It ain't *hands* we plan to lay on you, bitch." Both of them laughed.

Once the second killer had finished tying Dom's hands, he moved over behind Sarajane. She feared he would check her bindings, but instead, he slid his hand down the front of her blouse and grabbed a breast, fondling her. She didn't have to put on an act to show her revulsion, but she also was cognizant of the gun at her back. *Please, please, please, God,* she prayed, *don't let him touch me anywhere else.*

She gritted her teeth until they hurt. If she had to tolerate groping to keep his attention away from the only chance they might have of defending themselves, so be it. Still, she couldn't contain a shudder borne of fear and disgust.

Dominic came up out of his chair again in protest, but unfortunately, this time the chair was attached to his hands. Killer number one pushed him back down and his partner tormented both Sarajane and Dom by fondling her other breast.

He leaned down and whispered into her ear loud enough for Dom to hear, "Nice tits."

"Save it for later, Jackie. We gotta attend to business first." His eyes were glued to Sarajane's chest, watching his partner's hand intently.

She could read every salacious thought running through his sick mind. She decided then and there, if they didn't discover the hidden gun, she would kill them both before they could rape her. Under Oregon law, she and Dom were in mortal danger. No charges would ever be filed against her for taking action to save their lives. She would never submit to the Paired-Ups and she didn't plan on letting them kill the man she loved.

Jackie laughed. "You're just jealous, Shep, 'cuz you

didn't think to feel her up, did ya?"

His eyes on Sarajane's breasts, Shep said, "I didn't have a chance before the goddamned doorbell rang." He licked his big lips. "I think you know why we're here, don't you Missy Medical Examiner?"

Jackie and Shep. Just two serial killers from Big Sky Country, out to kill a few people and rape a couple of women in the process. "You want Luce Maguire," Sarajane replied, "and her boyfriend." No sense beating around the bush.

"Damn, you're one smart bitch," Jackie said. He looked at Shep. "We're gonna have some fun with this one."

Shep's gaze dropped once again to her breasts. He stared at them the entire time he gave his instructions. "You will call the Judge-bitch and give her some valid reason why you want her here. You will tell her to bring her boyfriend with her." He laughed and looked at his cohort, practically drooling. "This just gets better'n better! We tie up the boyfriends and make 'em watch before we off 'em all. Even the big shots never suggested any shit this good."

Jackie's evil eyes glowed with anticipation.

She had a triple whammy going on. The pain in her thigh was excruciating, her head hurt like the devil, and she was sickened by the brazen repulsive end the Montana pair had planned for her and her friends. Sarajane tried not to throw up.

Dom glared fifty-thousand-volt light sabers at them.

Shep finally lifted his eyes to look into hers. "Tell me what you plan to say to make sure the Judge-bitch comes right over."

Sarajane had already decided how she'd play this, but she faltered as she spoke, so the psycho pieces of dog crap wouldn't get suspicious. "I'll, uh, I'll tell her that, uh, that Dominic just got back in town and he's anxious to see them again." She shot a glance at Dom. "He's been away for years."

Shep turned his attention on Dom. "Where you been?"

In a tone as steely as his expression, Dom said, "Iraq. Afghanistan."

"You a soldier?"

"No."

Shep took a step closer, the gun in his hand pointed at Dom's head. "Why don't you knock off the bullshit, tough guy, and tell me why you were in war country."

"I was a priest," he said. "I offered spiritual comfort where I could."

"A fucking priest?" Jackie roared. "No shit!"

"Shut up!" Shep yelled at him, his eyes still on Dom. "Where's your collar? What do you mean you *was* a priest."

"I'm no longer a priest."

"You can't just quit being a priest," Shep said. "I went to Catholic school and Sunday mass. Priests don't fucking quit. They just don't."

"It's a process," Dom said. "I did what I had to do, and now I'm no longer a priest."

Shep squinted his eyes at Dom, as if trying to figure out what made him tick, or maybe if this unexpected turn affected what he and Jackie had planned for their day's entertainment. He looked at Jackie and said, "I never figured on killing a goddamned priest!"

"He says he's not a priest anymore."

"Still—"

"Still nothing. Let's get this show on the road. I'm getting hornier by the minute." He rubbed his bulging crotch for emphasis.

"Keep your hands off of her," Dom warned.

Jackie replied by slamming him up alongside the head with the butt on his weapon. "Don't tell me what to do, *Father*!"

The skin on the right side of Dom's forehead split from the impact and began to bleed profusely, as head wounds are prone to do.

Sarajane tried to send him signals, but he wouldn't turn toward her. The pain in her leg was getting worse. She had pills in her purse—Aunt Gennie had sent them along with Luce, bless her soul. The problem was, if she asked for an Oxy, would it dull her to the point that she wouldn't have good reaction time? If she didn't, would pain so debilitate her that she wouldn't be able to think straight?

She opted for a pill. "My leg is really hurting from when your Killzone crony shot me a few weeks back. Would you mind giving me a pill from the bottle in my purse?"

"What the hell's a crony?" Shep demanded, his evil eyes darkening with anger.

"It means buddy, pal…."

He stared at her for several long moments, apparently weighing the veracity of her response. Finally, he asked, "Where's your purse?"

"On the sofa."

"Go get it," he instructed Jackie.

Mumbling obscenities, Jackie left the room and was scrounging through her purse when he came back. "The bitch has Oxycontin. Score!"

"Give her one," Shep said. "She won't be needing more than that."

"Open your mouth," Jackie said, pulling a pill out of the bottle.

"Water," Sarajane said.

He looked about to refuse, but his gaze dropped back down to her breasts and his eyes, when they met hers again, had taken on a lewd glint. He started opening cupboards, looking for a glass.

"To the right of the sink," Sarajane said, wondering what was coming next. She tried to prepare….

He filled a tumbler, then moved to stand over her. He shoved the pill into her mouth so hard, she almost gagged on it. Then more than half the water spilled down the front of her, which must have been his plan. She was wearing a white cotton blouse and the moment it soaked up the liquid, it became transparent against her skin.

With a sickeningly lascivious expression, he repeated his earlier thoughts, almost rapturously. "Nice fucking titties."

This time he drew out the middle word, making Sarajane's skin crawl. All the horrible things she'd seen as an ME and not one of them left her feeling as dirty as—

Jackie-the-Jackass pervert put his hand on her again, fingering her nipples.

Beside her, Dom visibly swelled with rage. Sarajane steeled her thoughts against processing what was happening to her and sent him a look with a barely perceptible shake of her head. His face was flushed, his eyes blazed with hatred, but he got himself under control. The look in his eyes did not bode well for either Jackie or Shep.

Shep walked over and gave a look-see at what Jackie had been admiring. "I'm doing this bitch first, when it comes time."

"No reason we can't both do her together," Jackie responded, eyeing her mouth.

Sarajane understood in that moment that these two were worse than psychotic whack jobs, and even describing them as psycho-sexual perverted assholes didn't seem strong enough. Luce had never discussed the particulars of the first trial, but Sarajane didn't have to hear the details to know how horrific it must have been for the victims.

And now these two deviants discussed her promised rape as if they were going to stand in line for an ice cream cone—and as if she would stand still and let them have their way with her. Crazy, delusional bastards!

She had to keep her cool. She couldn't turn into a blubbering idiot or a cowering twit. She had work to do.

Her resolve to kill them grew.

# chapter 44

Shep grabbed the phone off the charger and hit the green button. "Gimme the number," he said.

"I have it in speed dial," Sarajane said. She told him how to access it.

"Remember I'm listening to every fucking word, bitch. Stray and I'll kill you where you sit."

He put the phone up to Sarajane's ear. After what seemed like an eternity, she said, "Hi, Luce."

She was silent for several moments. Dom had not expected her to turn into a quivering Caspar Milquetoast, but he also hadn't expected her to mouth off to the killers. On the one hand, he wanted her to shut the hell up. On the other, he was proud of her courage and stamina. Not many women could go through what she'd been through the past weeks and still maintain a spunky, defiant attitude. He just hoped she didn't back-talk one time too many and get them both killed before he figured a way out of this.

"Yes, yes," she said. "Guess what? No, no. Dominic just came into town, can you believe it?" Her conversation continued, peppered with short and long pauses.

"Yes. He wants to see you and JD both. Yes. Maybe you can come over here? Yes. Okay. So how long? No, no. Good. An hour?"

Shep shook his head ferociously.

"Uh, Yes. Can you make it in half an hour, instead? Or sooner? We have, uh, plans to go see his brother later. Okay. Yes. And JD's coming with you? Good. Yes, I understand. Yes. Sure, see you then."

Dominic decided the two killers were morons. They got their jollies from raping and killing, and obviously torturing, but they didn't have smarts enough to know how to tie knots and they didn't have a clue regarding the fine art of holding hostages. They could have put the phone on speaker and listened to what he assumed was Luce asking question after question to Sarajane's assertion that he'd just arrived in town and wanted to see them, when they'd all just spent two hours talking over pizza and beer. Or maybe Luce had handed the phone over to JD. Either way, Sarajane's every *yes, no, good,* and *okay* had to be in response to questions from someone, preceded and followed as they were by seconds of telling silence.

"Thirty minutes?" Jackie whined.

"She said it might be sooner," Sarajane reminded him.

"Oh, yeah?" Shep asked. "We don't have much time then. They tied up good?"

"Sure."

"Let's get the lay of the place." He sniggered. "Get it? *Lay?*"

Jackie wiggled his eyebrows in response.

"I wanna see what the bedroom's like. Long as we got comfort, we might as well use it, huh? Better'n the floor or the ground for a change." He looked from Sarajane to Dom and back to Sarajane. "You two kids play nice while we're gone. I hear even one chair scrape across the floor and I'm going to blow Father Boy-friend's balls from here to kingdom come, bitch. Understand?"

"Yes," Sarajane said meekly.

*What an actress,* Dom thought, impressed.

The killers left the kitchen and he tried to picture where they were at any given second.

"Dom," Sarajane whispered. "Are your hands tied tight?"

"Nah, I can get loose in a second."

"Do it now," Sarajane said, working at her own binding. "While you were at the door, I called JD and gave him a quick scoop. The cops should be all over the place by now." She slipped the cording off her hands and withdrew a pistol from her waistband.

"Where did you get that?" he asked, shocked in spite of his admiration for her cunning.

"From the drawer." She took a moment to secure one button of her jacket over her breasts, then she helped him get the last knot loose and motioned him to follow her to the back door.

Dom held on to her, in case her leg gave her problems. He hoped the idiots couldn't hear her foot dragging against the floor as she limped beside him.

Two officers in dusky-green uniforms, with SWAT emblazoned across their flak jackets, crouched just outside, around the corner of the house. One, who Sarajane recognized as SWAT team leader Blake Halloran, instructed them in a whisper to stay low under the windows and escorted them out to the front yard and out of danger. "JD and Luce are waiting for you down the block, near the ambulance," he told them.

"Thanks, Blake," Sarajane replied.

Dom scooped her up in his arms and carried her the rest of the way.

Once they reached the ambulance, still clinging to his neck, Sarajane said to JD, "I thought you'd be going inside."

"The LT won't let me near this case anymore since I'm one of the targets." He reached out and squeezed her arm with affection. "You did good, darlin'."

Sarajane looked over Dom's shoulder, in the direction of her home. "I hope they don't shoot the place up. Marsh will be royally pissed if they do."

"Sarie," JD said, "Marsh will just be relieved that you and his brother got out of there safe and alive."

"You doing okay?" Luce asked Dom, looking at his head.

"Thought I'd left the war zone behind me," Dom admitted, "but at least this saga has a somewhat happy ending."

"One of them came in an SPD uniform," Sarajane said to JD. "Did they…?"

JD nodded grimly.

"Oh, no!" Sarajane wailed softly. "Who?"

JD named an officer she didn't know, but it didn't lessen the loss of another good man. "They've killed for the last time," he said.

"I hope to God you're right," Luce said fervently.

"You need medical care," Sarajane said to Dom, frowning as she studied his head wound.

He knew the blood flow had eased, but he must look a sight.

"I think you might need stitches," she went on, worrying her lower lip.

"A butterfly bandage will probably fix me right up," he assured her.

"You should put me down. The EMTs need to tend to you."

He didn't *want* to put her down, but he couldn't very well stand there holding her all day.

She unclasped her hands from around his neck and he lowered her feet gently to the ground. She leaned against the ambulance for support. Still frowning, she said to JD, "Would you mind taking my gun? I'm afraid I might be tempted to kill those two assholes when they're brought out."

"I might be more than tempted," Dom said.

"What the hell?" JD asked at the same time Luce said, "What happened?"

"They planned to rape Sarajane and Luce, in front of us, then kill us all."

JD's face flushed with anger. He swore profusely, taking a step toward the house.

Luce grabbed his arm and begged, "Don't."

Dom ground his teeth together. "One of them man-handled Sarie and they both got graphic in what they planned to do to her."

"What?" Luce cried.

JD took another step.

"JD, *please*. Stay put!"

Sarajane looked at her friend then JD. "Look, they didn't finish what they started. We're all okay."

JD seemed about to argue, but Luce's hand on his arm stilled him.

Two EMTs came around from the other side of their vehicle. "Come around to the back of the ambulance," one of them said to Dom. "We'll take a look at your head."

The sound of two gunshots startled an assortment of birds into squawking protests as they fled the big cypress tree hiding the group from view of the bungalow. A flurry of gunfire followed.

JD quickly urged everyone behind the ambulance.

"Damn!" Sarajane muttered, hampered by her wound.

The six of them turned as one. Sarajane's leg gave out halfway around her pivot and she started to go down. Dom grabbed for her, scooping her up in his arms again. She didn't argue. She'd had it. For a change, it felt good to be protected. It felt *exceptionally* good to be secure in the arms of the man she loved.

Within minutes, the radio in the patrol car in front of the ambulance crackled—the serial killers were in custody. Not too long after, Jackie and Shep were paraded out in handcuffs. One had a bloody nose, the other bled from a wound in his upper shoulder. Both screamed obscenities far worse than the *bitch* they'd been prone to using earlier.

Even with dozens of armed police surrounding them, the pair lunged in unison as they passed near Sarajane and Luce. Well trained, every officer with a weapon put a bead on them and still they moved forward, their one-track dedication to their killing quest apparently giving them an adrenaline rush that was off the charts.

Dom backed up with Sarajane in his arms and put her down on the opposite side of the patrol car. JD shoved Luce in the same direction. As if by unspoken agreement, the two men met Shep and Jackie head on, with no interference from the SWAT or other officers. Dom took the one on the left, JD the one on the right. It only took two punches each to level the lunatics, who went down screaming more vulgarities, all prefaced by the f-bomb.

No one knew if the vile name-calling was directed at Sarajane or Luce. No one cared. Everyone just wanted the nightmare to be over. Enough people had died. Enough people had suffered.

The men in handcuffs were ignored when they began to whine and snivel that they needed medical attention. Even the EMTs newly on-scene walked into the fray as slowly as possible without actually standing still.

The other EMTs attended to Dom's head injury quickly and competently, suggesting he needed a CT head scan.

"Being hit with the butt of a gun can cause serious injuries," Sarajane informed him. "I just went through all this, remember?"

The EMTs seconded the observation, then indicated they wanted to treat both Dom and JD for skinned knuckles.

Dom and JD hemmed and hawed, resisting. "Don't forget how vile and filthy those pigs were!" Sarajane said, adding for good measure, "And bloody." She then began to recite a list of pathogens Dom and JD would be avoiding with a simple medical treatment now.

To their credit, neither Dom nor JD howled aloud from the sting of the antiseptic, but both their faces reflected they wanted to.

Sarajane and Luce exchanged a look and grinned. "Men!" they both said at the same time.

Dom asked that Sarajane be allowed to ride in the ambulance with him. JD and Luce followed in Dom's car after they retrieved Sarajane's crutches and purse and asked the investigating officers to lock up when they finished. Blake, who remained on scene, assured them he'd take care of it.

In the ER waiting room, Luce said, "A dozen bullet holes in the living room wall. One or both of those sick freaks fortunately had terrible aim."

"Not *so* bad," JD said. "One of them shot the other one."

"How do you know that?" Sarajane asked.

"Blake said none of his men fired."

Sarajane shook her head. "Remember what Forrest Gump said—stupid is as stupid does."

Luce half grinned, but Dom's expression grew as dark as JD's.

"Chill," Sarajane advised. "It's over. Finally."

Dom's frown diminished marginally. "I can patch the holes, since I'll be staying at Sarajane's until Chloe's brother and his girlfriend go back to California."

"Thanks," Sarajane said, "that would be great. Marsh has enough on his plate right now, and I don't think he'll be too happy about the condition of the place, especially when the forensics team is done with it."

"They know it's a cop's house," JD said. "They'll take precautions not to make a bigger mess than they have to. I don't think they'll have much evidence to collect, anyway. The bigger crime scene today will be where they hijacked the other patrol vehicle and slaughtered another police officer."

"Slaughtered?" Dom questioned.

"Don't ask," JD said bluntly.

"Oh, no," Sarajane said, her voice breaking.

Dom could only imagine they'd tortured the poor guy after stripping his uniform off. He worked furiously to silence the *what-if*s slithering around his brain.

For the second time in his life, he had the urge to kill.

# chapter 45

*O*nce they took Dom into the treatment area, no one was allowed back with him except family. Marsh came down from maternity as soon as JD called him.

"You aren't back twenty-four hours and look at all the trouble you're into," Marsh half-teased, standing over his brother.

"I think it's a good thing I was there, or they might have raped her first and *then* had her call Luce," Dom said, his voice tight with emotion.

"Don't think about what might have been," Marsh said. "Trust me when I say it'll drive you nuts."

"Been there, done that."

"Yeah, I guess you have."

"But this was Sarajane. I can't seem to keep the what-ifs at bay."

"Sarie seems no worse for the wear."

"You weren't there. Didn't have to watch one of them grope her, tell her in vile terms what they were going to do to her, then deliberately spill water down the front of her shirt so he'd have more to look at." Dom's eyes blazed in remembered anger. "The things he said…where he put his hands…."

Marsh studied him intently. "I'll be damned."

"What?" Dom ground out.

"You *are* in love with her."

"What are you talking about. I don't even really know her."

"She's still the same Sarajane you kissed after senior prom."

"How do you know about that?" Dom demanded, his face growing hot.

"I took her to that prom, remember? She was trying to get your attention. You danced with her a couple of times, and that was it. Damned near broke her heart. Later, before we split, I saw her kiss you, and you kissed her back." Marsh shook his head. "I never understood your desire to become a priest, but I supported it, regardless. Every man has a right to choose his vocation."

Dom stared at him, silent.

"She's a helluva woman, Dom. Other men have tried to woo her and gotten nowhere. For some reason, you're the one she loves and no one else will do. What are you going to do about that?"

Dom tried to get his big body comfortable on the gurney. "I don't have a clue," he said. "It's not like someone waved a magic wand over my head, converting me from a priest to a man who used to be a priest, and then gave me a set of rules to follow."

He might have said more, but the orderlies came to wheel him off for the CT scan.

Marsh had no idea, listening to his big brother mutter as they wheeled him away, that Dom even *knew* such language.

Sarajane would have paced the floor, waiting for word on Dominic's condition, if she hadn't been in so much pain.

Luce and JD both tried to talk her into seeing a doctor

herself in the ER, but she refused. "I've had enough of doctors and hospitals lately."

"Could you take another pain pill?" Luce asked.

"If I had one, I could." Sarajane had already looked in her purse, but one of the whack-job psychos must have pocketed the bottle, because JD said he hadn't seen it anywhere in the kitchen.

JD pulled out his phone and called the jail. After a brief conversation, which he conducted outside the ER, he came back inside. "A patrol officer is going over to the jail to get the bottle. He'll deliver it here."

Sarajane looked up at him with relief. "Thanks."

He sat back down next to Luce and took her hand in his.

"This just f-ing sucks," Sarajane muttered. Since no one sat beside her, she pulled out the chair and propped up her foot up on it.

"I'm so sorry you're in pain," Luce said.

"It's not the pain I'm talking about. It's everything." She glanced at the double doors leading into the treatment area. "I'm having déjà vu all over again."

They offered her weak grins in response to her half-hearted attempt at levity.

Marsh pushed through the double door moments later. "Not much to tell," he said. "They'll do the CT, then bring him back down and stitch him up while the radiologist reads the film." He grinned suddenly. "He's hard-headed. They're not going to find any fractures in that skull."

"Amen," Luce agreed.

Sarajane remained silent. She'd worry about Dom if she damned well wanted to!

Marsh laughed. "He wasn't happy about the CT at all…you should have heard him when they took him away. His *language*!"

"Your brother has a stubborn streak a mile wide," Sarajane said darkly.

"Then the two of you should be a good match-up,"

Marsh shot back.

She stared at him, stunned.

"Don't look so surprised," Marsh said, taking the seat across from her, next to her propped-up leg. "You think he's going to live the life of a monk now that he's no longer a priest?"

"I don't know what the hell he's going to do!"

Marsh quirked his lips. "Trust me, he's not."

"You know something we don't?" Luce asked, "Because I think Dom is hot to trot for Sarie."

Marsh shot her a look. "I don't know that I would have phrased it quite like that, but it definitely hits the mark."

Luce looked at JD. "I told you!"

"Look, I don't even know the guy," JD said, "but I would think he has some readjusting to do after serving at the altar for so many years. Give him some breathing room!"

Luce opened her mouth then snapped it shut.

Sarajane knew he had a point. She also knew what had transpired between her and Dom earlier. She suspected Dominic Fielding may have already had his breathing room, and now he had gotten his second wind. She wasn't about to share how the two of them had exchanged more than air earlier, so she changed the subject. "How's Chloe doing?"

Marsh smiled. "She's doing great. Her brother and Ally are upstairs right now. It's a happy, tearful reunion for both of them."

"The babies are so beautiful," Luce said.

"Yeah," JD chipped in, "they don't look like their daddy at all."

Marsh leveled a grin on him. "You're lucky that you're marrying a good-looking woman yourself," he shot back.

JD laughed.

Sarajane's gaze went back to the double doors. She should be with Dom, not out here listening to her friends exchange loving comments about their significant others. It made her want to indulge in a self-pitying sobfest.

The doors at the entrance to the ER slid open. Aunt Gennie, Rose, and Mags swooped in. "Sarie," Aunt Gennie cried, "are you all right? You have blood all over you!"

Sarajane looked down, belatedly realizing that her white shirt was stained red. "It's Dom's, not mine. One of those fu—, uh, bad guys hit him in the head and he's gone up for a CT."

"Bad guys? What in the world has happened now?" Rose asked. She turned her eyes on her grandson. "Marsh, you didn't say what happened when you called. Just told us you were here."

Marsh said, "Sorry, Gran. I did say everyone was okay, if you recall."

Rose sniffed in his direction. "Like that helps!"

Marsh and JD got up and made sure each of the older ladies was seated. The ER was busy, so the group huddled together while Sarajane told the story. She left out the mauling details and graphic sex talk.

"You girls and your guns," Mags said. "I'm thinking I should buy one myself. I could take a class on how to shoot it, be ready in case something happens…." She shook her head. "I never knew Salem was such a hotbed of crime!"

"You'd probably shoot your foot off, Mags," Rose said. "I'd recommend a taser."

Marsh looked at his grandmother in surprise. "And who do you think is going to sell her a taser?"

"You'll get it for her, of course. Gennie and I don't have to worry so much because *we* don't live in Salem …." She trailed off, letting the implication speak for itself.

"This entire fiasco has been an anomaly, Gran, and you know it," Marsh said.

"It's a changing world," Aunt Gennie said, as though she were uttering words of wisdom.

Everyone stared at her.

"Don't worry," she continued. "I haven't seen any-thing else untoward coming down the pike."

"Thank God for that!" Sarajane said, slightly amused by Aunt Gennie's dramatic pronouncement.

But after she thought about her aunt's words for a moment, she realized plenty had been left unsaid. Aunt Gennie had only addressed the fact of nothing else *bad* happening. That meant she probably had a lot more to say about what she considered *good* to be coming.

At the moment Sarajane decided to quiz her aunt further, the outside doors opened and a patrol officer she recognized as Dave Jernigan strolled in.

"Got your pills," he said, shaking the bottle in her direction. "Don't you people ever get tired of hanging out in the ER?"

As a group, they gave a bark of laughter. Dave had been with them the day of Luce's bomb threat. He'd been instrumental in discovering the Killzone website and helping to catch the serial pairs all across the U.S., Canada, and Mexico.

He went to the counter to request a glass of water. When he returned, he had a chilled water bottle, which he handed to Sarajane. To Marsh, he said, "I hope your brother's okay."

"He has a harder head than mine, so he should be."

"You can say that again," Sarajane added.

"He has a harder—"

"Stop!" She would have lifted a middle finger to her old friend, but both her hands were full.

"Okay if I go up and peek in the nursery window, see the new kids?" Dave asked.

"They're in with Chloe," Marsh said. "Just knock on her door." He gave Dave the room number. "I know she'd be pleased to say hello to you."

Dave nodded, asked Sarajane if she needed anything else, then strode on to the elevator.

"That kid is going to make some woman very happy

one of these days," Sarajane said when the doors had closed on him. "He's easy on the eyes, smart, and well-mannered. If I was ten years younger, I'd go after him myself."

"Go after who?" Dom asked, coming up behind them.

# chapter 46

No one had heard the double doors open or the big man walking across the floor toward them in his stocking feet.

Sarajane decided to remain silent.

Luce had no such compunctions. "Dave Jernigan. He's a patrol officer with SPD."

Dom scowled, his eyes on Sarajane.

She said, "You look cute in that hospital gown."

His scowl deepened.

Marsh asked, "What are you doing out here?"

"Waiting for them to read the damned CT scan!"

Rose jumped up to go to her oldest grandson. "You should be laying down. You have a head injury." She examined his wound. "How many stitches?"

"Eleven," he growled, his eyes still on Sarajane.

"Mr. Fielding!" a nurse called from the double doors. "You're not supposed to be up yet!"

Marsh rose. "Back you go, Dom. These people have enough to do without putting up with any crap from you."

Dom swiveled, unsteady on his feet. JD stood and

went to one side of him while Marsh took the other.

Sarajane's lips quirked in a grin. The big bad cops escorting the recalcitrant former priest, who stood a good inch or more taller than either of them, back to his hospital bed. She knew Dom was out of it, otherwise he would have realized his gown was flapping in the breeze, showing off his nicely built, brief-covered butt and some seriously muscled thighs and calves to one and all.

An hour later, they were told Dom was going to be admitted overnight. He didn't have a fractured skull, but the doctor wanted to make sure, after being struck in the temporal lobe, that he didn't suffer a epidural hematoma that went unnoticed overnight. The only person who argued about it was the patient.

"Before you go thinking you're going to spend the night up there watching over him," Rose said to Sarajane, her tone stern, "think again, young lady."

"That's right," Aunt Gennie chimed in. "You need your rest and he needs his. You'll see him tomorrow."

"But—"

"But nothing," Rose cut in. "Plans have changed. Kyle and Ally are going to stay at your house and Dom will take the attic, so we can take turns watching over him for awhile."

That brought Sarajane up short. Her and Dom under the same roof, for who knew how many nights? And days? And *nights*? Her pulse hammered wildly. Unbidden came, "The sheets need changing at my house."

"We went by there as soon as we figured out the new logistics. Kyle and Ally were totally agreeable, especially since your house is so close to Marsh and Chloe's," Mags contributed. "The police made a bit of a mess over there arresting those...those *animals*, but that nice lieutenant let us start putting things back together and we'll go finish up as soon as we leave here."

"But Kyle's always wanted to sleep in the attic," Sarajane said lamely.

They all stared at her.

Marsh finally laughed. "Kyle's a grown man now, Sarie. He'll live."

The next day, Marsh collected Chloe and the babies from the hospital first. It took a while for him to get his family loaded up, now that it had doubled in size. The matching carseats were installed properly and the babies didn't seem to notice they weren't in their hospital bassinettes anymore.

Once he got everyone settled in at home, he took time to have a cup of coffee and a slice of the still-warm coffee cake his grandmother had baked.

Two baby monitors sat on the kitchen counter. Companion monitors were set up in the nursery and in the master bedroom. He could hear the gentle nick of wood against wood as Chloe rocked Brenden.

His phone rang. After he said hello, Dom growled back, "I'm ready to go."

"I'll be there in ten," Marsh promised. "Fifteen tops."

Half an hour later, he and his brother sat at the kitchen table with Rose. She poured them each a cup of coffee and cut two more slices of coffee cake. "Hospital food should be illegal," Dom groused.

"They have a special menu you can order from if you don't have restrictions," Rose informed him. "We found that out when we spent so much time there with Chloe and Sarajane. They were trying to poison and/or starve the poor girls!"

"How is Sarajane?" Dom asked. His eyes went to the swinging door.

"Sleeping, as far as I know," Marsh said. Her door had been closed when he'd returned with Dom and she hadn't made any effort to come out. If she'd been awake, he was certain she'd already be sitting at the table with them.

Rose pulled out a chair and sat down with a cup of coffee and a slice of coffee cake for herself. "So, Dominic, tell me about this priest thing. Are you completely out of it now, or is there a process you have to follow?"

Dominic's back was to the door that lead from the kitchen to Sarajane's makeshift bedroom, so he didn't see it open. Sarajane stood there, propped up on her crutches. Marsh figured Gran's question had frozen her in place.

Dom washed down a big bite of his breakfast with a long sip of coffee. "Yes, I'm out, permanently. I've been laicized—"

"What does that mean?" Marsh asked.

"It means I've been reduced to a lay state, except for ordination. That can't be undone."

"This is confusing," Rose asked. "Can you explain it for us?"

"I can no longer perform priestly duties, like last rites, administering communion, hearing confessions, and the like. There is an exception, however, and that is, if a person is in danger of dying, I can minister to him. Or her."

"What about your vow of celibacy?" Marsh asked.

"Released."

Marsh glanced at Sarajane. Tears streamed down her cheeks.

Dom followed the direction of his brother's gaze.

Sarajane had disappeared and closed the door by the time Dom turned completely around.

"Where does that door go?" Dom asked.

"To Sarajane's room."

Rose put her hand over Dom's. "She heard, Dominic. All of it. Let her absorb it. And for God's sake, don't go into that room if she's not going to be the woman with whom you plan to share the rest of your life."

Sarajane propped the crutches up in the corner near the bed and limped back over to the side.

Dom had officially quit the church. He'd already

taken all the steps necessary to that end. He had been released from his vow of celibacy.

After living with knowing him to be a priest for so long, this new information was almost too sudden, too shocking, too good to be true. She couldn't take it in.

And God, was her leg hurting! The doctor had told her not to take more than two of the Oxys in one day. She had since called and asked what would happen if she *did* take two, if the pain became unbearable. "Just be aware, it will knock you out, so let someone know what you're doing," Doc had said, and added, only half joking, "so they don't think you've gone into a coma or something."

Sarajane had taken a pill an hour earlier, with no relief. She reached for the bottle and extracted another one. She downed it, then reached for the pad on the bedside table. She wrote: *Leg hurting. Taking 1 extra Oxy per doc. Want to sleep for a while. S.*

And then she snugged in under the covers, closed her eyes, and waited for the double dose to take her to dreamland.

Before she got there, she had a vision.

It involved a man and a woman—he in a black tux, she in a beautiful white wedding dress.

As sleep claimed her, she wondered, was it really a vision of the future, or was she just dreaming her dream again?

Sarajane hadn't come out a couple of hours later, so Rose crept in to check on her. She found the note and reported it to her grandsons.

In the meantime, the house alternated between quiet and active. The babies woke, got diapered, got fed. Kyle and Ally came and spent the time upstairs with Chloe and the babies. As Chloe had predicted, Marsh's upstairs study worked nicely for a second living room.

Rose and Mags fixed sandwiches for everyone and

Aunt Gennie made lemonade and iced tea. Marsh stayed out of the kitchen for a change, dividing his time between his brother, who had settled into the attic, resting, and his wife and babies.

Luce and JD showed up, Rose and Mags made more sandwiches. Mo and Quinn, the new grandparents, arrived shortly after that. Mo had made two lasagna casseroles, which Rose popped into the oven to warm. Aunt Gennie ran to the store for more paper goods and some soft drinks. After checking with Marsh, Dom, and JD, she also picked up a six pack of Fat Tire and another of Sierra Nevada. At Luce's request, she bought two bottles of wine.

It might have seemed like party time at the Fielding house, but everyone remained relatively quiet, even though they shared smiles, laughter, stories, and baby-holding.

After Sarajane had been asleep for eight hours, Dom made his way down two flights of stairs and stood outside her door. He knocked softly, but no answering response came. He opened the door and peeked in. She slept on, soundly.

He entered the room and closed the door behind him. With stealth uncommon for such a large man, he made his way to the table she had set up for her work and quietly moved it aside. He turned the easy chair toward the bed and settled in.

And then he commenced watching her. He didn't look at the clock, had no idea how long he sat there, but while he watched her, he also thought. And thought and thought and thought. She moaned in her sleep, uttering his name. Her brow furrowed and several tears slipped down the side of her beautiful face.

He leaned forward and put his elbows on his knees, clasping his hands. For the first time in nearly three years, Dom bowed his head. And prayed. The words came easily. Simple, yet profound, they flowed straight from his heart. *Lord, please guide me. Help me to be as strong a man outside Your house as I can be, as strong as I was when I ministered there. Help me be the man Sarajane needs me to be. Help me be the man I need me to be. Guide me, oh Lord.*

He paused a moment. *Thank you for my beautiful Sarajane, Lord. Please keep her safe from further harm. Let her heal, in her body, in her heart, and in her mind. Amen.*

He maintained his prayerful position for several long moments. When he looked up, Sarajane was staring at him. The love in her eyes almost undid him.

"You *are* the man I need you to be, Dom. You always have been."

Startled, he hadn't realized he'd actually prayed aloud. Then he remembered Sarajane had the *juju*. Was it possible…?

She put out her hand to him. "They say confession is good for the soul."

Dom rose from the chair and entwined his fingers with hers as he knelt beside the bed. "Then I have something more to confess to you. I love you, Sarie. I have always loved you and I always will. You make me complete."

"I love you, too, Dom." She scooted over and urged him to lie beside her.

"I don't want to hurt you," he said.

"You won't. I promise."

He laid there with her for hours.

Both of them fell asleep, holding each other. Content as they had never been before.

# chapter 47

*Six months later*

*t*he brides wore white. One had chosen a lacy confec-
tion, strapless with a beautiful beaded satin bodice and
a satin skirt overlaid with finely woven beaded lace.
Another had selected a more tailored style in long chiffon, also strapless with a rosebud bodice and a satin sash,
no less beautiful. The third had gone with a lovely taffeta
with a sweetheart neckline, narrow spaghetti straps, and
a knee-length tulip skirt.

The lone matron of honor wore a floor-length chiffon
gown with an empire halter in a shade of lavender that
set off her dark hair.

The three grooms and one best man wore black tux-
edos, each with a pure white rose boutonnière.

The ring-bearer babies had no idea they were ring
bearers. For the moment, they slept contentedly in a
double stroller.

The families and a limited number of friends had gathered for the early evening, black-tie triple summer
wedding in the large and amazingly gorgeous back yard

of Marsh and Chloe Fielding, the best man and matron of honor.

The families included The Girls, all of Marsh's brothers and sisters and his parents, Maureen and Quinn; Luce Maguire's parents, Thomas and Bertie; and Chloe's dad, Jack, and his wife, Ilene, who had brought their four children.

Others included a select few whom the six soon-to-be-newlyweds considered to be *real* friends. Freddy Nelson and his partner and Cameron Swift and his wife Anna, all from the ME's office. Marsh and JD's LT, Kerry Schaeffer and his wife; Sid Ralston, Luce's bailiff; and Blake and Connie Halloran, he from the bomb squad, she, Luce's court secretary. Kyle and Ally had invited two friends each and each of them had brought a spouse.

From the upstairs window, Chloe looked down on the gathering. She still couldn't believe her father and his family had come. In truth, even now, she was shocked that he had shown up at her door a week after she'd come home from the hospital with the babies.

Kyle and Marsh had paid him a visit, and though they refused to reveal what had been said to Jack Faust, whatever it was must have been powerful. Her dad had cried while he apologized to her for the years he had estranged himself from her and Kyle. He had missed so much, and he wanted to catch up, if she'd let him.

Chloe had cried, too. Hugged him and said she loved him. Her father had said the same, muttering a self-deprecating criticism of himself and his behavior. Afterward, he had been speechless when she introduced him to Brenden and Mary Kate, let him hold them.

Not four days later, he had arrived with his wife Ilene in tow. She, too, had apologized and said with sincerity that she wanted to make amends. Now they all saw each other at least once a week. Chloe's small half-siblings were enamored with the twins. Brenden and Mary Kate adored them in return.

Life was getting back to normal.

Luce and JD.

Sarajane and Dominick.

Ally and Kyle.

Chloe's heart filled to overflowing with love for all of them. They had so much to look forward to—marrying, having children together, spending the rest of their lives growing old together. Who would have thought, seven months ago when all hell had broken loose for all of them, that today they would be gathered for a triple wedding?

Mo Fielding, Marsh's mom, knocked on the door. "You girls ready?" she asked.

Luce, Sarajane, and Ally vied for space one last time in front of the full-length mirror in the spare bedroom where they'd all gotten dressed. One by one, they said, "Yes."

"You're all so beautiful," Mo said proudly. "I'm so pleased to see my family growing and happy like this!"

Ally, whose parents had died when she was a child, had been had been accepted unconditionally by the Fielding clan as part of the family. Ally dabbed away a stray tear and went to hug Marsh's mother.

"See you downstairs. Be careful coming down in those long dresses."

Ally clasped hands with her fellow brides and they stood before their matron of honor smiling. "This would not be happening if not for you," she said to Chloe.

Chloe opened her mouth to deny any credit, but knew in her heart that she was at least partially responsible. If she hadn't taken that class in criminal investigation, she might never have met Marsh, might not have become best friends with Luce and Sarajane, might not have gotten shot. And then her brother might not have visited and taken another look at life himself, realized what a prize he had in Ally. Everything happens for a reason.

Chloe moved closer to them and put out her own hands, completing the circle.

"Sisters," she said, "One and all. Now and forever."

They nodded, smiling, repeating as one, "Now and forever."

"It would have been so wonderful if Mary could have been part of this," Chloe said. "You all would have loved her so much."

"I'm here," Mary said, suddenly in the center of the circle. She floated slowly around, looking each of them. "Tell them for me, Chloe. They are beautiful and I love each and every one of the them."

"Mary!" Chloe cried out. The others looked around.

"Where?" asked Sarajane.

"In the center of our circle. She asked me to tell each of you how beautiful you are and how much she loves you."

"Mary," Sarajane said, "I can't see you, and I know Chloe already told you for me, but I want you to know again how much I love you, too. You saved my life and I will be eternally grateful."

"Me, too," murmured Luce and Ally fervently.

"Sisters now and forever," Mary quoted.

Chloe repeated her words. Then they all said it together.

"Let's go get hitched," Sarajane said. "I've got a wedding night to get to." She grinned and wiggled her eyebrows at her "sisters." Of the four of them, she would be the only one to take a husband to her wedding bed as a virgin. At least technically.

Chloe leaned forward and teased Sarajane. "I'm looking forward to playmates for Mary Kate and Brenden in exactly nine months!"

Sarajane grinned.

"I have a confession," Luce said. She put her hand just below the rosebud bodice where it flared into the chiffon skirt.

"No way!" Sarajane cried.

"When?" Chloe demanded.

Ally, slow to the party, said, "What did I miss?"

"I decided I couldn't wait any longer," Luce admitted. "I did the stick test this morning. I got a plus sign."

"You're pregnant!" Ally declared.

"Does JD know?" Sarajane asked.

"Yes. It was my wedding present to him."

"How far along do you think you are?" Chloe asked.

"Best guess, almost four months."

"You're not showing at all," Ally commented.

"I have the baby bump," Luce said proudly, turning sideways to give her profile. She tucked her hands low on her belly.

Chloe shook her head. "That's what happens when you're tall and willowy. You don't show so much when you're early into pregnancy. Me, I looked like I was six months along when I was still in the first trimester!"

"Having twins might have had something to do with that," Sarajane pointed out, amused.

"Well, I hope *I'm* not having twins!" Luce declared. "I'm worried enough as it is about taking care of just one."

"You're going to be a great mom," Chloe said, hugging her friend. "*All* of you are going to be great moms."

"It's a boy," contributed Mary, though no one but Chloe could hear.

Chloe laughed with delight.

"If we don't hightail it downstairs," Ally chipped in, "we won't have any dads to go along with us moms-to-be."

"See you down there," Mary said, and disappeared.

# chapter 48

*t*he other two brides and Chloe trailed Sarajane down the stairs, helping her keep her skirts high so she didn't trip. At the back door, Owen and Niall, Marsh's younger computer-savvy brothers, hit the PLAY button on the CD player that they had wired to provide surround sound throughout the back yard. A soft romantic piano piece wafted over the gathering. Under the direction of The Girls, they had put together an entire evening of romantic music.

Keeping with tradition, the best man, Marsh, escorted the matron of honor, Chloe, up the grassy aisle toward the three waiting grooms. She whispered in his ear when he leaned down to kiss her before they went to their respective stations, "Mary's here." She looked past him. "Jamie's standing next to Kyle—they're going to get married, too!"

The ring bearers, now awake, watched from their double stroller, parked next to their grandmother and their great-grandmother. They each had a bottle to keep them occupied, but they were more interested in watching their parents.

The wedding party had practiced the procession several times the day before, with the decision made previously that the oldest male groom would stand closest to the center of the altar. All the planning paid off. The segue into Mendelssohn's *Wedding March* coincided exactly with Quinn Fielding tucking his soon-to-be new daughter-in-law's hand into the crook of his elbow as they began to walk down the grassy aisle. Sarajane's limp was barely noticeable. Luce's dad, Tom, stood next in line and patted Luce's hand as she wrapped it around the crook of his arm. Jack Faust similarly escorted his future daughter-in-law, Ally.

Right behind Ally came Mary in the long white day dress she'd worn while earthbound. Even the violet ribbon at her waist matched the beautiful purple Siberian irises the brides carried. She floated down the aisle alone. Chloe's gaze flew to Marsh. He leaned over and said something to Jamie, who wore the Sunday best he'd had on the day of Mary's death.

Chloe glanced at Dominic and knew instantly that he also saw Mary coming up behind Ally. Dom took possession of Sarajane's hand and shot a quick look toward his right where Jamie stood, then looked back at Chloe, giving her a smile and a wink.

Chloe glanced back at Marsh, tears in her eyes. Even though he didn't need to, he stepped aside so Mary could stand by her beloved Jamie.

JD, Dominic, Kyle, and Jamie stood at the altar, each with his eyes on his bride, his heart on his sleeve. Marsh was no exception, even though Chloe had been his bride for almost two years.

A friend of Dominic's, a minister he had met in Iraq, performed the quadruple ceremony. Each couple had written their own vows and the repeating of those vows went off without a hitch. Mary and Jamie repeated each of them as they were given.

As decided ahead of time by the six mortals, "I now pronounce you husband and wife," was said to all of them simultaneously, followed by, "You may now kiss your bride." All four couples complied with zest.

The friends and relatives witnessing the event applauded vigorously. There were more than a few wet eyes in the crowd.

One tradition would be altered on this day. The five unmarried Fielding siblings—Owen, Niall, Kieran, Erin, and Tess—and Colleen Fitzgerald and Dave Jernigan would vie for the bouquets when it came time to throw them, competing with The Girls. The older generation had declared it would do the youngsters good to have some competition.

Following the service, and much picture-taking, chairs were rearranged and tables set up to accommodate a catered meal. Where the altar had been, wood floors were unfolded for a dance area. Kieran, the self-appointed family photographer, took as many pictures as he could. Some were flattering, others were not. All would be memorable.

Marsh and Chloe took the opportunity to sneak away to the side of the house. Mary and Jamie followed.

"I wish you'd been here when Marsh and I got married," Chloe said.

"You got married in a chapel," Mary reminded her. "I can only appear in this house."

"But never before *outside*," Chloe said.

Jamie chuckled. "Must have gotten special dispensation…."

Mary giggled.

"However you did it, you're married now," Chloe said.

Mary clasped Jamie's hand. "Soul mates, forever."

Jamie leaned over and kissed her. "Soul mates, forever."

"Literally," Marsh noted with affection.

Jamie and Mary laughed with delight.

"I wish I could give you a wedding present," Chloe said.

"Are you serious?" Mary chided fondly. "Brenden Jamie and Mary Kate Fielding? I think that's the best wedding present a newly married spirit couple could ever have."

"It certainly is!" Jamie agreed with enthusiasm.

"I love you, Chloe, and you, too, Marsh. Forever and always." She shared a private look with Jamie. "We're going to mingle for a bit now, pretend it's our wedding reception, too. Then we'll go. Don't worry about us, okay? Just enjoy the day and your family and friends." The ghost who could cry, had tears running down her cheeks. "Now scoot before a I make a blubbering spectacle of myself."

"Oh, you!" Mary replied, laughing.

The silliness between the ghostly newlyweds made Chloe and Marsh laugh, but they did as Mary asked.

Once veils were stored away inside, and people began to fill up their plates from the banquet table, Chloe and Marsh put the twins in their high chairs and fed them their dinner. The babies had taken extra long naps in the afternoon, so no one expected them to nod off too early, which was a good thing because they were quite popular with the crowd. Just in case, however, Chloe had engaged Colleen Fitzgerald to help look after them for the evening.

Colleen had been so patient instructing her and Marsh, along with Sarajane and Luce, on the finer points of infant care over the course of the first three days of the babies being at home. Ally had decided to sit in, as well, since she had no baby experience, either, and of course, all the side-liners had listened in.

Interestingly, Chloe caught Kieran's eye wandering to Colleen more than once. Finally, she took action. She grabbed Colleen's hand and pulled her over to her brother-in-law. "Kieran, this is Colleen Fitzgerald. Colleen, meet Marsh and Dom's younger brother, Kieran."

She left them to it. She glanced at Rose and got a nod of approval. Chloe grinned at her husband, who watched her make her way back to him with a raised eyebrow. "You are quite the matchmaker," he observed when she'd retaken her seat next to him, facing Mary Kate's high chair.

She picked up a spoon and a container of carrots, which happened to be Mary Kate's favorite vegetable at the moment. Brenden preferred sweet potatoes. "I'm thinking Dave and Tess might hit it off, as well."

Marsh laughed. "Who did you have in mind for Owen and Niall? And let's not forget Erin."

"Give me time!" Chloe lifted her lips to solicit a kiss.

Obliging her, Marsh murmured, "For you, my sweet, anything."

Over the sound system, Niall said in his super-sexy DJ voice, "Time for the beautiful brides and their ugly grooms to take their first married dance." The laughter from the gathering brought a grin to his face.

The four couples, three mortal, one ghostly, went to the dance floor as Bobby Vinton began to sing "My Heart Belongs to Only You."

Rose and Aunt Gennie insisted on taking over the baby feedings. Mags went to check on Owen and Niall, to make sure they weren't messing with the scheduled musical lineup. "Told you we'd bring the most romantic music ever to this shindig," Rose said, her eyes twinkling.

Marsh laughed, pulling Chloe up from her chair. They swayed to the tune in a secluded corner of the yard, alone and happy.

When the music segued seamlessly into the BeeGees hit, "How Deep is Your Love," he led Chloe to the dance floor where they could, as Mary would say, trip the light fantastic along with the newlyweds.

Had anyone asked, each of the couples would have had the same response to the second song's question: All the way to infinity and beyond.

# epilogue

*A note from Mary*

*f*ive months after our wedding, give or take a day, Luce gave birth to a son. Following in his father's footsteps, he was christened BJ. On his birth certificate, his name was recorded as Brian Joseph, after his grandfather and his daddy, respectively.

Nine months to the day after our wedding, Sarajane gave birth to twin girls. She and Dominic named them Sophie Rose and Annie Genevieve. Rose and Aunt Gennie were so pleased!

One year, give or take, after our wedding, Kieran and Colleen became another Mr. and Mrs. Fielding.

A year after that, Dave Jernigan made detective and Tess Fielding became the newest Mrs. Detective. Four months later, Luce gave birth to another son, TJ, this time named after her father, Thomas, and JD.

Owen and Niall, without any help from Chloe, have each found a woman they like, but haven't married yet, because they just aren't sure they're *in love.* They decided between them, if they don't know what love feels like, maybe they *do* need some help. They consulted Marsh and Dominic, who directed them to Chloe.

Erin was introduced to one of Dave's friends at his and Tess's wedding. She's pretty sure he is *the one*. She also consulted Chloe.

Not long after that, Chloe (with Marsh assisting) gave birth to their second set of twins. They liked to tell everyone that they both gave birth, since they both contributed to the process at the beginning and, as Marsh still explains it to one and all, he'd felt a lot of sympathy pains for the last three months of Chloe's pregnancy. The twin boys were named Sean and Liam.

I visited Chloe before she went off to the hospital. Jamie came with me. I didn't know if I should tell her that she wasn't quite done having babies yet. What decided me was that Chloe and I had never kept secrets. Once she knew, Chloe talked to Marsh about the possibility of building them a new house, one with no stairs.

I hadn't expected that revealing future events would result in Chloe and Marsh's family moving to another house, but it's okay. Kieran and Colleen are going to move into the MacFee family homestead. Colleen's pregnant and I have it on good authority the baby will be born right after midnight. So far, everyone who's been able to see me has been born during the night hours.

By the way, twins also run on Chloe's side of the family, which explains Kyle and Ally expecting their first set, a boy and a girl, shortly. Their names are still under consideration, but Jack and Jilly are heavy contenders.

I'm so thrilled I still have the ability to visit the earthly plane!

In between times....

Sarajane won the Megabucks lottery to the tune of four-point-five million dollars.

Dominic obtained his Master's while concurrently

acquiring his certification to become a physician's assistant in an OB/GYN practice. He was allowed to watch, but not deliver, his third daughter, Margaret Jane. We all call her Meggie. Mags is beside herself.

Chloe wrote a book about the Paired-Up Serials that became a best seller. It will pay for the new house with no stairs.

Luce has taken up editing, which turned out to be not only fulfilling, but lucrative because of the thousands of people who are self-publishing in ebook format. I've been wondering about trying my hand at writing. Luce has offered (through Chloe) to transcribe anything I put to paper.

Sarajane went back to work at the ME's office, but after winning the lottery, she decided to quit. She'd rather spend her time with her daughters and husband than going out to declare people dead, anyway, plus she still hates paperwork. And besides, she's pregnant again. With twins.

JD and Marsh remain partners in Persons Crimes. Neither one wants a promotion to lieutenant. Too much pressure, they say. Solving homicides and other violent crimes is a lot easier than supervising a bunch of detectives who know everything.

Rose, Aunt Gennie, and Mags frequent all the homes with babies regularly. They are so enamored with the growing family, they had a spacious triplex unit built, with a lovely courtyard where children can run and play and The Girls can cultivate a beautiful flower and vegetable garden. Being a grandma has never been so much fun, or so rewarding!

I agree, even though I'm still restricted to visiting only the house where I died. No matter, this house will always be full of love, laughter, and babies. The Fielding family and their friends make sure of that.

And down the road, Mary Kate, being the eldest daughter of my great-great-great niece Chloe Faust Fielding, will inherit the homestead in the MacFee family tradition when she's old enough.

Chloe wants to see her daughter living there while she and Marsh are still alive and young enough to enjoy visiting *their* grandchildren where it all started for them....

# Author Note

I hope you enjoyed reading the further adventures of Chloe and Marsh Fielding and their friends and relatives. Once I met Luce and JD and Sarajane and Dominic in the pages of *Chloe's Spirit*, not to mention Rose, Aunt Gennie, and Mags, I just couldn't let go of them. *After-stories* also gave me an opportunity to bring Mary back and right an injustice to her and Jamie.

I did take some authorial liberties with some of the events and procedures in this book. For instance, I'm pretty sure there is not a hospital anywhere that would allow someone in ICU to go visit the baby nursery, in a different building, in the middle of the night. Or any time, for that matter. Don't you just love fiction?

Hats off to the men and women who go to work every day, protecting the citizenry and solving crimes, and to the EMTs who respond to medical emergencies and save lives in the process. Any errors pertaining to medical issues or police procedure are mine alone.

## Afterword

If you missed reading
CHLOE'S SPIRIT,
and you want to find out
how the story began,
the paperback is available
with *free shipping*
on the author's website:
**annsimas.com**


The digital version is available at:
**amazon.com**
or
**barnesandnoble.com**

**And a glimpse at an upcoming
romantic suspense by
Ann Simas…**

A stalker, a found sister, a new love…

FIRST Star

Alexandra Dumont's best friend had come up with some corkers in the past, but this scheme to "man-hunt" at the grocery store, based on some article she had read in a women's magazine, was too much. "Dani, this is not one of your better brainstorms."

"Of course, it is. Would I have thought of it if it wasn't?"

"Yes," Alex said, her tone dry. "As the master of convoluted thinking, you would."

Dani grabbed Alex's hand and tugged her out of the ancient Volvo. "Come on—our destiny awaits."

"If someone notices what we're doing, and how stupid we look doing it, you're getting full credit," Alex hissed as they passed through the glass doors of the supermarket.

"We're just shopping." Dani reached for a shopping cart. "Looking over the merchandise."

"You mean the men," Alex said, amused despite her reluctance to dive into Dani's wacky plan head first.

"C'mon, Alex. Cruising the grocery store aisles on Friday night is much safer and a lot less smoky than hanging out in singles' bars."

"I don't hang out in singles' bars, and they don't allow smoking in public places anymore, remember?"

Dani perused the rack of paperbacks briefly, grabbed one, and tossed it into the cart. "I remember and I don't, either—we're not cut out for the bar scene, but if we don't try something, we're going to miss out on all the guys. We'll end up as old maids."

Alex laughed. "We're thirty-one. By today's standards, that's not even middle age yet! Besides, I've gone the marriage route once. I'm not looking for a repeat performance."

"Still..." Dani guided the cart over to the sundries and loaded up on toothpaste, deodorant, and two different flavors of antacid.

"You wouldn't need something for your stomach," Alex said, unable to keep the laughter out of her voice, "if you didn't come up with hare-brained ideas like this."

Dani smirked over her shoulder at Alex. "Check out the guy at the wine display."

Good-naturedly, Alex humored her friend.

"He's got a little paunch," Dani said, "but he has dynamite hair."

"He's got a beer belly," Alex corrected. "And the start of a bald spot on his crown."

"Spoil sport."

"I'm streaming an episode of *X-Files* tonight. I could be home in my jammies instead of cruising the aisles of the grocery story with a crazy woman," Alex said.

Dani lowered her voice in an apparent attempt to mimic Agent Fox Mulder. "The truth is out there, Alex Dumont. Thirty-one and no man."

"And as Fox would also say," Alex shot back, "Trust no one." She wanted to believe there were still some good men left, but she had no hopes of finding any of them at the grocery store.

Dani shrugged. "What's paranormal video compared to this?" As they made the frozen food aisle she said, "My cousin met her fiancé in the grocery store. He's a foxy Italian if ever there was one."

"He's the baker where she works." Alex almost choked on her laughter. "And he's a couch potato when he's not at work."

Dani shrugged, unconcerned. "He's cute, though."

"Maybe in his baby pictures."

"Well, he might have a brother who's okay."

"Dani—" They rounded the corner of the cookie-and-cracker aisle and came up short. A little girl of about three sat on the floor, alternately sobbing and shoving cookies into her mouth from the Oreo's bag in her lap. Under her free arm, she clutched a doll that drooped as only a doll that's been well-loved can droop.

Alex knelt down next to the child, who gazed up at her with the largest cornflower-blue eyes she had ever seen. Huge alligator tears overflowed their depths and streaked down round little cheeks gooey-brown with cookie. "Hey, sweetie, what's the matter?"

Instead of answering, the child shoved her hand into the cellophane package for another Oreo, then stuffed it between chocolate-circled lips.

"Don't put the whole cookie in your mouth at once," Alex warned gently, grasping the girl's chubby arm. "You might choke." The child blinked up at her, and her body jerked with something that was part hiccough, part sob, part crunch.

"What's your name?" Alex tried again.

Another sob.

Dani leaned over the basket. "What's your name, kiddo?"

The child never took her eyes off Alex. "Emlee," she mumbled around a mouthful of cookie.

"Emily?" Dani asked.

The little girl nodded.

"That's a lovely name," Alex told her. "Are you lost?"

Honey-colored curls bounced as Emily shook her head. "Daddy and Meggie's losed," she informed them seriously.

"I see." Alex shot an amused glance at Dani. "Well, I think we can help you find Daddy and Meggie."

Emily dipped her hand back into the Oreos package.

"Would you like us to help you?"

Emily's curly head went up and down.

"Up you go, then." Alex grabbed the bag of cookies

before they spilled to the floor and reached for the child's free hand before she thought. By the time she realized her fingers had connected with tacky chocolate, it was too late to recall the gesture. She ignored Dani's muffled laughter. "Would you like to ride in the cart or walk?"

Emily appeared insulted by one of the options. "Walk."

Since the child was in danger of losing either what was left of the Oreos or her doll, Dani offered another solution. "Do you want me to carry your cookies?"

The little girl screwed up her face at the suggestion.

"Would you like your dolly to ride in the basket, then?" Alex asked. "So you don't drop the cookies?"

Impossibly long lashes swooped down in a slow blink. A fat tear was released over each chubby cheek. "Guess so."

Even as the child handed over her doll, her frown of concentration told a different story than her acquiescence. Once relieved of the burden, however, she rearranged her cookies and offered her rescuers a tearful, if chocolaty smile.

Alex reached discreetly into her purse for a tissue, but nothing short of soap and water was going to get the goop off of her hands. Resigned to a temporarily sticky situation, she walked with Emily and Dani to the Customer Service counter, where she explained the situation to the clerk.

Emily seemed awed by the fact that her name blared over the PA system. "That's me!"

"Yes, it is," Alex agreed, trying not to laugh. "Have your Daddy and Meggie ever been lost before?"

Emily's head bobbed up and down with enthusiasm. "Lotsa times, but I always finded them before."

"And this time you didn't."

"Uh-uh."

"Hey, you're the chick who writes about the building stuff for the newspaper!"

Alex had all but forgotten the young man behind the customer service counter, whose name tag read JAMES, but being called "chick" brought him back into focus. She had to bite her tongue to keep from telling him she wasn't remotely related to the poultry family. "Yes, but I write about the housing market, in general, not just building."

He shrugged. "Whatever. It's cool."

Alex offered him a tempered smile, hoping to dissuade further conversation without being rude. "Thank you."

"I've been thinking about starting up my own construction business," he said.

She shared a look with Dani. This wasn't the first time someone had confided such plans to her, but these days, she had grown particularly leery of men she didn't know showing interest in her. "It's hard work, and the market isn't recovered yet," she said, feeling foolish for the twinge of paranoia that caused her to be so short with the guy. He was little more than a kid with a dose of macho swagger thrown in, not a stalker. Still, annoyance caused her to persevere in gloom-and-doom mode. "It's not likely to experience a full recovery for years."

"I'm taking some business management classes," he boasted, totally ignoring her grim forecast.

"That's good," Alex said, and breathed a sigh of relief when two voices, one deep and masculine, the other youthful and scolding, called out "Emily!" simultaneously.

Alex and Dani turned in unison.

"Uh-oh," Emily said. She held up the Oreo bag to Alex.

The way she said it, Alex was certain, as she accepted the bag and dipped her hand inside for a cookie, that the little girl must fear a horrible punishment. Instead, the man who had called her name scooped his daughter up into loving, nicely-muscled arms and hugged her.

The idea of noticing the muscle tone of a man's arms

was so foreign to Alex, for a moment, she didn't even realize that she'd been *looking* at his arms. Belatedly, she wondered why he wasn't wearing a jacket when it was still cold out. She bit into the Oreo without realizing it.

"The ladies founded you," Emily said to her father, patting his cheeks with gooey hands.

The man didn't so much as cringe. It made Alex feel silly for worrying about the cookie stuck to her own hand.

"Yes," he said, looking first at Dani, then at Alex, "I guess they did."

Alex couldn't remember when she'd ever seen such expressive eyes. The color of a fine whiskey, they were filled with exasperation, amusement, and gratitude. She tore her own gaze away just to regain some composure.

The little girl—Meggie—who could only be Emily's older sister, tugged on the younger child's leg. "Emily, how many times has Daddy told you not to wander off? You know bad people might hurt you or take you away."

Startled, Alex looked down at the other little girl. With her lecture complete, the child eyed Dani and Alex suspiciously. The kid sounded more like a mother than an older sister. If Alex was any judge—and she wasn't—the girl looked to be about five and had eyes just like her father's. Wheat-colored hair trailed down her back in what must have been an immaculate French braid at some point during the day but now looked like she had stuck her finger in a light socket.

"I goed to get the cookies," Emily said in her own defense, reaching for the Oreo bag, which Alex handed over. The toddler extracted an Oreo from the bag and shoved it into her father's mouth. "Your fabe-rit."

"Thanks," Daddy mumbled around the cookie.

"We were going to get cookies," her sister chastised.

"Now we won't have to," their father cut in cheerfully, still chewing.

They both looked at him and grinned, hero worship rampant in their identical expressions.

"Thanks for helping the squirt," Daddy said to Alex and Dani.

Alex had to clear her throat before anything would come out. "You're welcome."

"No problem," Dani said, casting a speculative look at Alex.

"Since you have your cookies, Emily, I guess we're ready to go," he said. "No more for now, okay? You're going to get a tummy ache."

"She's a mess," Meggie said with resigned disgust.

"Reminds me of another three-year-old I used to know."

Meggie flashed him a smile that was part angel, part devil. "I know."

He laughed and no matter how much Alex wanted to, she couldn't keep her eyes off of him. It was a full-throated sound that made her want to laugh right along with him. His eyes sparkled with humor and affection as he ruffled his older daughter's hair.

"Daddy," she protested, "you'll ruin my braid."

"Sorry, punkin," he said, as if every hair on her head was perfectly in place. "Thanks again, ladies."

Dani said goodbye, but all Alex could do was follow her friend away in silence, looking over her shoulder once as the hunk with the two beautiful daughters made for the checkstand.

"Whoa!" Dani breathed several moments later. Her hand fanned through the air in front of her face, as if she'd just eaten something hot. Extremely hot. "Can you believe that guy? How come the good ones are always married?"

"It's *not* always the good ones," Alex reminded her.

"Don't be such a poop, Alex." Dani stopped and planted her hands on her hips. "You can't judge all men by a couple of bad experiences."

"Watch me."

"Are you going to tell me you didn't find 'Daddy' just a *little* bit attractive." For emphasis, Dani held her thumb and forefinger about half and inch apart and directly in front of Alex's nose.

Alex forced herself not to check the man's progress with his daughters. "Maybe a little," she hedged.

"OMG, Alex, admit it! He's sexy."

The urge was too great. Alex glanced toward the checkstands. Even with an Oreo smear across his cheek, he reeked of sensuality. His twinkling eyes and the way he treated his daughters only seemed to enhance it. "He's sexy," she grudgingly admitted.

Dani laughed. "You're too much. We come to the grocery store to man-hunt and you—"

"*I* am not on a man-hunt," Alex corrected her.

Dani laughed again. "I give!" They went to the end of the aisle and around the corner to the next one, where she reached for a package of pasta, tossing it into the basket. It landed with a soft thud.

"Oh, no, Emily's doll!" Alex cried. It was apparent the little girl had loved this battered doll to death. She would be heartbroken without it. Memories crowded in on Alex. Memories of her own childhood, when the only friend she had was a raggedy doll that listened and commiserated and never talked back. "I'd better return it to her."

By the time she reached the checkstands, the man and his daughters had disappeared. Alex hurried outside, scanning the parking lot. With his size, they should have been easy to spot, but Alex saw no sign of them. Disappointed, she turned to go back into the grocery store just as a truck pulling out of the lot caught her eye.

Illuminated in the light spilling from the standards around the parking lot, she recognized "Daddy" behind the wheel. She made a mental note of the company name lettered on the door. Sagen Construction.

Back inside, she clutched the doll under her arm. Emily would be relying on her to take care of it.

"Well, what did you think of your first Friday night at the grocery store?" Dani asked on the way home.

"I've been to the grocery store on Friday night before."

"Yeah, but not as a substitute for a singles' bar."

"Thank God."

"Does that mean you won't go with me again?" Dani maneuvered the last corner before Alex's house. "That guy looking over the tomatoes had possibilities."

"Dani," Alex said with great patience and fondness, "any man who squeezes a tomato like it was a squish ball is not a likely candidate for a long-term relationship."

Dani thought about that for a minute before she glanced down at the front of her sweater. "I guess you're right," she conceded. "I haven't got much as it is. He might mush 'em into pulp."

Alex was still chuckling later when she curled up under the covers with Emily's doll.

# About the Author

 Ann Simas lives in Oregon, but she is a Colorado girl at heart, having grown up in the Rocky Mountains. An avid word-lover since childhood, she penned her first fiction "book" in high school. She particularly likes to write a mix of mystery and romance with paranormal elements. Her books are available in both digital and print format, with autographing and free shipping directly from her website for paperback books.

An award-winning watercolorist and a budding photographer, Ann also enjoys needlework and gardening in her spare time. She is her family's "genealogist" and has been blessed with the opportunity to conduct first-hand research in Italy for both her writing and her family tree. Some of her Italy photos are displayed on her home page at **annsimas.com**. The genealogy research from century's old documents, written in Italian, has been a supreme but gratifying and exciting challenge for her.

Contact the author via:
Magic Moon Press
POB 41634
Eugene, OR 97404-0386

*Or visit:*
**annsimas.com**

**Thank you for purchasing this book!**

Please consider leaving your comments
regarding *Chloe's Spirit Afterstories*
or any book by this author on either:
**amazon.com**
or
**barnesandnoble.com**


You may also email the author at:
**annsimas.com**